MW00974004

The Glass Run

B.C. Reynolds

The words in this novel attributed to Jesus are not quotations from any Bible translation. They are, instead, paraphrases of words or statements that Jesus might have used.

WestBow Press books may be ordered through booksellers or by contacting:

WestBow Press
A Division of Thomas Nelson & Zondervan
1663 Liberty Drive
Bloomington, IN 47403
www.westbowpress.com
1 (866) 928-1240

ISBN: 978-1-9736-4258-9 (sc)
ISBN: 978-1-9736-4257-2 (hc)
ISBN: 978-1-9736-4259-6 (e)

Library of Congress Control Number: 2018912182

Print information available on the last page.

WestBow Press rev. date: 01/21/2019

Dedicated to my entire family:

Without their help, encouragement and support, this book would have never been written.

And so we must fall,
from beginning to end.

Falling each moment,
only to fall, yet again.

B. Craig Rey

Contents

CHAPTER 1

"Ma'am?"

"Ma'am?"

Molly didn't answer right away. She sat behind the wheel of her old 2059 blue sport coupe and stared down the hill. She could see another eighty or one hundred yards or so of the paved driveway that stretched out before her. The driveway was lined every fifty feet on both sides with beautiful magenta colored crepe myrtles that were in full bloom. Her mind wandered in several different directions as she listened to the tune on her vehicle's interactive allcomm system. She was fairly familiar with the song because it was by one of the old alternative Christian music groups she liked by the name of Deep Call. She sang the lyrics quietly to herself at those times when she knew them. At other moments during the song she was completely unsure of the words. During those times she hummed along to the tune as much as she could while tapping the dashboard near the steering hologram of her vehicle to the beat of the song.

To build a wooden tower,
starts a journey, to set the world free.

To gaze upon that tower,
and realize the fate, that was meant for me.

She sang the words softly but still loud enough for the security guard to hear. He rolled his eyes and then spoke a lot louder than was necessary.

"Ms. Mahan!?!?"

Molly jumped slightly in her seat and came quickly back to reality. "Yes? I'm sorry. I think I sort of spaced out there for a few seconds."

"No worries ma'am. Happens a lot around here. Your invitation checks out just fine. Here is your visitor's pass, your parking pass and a map of the campus."

"Oh, OK. Thanks. Ummm, what do I do now? I mean where should I go?"

The guard gave a quick roll of the eyes again but smiled politely and said to Molly, "No problem ma'am. Just follow this driveway around that curve down there. As you come out of the curve you will see the campus spread out in front of you. They are expecting you at the Administration Building. That's the blue building on the far right side of the campus. Park in the lot between gold and blue. That'll be parking lot number three. The main entrance to the blue Administration Building is in the center of the building facing the parking lot."

"Umm," Molly stammered. "Wait, what? Blue, what? Admin building? What does gold mean? Are you sure that --"

"Don't worry ma'am. Just drive around to the end of this driveway and consult your map. You can't miss it."

As he finished talking to Molly he was already looking behind her car and waving for the next vehicle to approach his guard hut. Molly quickly checked her rearview camera and saw a line of at least six vehicles behind her. She felt her face flush embarrassingly as she realized that she was holding the line up.

"Eh, thanks, I guess," she muttered as she pulled away from the guard hut.

Molly cruised slowly down the driveway trying to stay on the pavement as she fought with the map. The map won and she flung it half opened onto the passenger seat next to her.

As she drove she muttered quietly under her breath. "Blue, gold, admin buildings, what lot number did that guy say, three? Or maybe two? Why can't they just make this easy? I didn't want to come to this thing anyway. Waste of time if you ask me. I'm really gonna make Emily pay when I get back. I'm still on the driveway and I'm already lost. What building did he say, blue, purple, beige? I can't believe this. I have no idea what is going on around here."

Molly quit talking to herself as she pulled around the curve in the driveway and felt her jaw fall completely open. The driveway dropped down slightly and there before her was the entire three hundred fifty acre campus of Historelational Interactive Systems: A Quick Family Enterprise, known simply as HIS by the employees who worked there.

A short, polite (yet annoying) beep from the vehicle behind her brought her back from gazing down the hill at the campus and for the second time in less than ten minutes she felt her face flush with embarrassment. She drove ahead a few feet and pulled over to the side of the road. She waved to the driver of the vehicle behind her to go around her and at the same time fumbled to get the map and open it again. However instead of going around and passing her, the car pulled up next to her and stopped. The driver pantomimed that he wanted her to open the driver's side window.

"Now what?" she wondered. "Is this guy really going to chew me out for being a little slow?"

She verbally instructed her vehicle to let her window down and the driver in the other car did the same. She could see that he was a large, middle aged man, going gray at the temples.

"Hey," he shouted. "Looks like you're a bit lost. Your first time here I'll bet, right?"

Molly could tell that he wasn't angry at all. In fact he was smiling at her pleasantly.

"Uh, yeah," she managed to stammer.

"You going to the the big announcement?"

"Oh, uhh, yes I am. Not really sure what it's about, but yes I am supposed to be covering that."

"Ahhh, you're with the media huh? Me too. Look I've been here a couple of times before, just follow me."

Without waiting for her to respond he pulled out ahead of her. Before Molly could reply or follow him another car, the next one in line behind the mystery man, pulled in right behind him and effectively cut her off from following behind him. She could see that the driver of that vehicle had the auto drive engaged and was not paying attention to any other vehicle around. Molly carefully looked behind her and could see that there was a nice sized gap between her car and the next one approaching. She pulled back onto the driveway and followed both cars in front of her. The man who had offered his assistance was just a little bit ahead of the car in front of Molly and she had no trouble keeping his car in sight. One by one they reached a fork in the driveway. At this point all vehicles would need to follow either the right or left split in the driveway. The nice man took the right path and the lady in front of Molly chose the driveway leading off to the left. As Molly approached the point where the driveway split left and right, she could see plainly that there was a very large, well placed sign with directions on it. The sign was placed right at the intersection or split point between the right and left arms of the Y in the driveway. She slowed and read the sign quickly. The sign was painted a forest green color. A bright yellow arrow pointed to the left path. Next to that arrow were listed the buildings and parking lots on the campus that could best be reached by taking the left path. The arrow clearly indicated that anyone trying to reach the Green Building (Supply and Storage), Rose Building, Silver Building (Company Recreation), Parking Lot #1 and Parking Lot #2, should take the left hand driveway. Likewise there was a second bright yellow arrow on the sign pointing to the right path of the driveway. Next to that arrow were listed the Blue Building (Administration), Gold Building (Research and Development), Parking Lot #3 and Parking Lot #4. The message was clear that anyone trying to reach those buildings or parking lots should take the right hand part of the driveway.

For a brief second, the investigative reporter part of Molly wondered why all of the buildings were listed by not only color, but by their function as well. All, that is except the Rose building. It was listed by color only with no indication of exactly what it's function was. That was only a fleeting thought however as Molly's brain made the connection between the color names of each building and the buildings themselves. At this point in the driveway she could clearly see all five of the buildings. All buildings were different in size and shape, but all were made with tinted glass outer surfaces, each of a different color.

Molly quickly caught up to the smiling man who was just pulling into the parking lot clearly marked as lot #3. Lot #3 was located between the Gold R & D Building and the Blue Admin Building. She smiled to herself as she thought of her confusion back at the guard hut. She had not understood the directions that the guard had given her and in her mind she had wondered why the directions seemed so difficult. It was evident now that the directions had actually been extremely clear and obviously intended to put any visitors at ease. It had not been the guard's fault that she had become flustered. She realized that it was her impatience and lack of concentration that had led to the confusion. She reminded herself to slow down a bit and not to jump to conclusions like she usually tended to do. She knew that she owed that security guard an apology and made a mental note to do just that. She also reminded herself that even though she had not wanted this assignment, and still didn't really want to be here even now, she had a job to do and she needed to concentrate on doing that job to the best of her ability.

Chapter 2

Molly parked in the first available space she located. She took a few moments to set the parking pass she had received at the guard hut to hover mode so that it floated freely about two inches above the dashboard. She gathered up the visitor pass, her purse, her wrist write recorder, her All Contact Communicator (called an allcomm for short) and a few other items she thought she might need.

As she got out of her vehicle, she noticed the smiling man walking toward her.

"Lock," she said to her car and waited a second to hear the three toned chime that assured her that her vehicle was locked and would stay so until she gave the verbal command for the car to unlock itself. All voice commands were of course on a voice recognition basis and so only she could lock or unlock her car. She was aware that emergency personnel were in possession of override codes, but for today, she was confident that her car was locked.

"Hello. Glad to see you made it," the friendly man said. "My name is Garth. Garth Perry from WCRS news in Charlotte."

"Hello. I'm glad to meet you. My name is Molly; Molly Mahan."

The look of non-recognition in his eyes told Molly all she needed to know. She laughed and said, "That's OK, I know that no one around here has ever heard of me. My business partner and I operate a small, and I do mean very small, scroll site. My dad started it way back in the days before scrolling even existed. They used to call it blogging back then I think, or something like that."

"Oh wow!" Garth exclaimed. "That's pretty wild. I'm a lot older than you are so I know all about blogging. Or at least I know what it was used for back in the olden days. So what do you scroll?"

"Just about anything that is news is going to be scrolled somewhere on our site. We scroll news of items about any topic we think people might want to learn about. Of course it is filtered through just the two of us so we sort of pick and choose what we think our readers are interested in knowing more about. Emily takes care of things like politics, foreign interest stories, fashion and a few other specific areas of interest. On my side of the fence I take care of articles relating to sports, history, religion, academics, human interest stories and things like that."

Garth looked at her with a strange look and finally said, "Did you just say religion?"

Molly knew what reply was coming next but asked anyway. "Yes, why?"

"Why?" Garth answered. "Because nobody talks about religion anymore. At least not anybody I know. Man, if I even had a thought about the word religion, I think the other people I work with would think I had lost my mind. Religion is, well not just old fashioned, but simply just off of everybody's radar these days."

Molly sighed and said, "I know. I know all about that. Being an independent scroller I can still say whatever I want to say. Well almost. I can't get fired by anyone because I'm a part owner. But I know what you mean, everyone seems to be afraid to talk about it because someone might get offended or something."

"Well you do know that there are laws about that sort of thing don't you? I mean I guess religion is all well and good but you can't talk about it to just anyone. That falls into the public humiliation laws that were passed, oh when was that, maybe twelve or thirteen years ago? I'm surprised no one has shut you down yet."

"The law that you're referring to was passed ten years ago to be exact and yes, the government has suspended our license. Not just once but twice. Fortunately however, we managed to reorganize both times and come back into the world of the living; and hard as it might be to believe, we're still here".

Garth laughed one of the most pleasant laughs that Molly had ever heard.

"Well OK, but you better be careful who you say stuff like that too.

Personally I really do not care one way or the other. However there are plenty of people around who do care and they would turn you in and rat you out to the authorities in a heartbeat."

"I know, like I said, it has already happened to us twice. But you know what is really frustrating about that law. Seems like anyone can say anything they want to about most religions and no one really cares. They just look the other way. However if someone mentions Christianity, or Jesus, out pops that law and businesses get shut down, people get arrested or at the very least get looked at like they are carrying the plague or something"

Garth looked shocked. He glanced around the parking lot to make sure no one else was within hearing range.

"You one of those Christian types?"

Molly was instantly on guard. Even though she was not ashamed of Jesus, she knew enough about recent politics to be careful. Especially around people that she did not know well. She looked at Garth for several long moments but did not say anything.

Garth looked very uncomfortable. He glanced around again to see if anyone had heard their conversation. Finally he managed to say. "Well it's OK with me whatever you believe. Like I said, I don't care at all either way. But I really don't feel much like spending any time in a jail somewhere so if it's all the same to you, let's not bring that up again."

Molly nodded slowly. "I understand. No problem."

Garth changed the subject masterfully. "Well we'd better be getting on into the program. I think it is supposed to begin in about half an hour." He could see Molly eying him curiously so he quickly added. "You said you've never been here before right?"

"That's right. This is my first time here."

"Well I've been here three or four times for various reasons. Usually rollouts of their new products and stuff like that. Pretty much like what is going on here today I guess. Man, these guys throw a spread like you would not believe."

"You mean food?"

"Oh yeah, you better believe I mean food! These people really know how to have a good time and when they bring us media folks in here like you and me to cover their new products or whatever, man they feed us like nobody's business. That's why we need to get in there a little early. See all those other people going in there?"

Molly looked over towards the entrance where Garth was indicating with an outstretched hand and nodded as she saw about twenty or thirty people heading for the entrance.

"They're probably all media types too. Just look at 'em' rushing in there. They're all greedy little piglets. Rushing in to eat up all of the food before we get in there."

"But Garth, we're both with the media as well."

"Yeah I know but we're not greedy piglets. Everyone else is, not us. Now let's get going before it's too late. I haven't eaten yet today."

Molly could see that he was kidding and she laughed as she saw a smile start to spread across his face.

"You're not fooling anyone with all that nonsense about members of the media," Molly whispered. "I'll bet you're friends with just about everyone in there."

Garth winked and said, "Well you never know. I might know a few people here or there. Now can we get going please? Starvation is not high on my priority list today."

Together they walked toward the entrance of the blue building that Molly knew now was used for administration purposes such as today's product rollout.

As they walked Molly said, "I tried to do a little research on what this is all about but I couldn't find much of anything about it. Do you know why all of us have been invited here today?"

"No clue. But now that you mention it, this does seem rather strange. The other times I've been here it has only been myself and maybe four or five other members of the media. And it seems as though I was always invited with plenty of advance notice. I also recall that there was always a lot of hype and fanfare involved with those previous rollouts as well, not all hush hush like today. I have no idea what they are going to reveal to us today but this just somehow has a different feel to it. Oh well, I'm sure we'll find out soon enough."

CHAPTER 3

Approximately three weeks earlier, Molly had received an invitation to the product rollout that was apparently what today's big event was all about. At that time, she was aware of HIS, as was everyone else on planet Earth. Even though she had heard of them and knew that they were involved heavily with cutting edge gaming techniques and forward thinking technology, she realized that her knowledge of HIS was really very limited. So in the days just following the receipt of her invitation, she dove into researching the huge family run company that had just issued her an invitation to their latest product rollout. What she found amazed her.

HIS was indeed a giant of a company but she was stunned to discover that they were rated as being number three in the entire world at research involving innovative electronics. She did not really know much about that sort of thing but she couldn't help but be impressed. After all there had to be thousands of companies all around the globe doing this sort of work, and these guys were rated number three? Wow! Further research showed her a lot more about the company. HIS had been started many years ago by someone named James Quick. It seems that James Quick had been one of the leading designers of early interactive electronic games. Used initially for personal recreation, these games had become so intricate that they had become almost addicting to many people. They had evolved from just simple games to items and implements that were used every day by people all over the world. James Quick had begun his career working for a company by the name of Interactive Explorative Gaming Concepts. He had been paid well for his imaginative and creative efforts but the individuals who owned the company he worked for had made much more money than he had by using many of his ideas. This eventually caused friction between Quick and the company owners and eventually things had become so bad that James Quick had resigned from his position. The company that Quick had worked for had been located in England and apparently James thought that he was in need of not only a new company to work for, but also a new country to work in as well. Through a friend of a friend, James had relocated to The United States and gone to work for several electronics research companies before finally starting his own company. He settled in what was then called the Research Triangle area of North Carolina. The Research Triangle was situated in the area between three cities that formed the points of the triangle. Those cities were Chapel Hill, Raleigh and Durham. Those three cities were home to three very good, and very well connected research universities, The University of North Carolina, North Carolina State University and Duke University.

Not surprisingly James Quick named his new corporation "Quick Games." With his genius for electronics and his uncanny knack for knowing what the gaming community wanted, Quick Games rapidly became the dominant gaming company in the United States and rose to be rated in the top five world wide. When James retired at the age of seventy, his son Harrison took over as the President and CEO of Quick Games. It was under his leadership and foresight that Quick Games morphed from being only a company that invented interactive games, to a corporation that also delved into cutting edge technology in a variety of fields. They quickly became one of the leaders in smart equipment and awareness technology. They developed and built vehicles, household appliances, farm equipment, aircraft, communication devices and even medical equipment that utilized advanced intelligent technology that was years ahead of most of their other competitors.

Quick Games had its corporate headquarters just outside of Durham but their Research and Development Department was located on the Southeast side of Raleigh. The distance of almost fifty miles between the two locations was a minor nuisance at first but finally began slowing production down to a crawl. Harrison Quick realized that the solution was to move the two units closer together. He found some suitable acreage about twenty five miles north of Greensboro and decided to move all aspects of Quick Games to that location. It wasn't quite in the research triangle but it was close enough. The property was beautiful farmland when he first found it and bought it from an eighty four year old farmer named Garvey Graham. Mr. Graham's wife of more than forty five years had passed away a few years previously. The Grahams had no children so when Harrison Quick came by with a checkbook and asked about purchasing the property, a deal was made in just a short amount of time.

Mr. Graham retired to Florida to be near his brother who had retired there two years earlier. He received a great payout from the purchase of his farm. He tithed ten percent to his local church, bought a condo near the outskirts of St. Augustine (paying in cash of course) and still had enough to allow him to live easily with no debt for the next twenty years, if he needed to.

It took Quick Games several years to plan and build the facilities on their new campus. The campus that Molly had entered looked very much like the original campus design that Harrison had planned years earlier. The five main buildings with their variety of tinted glass facades were much like Harrison's original plan. Since that time there had been only one major addition to the campus's outward appearance. The buildings were spaced with three buildings on the West side of the property and two buildings on the East side. When Harrison took over as President and CEO, the area behind and between the two groups of buildings had a few trees scattered here and there but was mostly covered in a grassy low lying area, once known to the employees as "the swamp".

Harrison converted most of that area into a picturesque twelve acre pond. Around the pond was a paved walking path that completely circled the pond but also wandered lazily through some of the wooded area that had been left in its natural state.

Employees at Quick Games worked hard and most of the time worked under a lot of pressure and severe deadlines. Both James and Harrison Quick recognized the need for a little downtime for employees during the work day and the walking path was open to all employees so that they could get out of their work stations and clear their heads when needed with a stroll around the pond. This same reason was also why the Silver Building was designed as a recreation and leisure area for employees. That building housed several game rooms, a small (but always well stocked) snack bar, comm/video rooms, meeting space, lounge, workout facilities and in the basement, a four lane swimming pool. Harrison had always believed that if he took care of the people who worked for him and respected them as individuals that they would, in return, give him their best effort every day and work hard to produce high quality products.

Though not a good athlete himself, Harrison had always been a huge sports fan. Even as a young boy he had loved growing up in that part of North Carolina which for years had been such a hotbed of collegiate athletics. He never really had a favorite team, but he did have a favorite sport, and that sport was baseball. He loved all sports but in his mind, baseball was king. Though his work schedule was incredibly wearisome, Harrison tried to get to as many college baseball games as he could. He made certain that he never went to a game where any of the three nearby universities were playing against each other. He just couldn't bear the thought of cheering against one of his three favorite teams.

Harrison Quick had only one child, a son named Dylan. Dylan's birthday was in October and the year he turned seven it was Autumn of course and not baseball season. Harrison was determined to give Dylan a birthday present that he would always remember and decided to introduce Dylan to collegiate sports in person rather than just on a vid/comm or holo/comm. Dylan's birthday that year fell on a Saturday. Both Duke and N.C. State's football teams were playing away games that day but UNC was in town. It was homecoming weekend and the Tar Heels were scheduled to play a non conference game against The University of Georgia. Dylan had already caught some of his father's exuberance for sports so when the big day came he was ready to go several hours before game time. Later in life Dylan would always refer to that day as the day he became a Tar Heel. As Dylan grew older there was never a doubt in anyone's mind about which college he would end up attending. He was a better athlete than his father and played on varsity squads in high school both on the soccer team as well as the baseball team. He was a good athlete, but not good enough to receive an athletic scholarship from the school that he knew he really wanted to attend. He did receive a few scholarship offers from some of the smaller schools but he was a Tar Heel through and through. The Quick family could of course have paid for Dylan's way through any college easily, but they didn't have to. Though Dylan was not good enough to receive an athletic scholarship, he was way past good enough to receive academic scholarships. During his adolescent years the other love of his life, other than sports, was academics. He excelled in the classroom and made the highest grade possible in every class he took in elementary, middle and high school. The old SAT and ACT tests had been discarded long before Dylan was in high school. Teaching professionals had finally realized that those sort of exams were not really indicative of what individual students were capable of. In place of those exams a more equitable exam had been developed by academic researchers from Princeton and Emory Universities. The new exam, called the RACER (Reactive Academic Capability Exam Response) had been the benchmark since long before Dylan was born. The highest score possible for an individual to achieve on the RACER was five hundred. Dylan took the exam twice and received five hundred both times. His favorite subjects were math and science and when he entered the University of North Carolina, he immediately began to take as many classes in those two departments as he could.

To no one's surprise Dylan Quick graduated from UNC at the top of his class. Two weeks after he graduated he traveled to England with two of his college buddies, Frank Clement and Jeremy Levy, to attend a month long course titled, "The Future Longevity Outcomes of Diverse Mathematical Systems".

That course was offered at Cambridge University and taught by Dr. Brad Raymond, one of the world's leading theorists in analytical mathematics. Of the fifty five students who had been accepted into that prestigious month long course, Dylan was the only one to receive a perfect score from Dr. Raymond, the first time that Dr. Raymond had ever given a perfect score to anyone in any of his courses.

Dylan returned to the U.S. in late summer, just in time to begin taking graduate courses at Georgia Tech. Against the advice of several of the faculty at Georgia Tech, he finally obtained permission to take classes toward two graduate degrees simultaneously. His areas of concentration while in Atlanta were Non-Dimensional Nuclear Bionics and Interpretive Micro Physics. He flew through all classwork and completed both graduate degrees in only eighteen months. From there he attended CalTech and received a PhD in Applied Cosmotic Engineering, again finishing in just eighteen months.

He was still only twenty five years old when he took a job at Quick

Games in the Research and Development Department as a research assistant. Even though he was way ahead of most of the other workers at Quick Games, he had agreed with his father that he not be shown any kind of partiality simply because he was the President's son. Undoubtedly there were a few unkind words whispered about special treatment and things like that but many of the employees at Quick Games had known Dylan since he was a baby so those comments were small in number. Most of the employees also knew of his intellect and his education and were well aware of the fact that even though he was starting his career as an assistant, he knew more about what they were doing then almost all of the rest of them put together. Dylan worked as a research assistant for only three and a half months. At that time everyone in the company agreed that it was a waste of time for him to remain in that position. Harrison had originally planned for Dylan to spend at least a year as an assistant so that rumors of favoritism could not be spread but he finally agreed that Dylan's skills were wasted there. Quick Games gave him his own office, his own laboratory and an assistant of his own. He had no supervisor other than his father and a man named Reid Corder. Reid Corder was Harrison's oldest and best friend and was the Vice President of Quick Games. He and Harrison Quick had been roommates together in college. On paper, Reid was Dylan's supervisor, but that existed only to allow the auditors to see a clear line of command and supervision. In reality, Dylan had received the following instructions from Harrison. "Go see what's out there. I want you to dream it, invent it, develop it, build it and then, if possible, have it make a little money for Quick Games."

Dylan had always tried to follow those instructions and in fact, some of his creative thinking and ideas had made quite a lot of money for Quick Games and everyone who worked there. Largely due to Dylan's imaginative thinking, Quick Games had a worldwide reputation for dreaming of impossible things, and then seeing those things become reality. Every year some of the best and brightest people in the areas of mathematics, artificial intelligence, electronics, graphic design, technology and cutting edge software applied for positions at Quick Games. In fact the HR department rarely had to advertise for open positions. When a position became available, they usually just selected from among applications that they had received previously from some of the best minds in the world.

It seemed as though everyone wanted to work at Quick Games. They had a great reputation for being that rare combination of great working conditions, treating their employees as valued individuals and making a difference on the worldwide stage, not just in the gaming community but in all other sectors of life as well.

On a chilly cloudy day in early March when Dylan was twenty seven years old, he received a message on his allcomm to come immediately to his father's office. The message said that it was not exactly an emergency but that he should make every effort to come as soon as he could. Dylan had to run over from his lab which at that time was located in the gold research and development building. His father's office was located in the blue administration building. Halfway between the two buildings he was joined by Reid Corder who had received a similar message. Corder had been in the green building going over some audit results on supply management and comparing those results to recent company purchases when he received his message. Both Reid and Dylan possessed very healthy competitive natures. As soon as they met up between buildings, they began walking fast, then faster and finally sprinting alongside of each other in a friendly foot race. They arrived with Dylan just a few steps ahead of Reid who was older than Dylan by quite a few years but still in fantastic physical condition. They both had to slow down a little in order to open the door.

"What's up?" Reid asked. He was completely out of breath but he managed to get that question asked.

"I have no idea," Dylan replied. "I guess you got a message on your allcomm too?"

"Yeah," Reid panted out a reply. "But my message just said your dad wanted to see me as soon as possible. No info other than that, no details at all."

"Same here. I have no idea what this might be about."

They entered the building and found one of the HR assistants waiting for them at the door. Dylan knew the man's name was Rick but couldn't recall his last name. Not that it mattered at the moment.

Fearing the worst, Dylan shouted to him as he and Reid raced through the doorway, "Rick, what's happened? Is everything alright?"

Rick shook his head and said, "I have no idea. Harrison just sent me to find you two and I was just heading out. He's waiting for you both in his office."

Harrison Quick's office was located on the third floor so Reid headed for the elevator. Dylan was a lot younger than Reid and was in the better physical condition of the two men so he headed for the nearest staircase. Dylan arrived at his father's office a few seconds before Reid did. He was breathing hard but winked at Reid and said, "Got ya."

They knocked on Harrison's door and then entered the office together. They found Harrison sitting at his desk holding his head in his hands.

"Are you OK Harrison?" Reid asked.

At the same time, Dylan took several rapid strides across the room to stand beside his father.

"Dad," Dylan yelled. "What's wrong?"

He reached for and grabbed his father's shoulder. Immediately he could feel that his father was shaking slightly.

Harrison Quick looked up at his son and then looked over at Reid. He placed his hand on Dylan's shoulder and then squeezed it tightly.

"I've just returned from my annual physical and I'm afraid I've got some bad news; some really bad news."

He paused for a second and Dylan and Reid shared a concerned look between them.

"The Doc says that I have cancer; the non-curable kind."

Dylan involuntarily recoiled a step as if he had seen a monster. Reid had started to take a step forward but froze in mid step. For a long moment no one spoke and in fact it seemed that for a few seconds none of them even took a breath.

Finally Dylan choked out a whisper. "But dad, last year you were just fine. You've always been fine. You're always in great shape. How can you have cancer? How did it come up so quickly?"

Harrison chuckled a little and said, "Now listen, I can only answer one question at a time. Let's just slow down a little and we'll talk it through. It's all going to be OK. I'm going to need to rely on the two of you a lot more than I usually do, starting right now. But we're a team and I don't want either of you to worry too much. Worrying won't do any of us any good and it certainly won't help Quick Games in any way. Everything is going to be alright. Everything is going to be just fine."

Chapter 4

The cancer never had a chance to take its toll on Harrison Quick. Instead, he suffered a massive stroke late on a cloudy afternoon. The stroke occurred just four months after the conversation he had had with Dylan and Reid about his cancer diagnosis.

Three days after that, he passed away without ever regaining consciousness.

The company he left behind was just too large to shut down completely so on the day of the funeral there remained behind at Quick Games a skeleton crew. About seventy five percent of all Quick Games employees attended the funeral. Dylan hated funerals. He guessed that everyone else did also but he just would rather eat nails than attend a funeral.

He had never really known his mother. She had died of Pneumonia when he was three. His father had always told him that neither she nor anyone else knew she had it until about four days before she passed away. By then it was too late. Dylan had been told that she had been a very strong proud woman who just did not like to go to see doctors. Apparently she had believed that she just had a bad cold and was determined to try and suffer through it. When she finally collapsed at home one Saturday afternoon, Harrison had rushed her to the hospital, but too much damage had been done. She went into a coma that night and never came out of it. Now his father was gone too.

Dylan knew that he was the sole heir of all that Harrison had, which included the entirety of Quick Games. He understood that he could not just sulk and feel sorry about his father's death because all of the employees and their families relied on their Quick Games jobs and the paychecks that came with those jobs. Dylan knew that those paychecks needed to continue on at a regular pace regardless of funerals and other disasters. He understood all of that, but he still had to just get away and clear his head a little.

The day after the funeral Dylan met in his home with three of Quick Games' lawyers, Reid Corder and Miranda Saylor. Miranda was Vice President in charge of the Business office at Quick Games. As he left the funeral he had asked them to come to his house the next day at 4:00 PM.

"I'm sorry," he started. "I know that I am leaving you guys out on a limb, and I know I need to be responsible for a lot of stuff right now. But I just can't. Not now. I can't be responsible, I can't go on like nothing has happened, I don't think I can do much of anything at this time. I can only hope you all understand. I need to get away from here for a few days. Reid, I will call in to you every other day or so to see if everything is OK but please don't any of you try to reach me."

Everyone said that they understood and that they could hold the fort until he could get back. They were all aware that Dylan was never really involved in the day to day operation of Quick Games anyway and that life within the company would go on. They had lost a leader that everyone loved deeply. But the operation of Quick Games was not in jeopardy in any way. Dylan signed a few papers for the lawyers, said his goodbyes and three hours later was in his vehicle on his way to The Great Smoky Mountains. His destination was a remote area just across the state line between North Carolina and Tennessee. Harrison had owned a large cabin in Tennessee on (as he used to say) "forty five of the most beautiful acres this side of Heaven." The property had a clear stream running through one corner of it and in that stream, Harrison and Dylan had caught many trout that had ended up as dinner that night. The cabin was fully stocked with almost any kind of fishing gear imaginable. Dylan doubted he would do any fishing at all this trip. He just needed to get away.

He drove back onto the Quick Games' campus twenty two days later. As he entered the gate he stopped for a brief chat with long time security guard Sam Donman who was manning the guard hut that morning.

Everyone at Quick Games was on a first name basis with everyone else, regardless of position or company hierarchy. The one exception was that all of the technical employees or researchers who actually had Medical or PhD degrees were usually referred to as Doctor by those working for them.

"I'm glad you're back Dylan," Sam said when Dylan rolled up in his off road vehicle. "You were awfully busy at the funeral so I didn't get the chance to tell you how sorry I am about your dad. He was a great man and we are all going to miss him terribly. As a matter of fact, we already do."

"Thanks Sam," Dylan replied. "I appreciate that. And you're right, he was a great man. A very great man and I miss him so much I can hardly stand it. I really don't know how I'm going to get through this first day back."

"Well if there is anything you need, don't hesitate to ask OK?."

"Thanks again Sam. Everything been OK around here the last few weeks? Anything I need to know about?"

"Well it's really been kinda quiet. At least from where I sit it has been. I really don't know about anything going on as far as major decisions or anything like that. Those things are way above my pay grade."

"Sam I've known you since I was about five or six years old and I know one thing for sure about you. You make it your business to know just about everything that goes on around here. And I mean that in a good way. You've got your finger on the pulse of the whole operation. Probably even more than dad did. So let me ask you again, anything going on I need to know before I walk into a hornets nest of some kind?"

Sam chuckled quietly and then said, "Well like I was sayin, it really has been pretty quiet around here."

"But --?"

"Well, I have heard a bit of buzz about a few people getting their noses out of joint about a decision that Mr. Corder made two or three days ago. I guess he has the right to do it now but it just seems to be a bit early for some people, including myself."

"What kind of decision Sam?"

"Well it seems that he, Mr. Corder, moved your dad's belongings out of his office and put them in storage for you to go through later. Then he moved himself and all of his stuff into your dad's old office. Kinda set himself up to replace your dad. I guess he probably will be the logical replacement but it seemed like maybe that could have waited a bit if you know what I mean."

Dylan was still and thought for a minute and then said, "Yeah I guess I'm with you. Seems a bit premature to do that. While I was out of town I was sort of thinking that there might be someone else who might fit into that position. Well listen, it's probably just fine so let's keep this conversation just between the two of us alright?"

"Yeah that's fine with me Dylan. Anything you say."

Dylan started to pull away from the guard hut and Sam called after him. "Remember, you need anything, you just let me know."

Dylan waved and headed down the driveway, further into the Quick Games campus.

The next day, Reid Corder found Dylan in his research lab. The two men embraced in a friendly hug and then sat down in chairs facing each other.

Reid started the conversation. "I heard you got back yesterday. I went looking for you but someone said that you only stayed around for an hour or two. You look good. Everything OK?"

"Thanks Reid, yeah I'm alright. I had a lot of time to myself these past few days and even though you and I spoke almost every day, it was still good for me to get off by myself for awhile."

Reid smiled at him and said, "And now you're ready to come back? Are you sure you still don't need a little more time? We can take care of the shop for a while longer, no sweat."

"No thanks," Dylan laughed. "I love it up there at my dad's mountain place but it's time for me to get back. I'm ready to get back into the game."

"Well I know you will miss him for a long time. And all the rest of us will too. He and I were best friends for so long I can't even remember a time when we weren't friends."

Reid started to get up and leave. "Well as you said, we all need to get back into the game and I have about a thousand things that need my attention so I'll let you get settled back in. Let me know if you need me for anything."

Dylan held up his hand to indicate that he wanted Reid to stay.

"Hang on a minute Reid if you don't mind. There is one thing I think we need to discuss. Do you have just a few minutes to spare?"

"Sure," Reid replied and sat back down. "What's up?"

"Well I don't really know quite how to say this so I am just going to trust our friendship and blurt it out. OK with you?"

"Blurt away," Reid said.

"I heard you moved dad's stuff out of his office and moved yours in. Is that right?"

Reid shifted in his seat uncomfortably. "Well yeah, I did do that. I was going to tell you all about that but just thought I would wait awhile is all. I sort of figured that we all knew that Harrison would have expected me to take over in his shoes if something like this happened. You're OK with it, right?"

"Well," Dylan replied. "I'm not sure I am OK with it. In fact, I am pretty sure that I'm not OK with it. I know that you were always dad's right hand man, but dad really wanted me in that position. He wanted me to become President and CEO and he hoped that you would help me as my right hand man just as you did for him."

For a full minute there was no sound in the room. The two men looked at each other, each keeping their own thoughts to themselves until finally Reid spoke up. "Well," he started slowly. "This is a bit awkward isn't it?"

Both men smiled but the smiles were built of uncomfortableness rather than of warmth. Reid shifted in his chair and then continued. "I guess I assumed that you already knew that Harrison had asked me to take over for him if the time came. I know that he was your dad Dylan, but you just aren't qualified to take on this role for the company. You're a brilliant researcher but you are very young and you have had virtually zero experience running the business side of things here. I think that the company would be better served if you stayed in R&D and worked the research side of things. Don't you really think so too?"

"I've thought about that a lot Reid but I just don't see it that way. I realize that my experience on the business side of things is limited to almost nothing. But dad shared with me every single major decision he ever made and more importantly he shared with me the reasons why he made each decision. Without actually sitting in his seat, I feel that I know more about this company than anyone else. Even you."

Reid was quiet for a moment and then smiled at Dylan.

"There is a huge difference in hearing about how to run a company from someone and actually running a company. There really is no comparison.

Look we shouldn't be arguing about this. Instead we should be forming a bond as much like the one your father and I had as we can. Let me handle the day to day operation of the business. You take care of the research department. Trust me, if we work things out that way, all will be well and this company will be leading the competition long into the future."

Reid rose from his seat and reached over and patted Dylan on the shoulder. "Trust me Dylan, this is for the best."

Dylan grabbed Reid's hand in his. He stood up, looked Reid in the eye and said, "Reid you have always been like a second father to me. However I know that dad wanted me to take over for him. He told me that on several occasions and with his death, I think the best way to handle this is for me to try to do what he wanted me to do."

"I don't know what he told you Dylan, but I can tell you this. There were many times he told me that he wanted me to run things around here if something happened to him. He set you up in research because he knew that was the best place for you. It still is. Now we need to get this past us and move on for the good of Quick Games. I don't want to have to fight you on this. It would be better for everyone if you would just accept what's happened, get back to work on whatever it is you are working on these days and let me get on with running the company."

"I really don't want a fight either Reid. But I am prepared to take this to the board and senior management if I need to."

"Dylan let me give you some advice here, just between the two of us. I already am the acting President and CEO and everyone here has acknowledged that. Don't try to take this to the board. You will lose that fight. Your reputation will be dragged through the mud, both within Quick Games and throughout the outside gaming and business community as well. That is only going to serve to harm our company and I know that neither of us wants that to happen. Don't do it. Please!"

Just three weeks later the board met along with all department heads and other key senior management employees. The fight that Reid had predicted never occurred because of two key factors. Factor one was that if a vote had been taken it was likely that Dylan might have won in a landslide and possibly might even have won by unanimous vote. That is how popular Harrison and Dylan both were with the employees of Quick Games. Factor two was that just four days prior to the meeting, Harrison's will had been made public. In his will he clearly had stated that it was his wish that his son Dylan become the next President and CEO of Quick Games.

The night after that meeting Reid invited Dylan out for dinner.

"Thanks for accepting my invitation Dylan," Reid began. "I appreciate that."

"Well thanks for inviting me. I know that we need to discuss a lot of things and we need to find some way to move ourselves, our friendship, our business relationship and most of all, Quick Games forward."

"I couldn't agree more. In fact that is exactly what I wanted to discuss with you tonight. OK with you?"

"Yeah sure," Dylan replied. "What exactly did you have in mind?"

"Well, I've asked our waiter to give us about fifteen or twenty minutes before he comes over to ask for our orders. I think we can wrap this up and move on pretty quickly."

"Alright, go ahead," Dylan answered.

"OK, so the way I see things is that one of two things needs to happen right away at Quick Games. One would be that I make a statement and publicly acknowledge that I understand that you are the President and CEO and I will remain in my current role as VP. If you will agree to that. If that can't happen then I need to move forward with the second thing which would be for me to resign and leave Quick Games in the next few days, or maybe even tomorrow. In the end, this is going to be your decision, but I would like you to hear what I want first."

"Agreed, keep going," Dylan said.

"My wish is to stay. I really thought that I would be the logical choice to replace Harrison as the head of this company. But it has been decided that you are to be that person. I need to swallow my pride, which I am trying to do right now, and get on with my life. I think that I can be of use to you as the second in command and I would like to be that person, if you will allow me to be. You have so much talent and I truly think that you will be a great President and CEO. You have a lot to learn about the daily workings of any company or organization. But I think that you are quite capable of learning all you need to know and with me beside you while you are learning, I think that we will make a good team, just as Harrison and I were."

"Wow Reid!" Dylan exclaimed. "That was really well put. Of course I want you to stay. I've never wanted anything other than that. What I have in mind is that I will be President and CEO and will accept all of the responsibility that the position holds. But I really do want to spend most of my time in the research lab. I want you in charge of all the daily operations of the company. I also think we will make a good team and that is the way I see our company set up as we move forward."

"Well in that case I think we are agreed. You are the President and CEO and I will remain as the Vice President and handle most of the day to day business operations."

The remainder of the dinner went well and both men were relieved enough to talk about a few plans that they wanted to see put into place as the company moved forward into this new era following the passing of Harrison Quick. One important decision that was decided upon during dinner was a name change for the company. Both Reid and Dylan had been toying with the idea of changing the name of the company to something that indicated Quick Games' direction away from gaming research and moving into cutting edge research. Everyone knew that the research that Quick Games was doing was so far out in front of anyone else there was not even a name for it. Dylan called the research arm of the company "Research Out." The implication was that it was light years ahead of research of any other company on the planet. Most companies had to rein in their researchers in the quest to find or make something that in turn would make the parent organization money. But Harrison and Dylan had decided long ago that at least some of the research being done inside of Quick Games would be research simply for research sake. Research with no boundaries whatsoever. If it ended up making some money for Quick Games, so much the better. But the Research Out Department was not designed solely to make money. It was to discover things that no one else had ever found and go in directions that no one else had looked into previously.

Both Dylan and Reid had ended their dinner on a high note with both of them feeling that they were back in places they wanted to be in. They had also agreed on a new name for the company that would indicate to the world the new and improved company mission. Historelational Interactive Systems was the new name. It would remain as a family owned and operated business and the new mission would change from inventing gaming systems to putting much more effort into inventing more practical components that would affect everyday life. The research department was focused heavily on artificial intelligence that would guide the next generation of everything from smart vehicles and medical equipment to everyday household items.

Dylan remained President and CEO of the entire company but he was quite content to let Reid make almost all decisions regarding the day to day operation of the company except for research, which Dylan would continue to run.

On the day that Molly drove onto the company campus, Historelational Interactive Systems, now commonly referred to as HIS, had been run this way for almost seven years. Reid continued in his role and had been very effective at leading the company through some very dangerous business waters and the company had thrived. Dylan had held the research and development department under his wing for a little over two years when he suddenly handed over all operations of the R&D department to one of the long time researchers, Dr. Karen Way. He then proceeded to virtually lock himself in his lab with four or five assistants working on things that only they knew about. Questions from other employees about what they were working on usually got stiff looks from them or comments like, "Oh, just something that Dylan thought up."

Reid and some of the other senior staff seemed to be aware of Dylan's line of research and experiments and they rarely interfered. The accounting office was also quite aware and alarmed by the continued increase in the budget for line items only listed as belonging to Dylan's lab. But the company was still making lots of money so no one complained too much about it all.

Then Dylan announced that a breakthrough had occurred and invitations were sent out to reveal to the public just exactly what it was he and his fellow researchers had been working on.

Chapter 5

Molly and Garth walked to the entrance and went inside along with four other people who had arrived at the entrance from their vehicles at about the same time. Just inside the large foyer two tables had been set up. One table had been set up on the right side of the foyer and one on the left. Each table had a young lady sitting just behind it. Three people were already standing at the table on the left talking to the young lady who was seated there so Molly and Garth gravitated towards the table on the right. One of the other people who had entered with them also joined them in walking up to that table. As they approached, the young lady who was seated there rose from her chair and smiled the brightest most cheerful smile Molly had ever seen. In fact Molly stopped dead in her tracks a few feet from the table as she realized with a jolt that the person who was now standing on the other side of the table and smiling at her was probably the most beautiful woman she had ever seen in her life. She suddenly felt very self-conscious about her own looks. She had never thought of herself as homely or not good looking but neither had she ever thought of herself as beautiful or even pretty. Standing next to this woman she felt like she should join a convent and never try to date anyone again. What would be the point when women like this were her competition. Immediately she felt guilty of trying to compare herself with this woman. She uttered a quick prayer of apology to God just as the most beautiful woman on the planet started to speak.

"Hello, welcome to HIS!"

Molly knew that the lady had spoken these words but it seemed to her that the words just sort of beamed themselves out of her mouth. She cringed again knowing that she needed to just get over the fact that this woman was prettier than she was.

"I hate when that happens," she thought to herself.

"My name is Becca, Becca Knight. Welcome to HIS and the new world."

Molly started to extend her hand to shake Becca's outstretched hand but Garth bumped his way in between Becca Knight and herself. In the process Garth had inadvertently bumped Molly's hand away and almost knocked Molly several feet to the left of where they were standing. Molly started to say something to Garth but when she looked at his face she could tell that Garth had forgotten completely about Molly. She realized that at this, sort of awkward moment, Garth did not even know that Molly Mahan even existed. At this particular minute his entire universe was consumed by Becca Knight.

"Hi," said Garth. "I'm Garth Perry from WCRS. I've been here a few times previously for various events but it's been awhile. I don't believe that we have ever met. I know I would remember a monumental occasion like that."

Molly rolled her eyes skyward as Becca said, "Oh yes Garth, I think I do recall that you have been here before. It's great to see you again. How have you been?"

Molly could tell that Becca had no idea who Garth was but Garth beamed with pride as Becca welcomed him.

Becca looked at Molly and introduced herself again and held her hand out. Molly stammered, "I, I, I'm Mmm, Molly Mahan. I'm fr, fro, from Truth Scroll. I know you've never heard of it, it's just a small independent scroll site."

Molly experienced a moment of panic and thought to herself. "What if this is all some sort of mistake. What if I really don't belong here. They'll realize it any minute now and I'll be tossed out of here like last week's leftovers." She looked back at Becca and quickly said, "I was invited."

Becca laughed pleasantly and said, "I'm sure you were. Welcome Molly, we're glad you joined us today."

Becca then turned her attention to the other person who had walked over to the table with them. While Becca and the other person, whose name apparently was Mike Standling, were talking Molly glanced sharply at Garth. Garth, who had the most cheesy grin imaginable spread across his face looked over at Molly. When he saw the look she was giving him he dropped the smile and sheepishly said, "What?"

Molly hissed her answer. "What is this? Are we in fifth grade?"

"What are you talking about?" Garth asked.

"Oh come on. You almost dropped your teeth when 'little miss perfect smile' over there was talking to you. In fact I'm pretty sure you drooled on your tie."

Garth grabbed his tie in both hands and held it up to his face. "I did?"

"No," Molly confessed. "But you might as well have."

Now they both realized that Becca was talking to all three of them again. "Well welcome all of you. If you'll just let me see the invitation that you received in the mail, your security pass that you should have received at the guard hut when you entered the campus and your driver's license we'll be all set."

All three of them produced these items for Becca to examine. While they were doing that two other people arrived at their table. Becca looked up from the items she was examining and smiled at the two newcomers. "I'll be right with you," she said.

"Ok, Mike you are with our scientific group right?" Becca asked.

"Yes, that's correct," Mike responded.

"Well sorry for the mix up, but the area to sign in for the scientific group, along with the technology group is at that other table over there."

As she spoke she turned and pointed to the table on the other side of the foyer.

"This table is to sign in our guests from the media and our visiting historians. We were supposed to have signs up clearly marking which table was for which groups. I guess someone didn't get the memo to get that job done this morning. Sorry about that."

"Not really a problem," Mike Standling said as he started walking over toward the other table.

"Don't worry, you have plenty of time before the presentation begins," Becca called after him.

He was already halfway across the foyer but he waved over his shoulder to let her know that he had heard her.

Becca raised her voice just a little more and cheerfully called out again. "And there's plenty of food left!"

Becca looked back at Garth and Molly and chuckled. "Sorry about that, but I can see that you are both with the media so you are in the right place." She handed back to each of them their individual driver's license and personal invitation. Next she pressed a tiny icon on the reverse side of the name badges. This activated the hover mode on the badges. She then gave the badges to Garth and Molly.

"Please put these on while you're here. I know this is probably overkill but it will just make it easier for everyone to figure out who everyone else is. We're expecting a pretty large crowd today."

Molly and Garth took the badges from Becca. They each held them above their clothes, just below the collar lapels on their left side. When they took their hands away from the badges, the name badges remained in place hovering about a quarter of an inch above their clothing. The badges would stay in place until the hover mode imbedded in them was deactivated.

Becca continued to talk to them as she turned halfway around and pointed to the back of the foyer. "Now, if you will just go through that doorway you'll be all set."

Garth and Molly looked to the doorway she was indicating.

"That door will lead you into meeting room A. That's where all the food is. Help yourselves. Everything is really good and most of it is homemade."

As she said that, Molly thought she saw Garth drooling again.

Molly was genuinely surprised. "Homemade?" she asked

Becca obviously had already been asked that same question about twenty times that morning and she beamed with pride and said, "Just about everything in there was made by our employees. We have some insanely good cooks around here. But don't worry, I'm not one of them. I did make some brownies but that's about all I can do while making sure it's still edible. Look for the blackberry cobbler. Stella Barnes from bookkeeping made that. It's to die for. There should be some left. Dylan made this into a fun competition for us and we do this at least once or twice a year. He and Reid are going to be the taste test judges and the winner gets two days of their choosing at Reid's condo on the Outer Banks later this summer. I think Stella might as well make her plans right now. That cobbler is soooo good! I would also recommend the chocolate pound cake. Caroline Gretch made that. She got the recipe for it from her grandmother, Nanny Jones or Johnson or something or other. She guards that recipe like it's part of the crown jewels."

Becca laughed and Garth fell in love again. Molly could not help but think that Becca was even more beautiful when she laughed. "How can that be?" Molly wondered. "Oh well, God makes us all special in our own ways with our own gifts I guess. But I sure wish he would have put some of what she's got in my basket when he was passing the individual gifts out."

She instantly felt guilty again. She thanked Becca and started walking toward the meeting room with Garth in tow. "Gifts, smifts," she thought. "Let me at that cobbler."

CHAPTER 6

Molly and Garth found meeting room A to be exactly as Becca Knight had said it would be. The walls were lined end to end with tables covered with dark gray clothes embroidered with the HIS logo in a medium blue color. Each table was covered with a huge variety of food types. There were cakes, pies, breads, homemade ice cream, fritters, fondues, candies and almost anything else that was guaranteed to add a few inches to any waistline if consumed in quantity.

One table stuck way over in the far corner had a sign suspended above it that labeled the food on that table as "Rabbit Food!"

There were five or six people standing around that table trying to be careful of their calorie intake. Molly could see that they were putting slices of carrots and small pieces of broccoli on their plates.

As Molly and Garth entered the room they could see that there were already forty or fifty people in the conference room. Almost all of them were camped out near the tables that held the cakes, pies, cobblers and other foods noted as not being too kind to one's waistline. From the look of the feeding frenzy going on at those tables it was immediately apparent to Molly that most of the people in the room had never even heard of a calorie.

Garth took in the whole scene at a glance and said, "I'm thinking of two things right now. The first thing on my mind is that I am wondering what the total number of sugar grams might be in this room right now if you added all of these goodies together."

"And what's the second thing you're thinking about?" Molly asked.

"The second thing I'm thinking is that right now I really couldn't care less how much sugar there is in here. I've got to find that cobbler."

Garth went off to sample as many items as he could while Molly was left to herself. She noticed that each item had a nameplate on the table next to it. She guessed that these were the names of the HIS employees that had made the goodies. She tasted just a small amount of raspberry flavored ice cream that said it was made by Dr. Jonathan Goldberg and also managed to try a chocolate and caramel cookie that had been made by Mrs. Claudia Doorman. She then spent about fifteen minutes wandering around the room, tasting a few items here and there but mostly just people watching. She could see that almost everyone was wearing colored name badges similar to the one she had been given at the sign-in table. The name badges all seemed to be divided up into four colors. There were name badges in orange, light green, maroon and navy blue. Molly's was one of the blue ones. After about twenty minutes she found that she had strolled all the way around the room and was now back at the place where she had started.

"Oh, why lookie here," she murmured to herself. "There is still a good amount of Dr. Goldberg's ice cream left. I wouldn't want him to think that nobody liked his ice cream. I'll just help the man out by having a bit more."

Molly managed to get quite a lot more into her plastic dish than just the 'little bit' that she had planned. But no one seemed to either notice or mind. There were obviously plenty of treats for everyone.

Just as she finished her ice cream and threw the dish and spoon into the recycler that was slowly cruising around the room, the lights blinked very slowly, fading in and out for about fifteen seconds. As everyone in the room settled down and became relatively quiet the lights went down to a very low level. There was still enough light to see by easily, but it was also plenty dark enough for everyone to notice that one of the walls (the wall directly behind the cookie table) was beginning to glow. Molly quickly realized that the entire wall was a huge comm screen built right into the wall. The wall was the screen and the screen was the wall. Gradually a face appeared on the wall. It looked like a live feed from somewhere but Molly could not tell for sure. The face was of a very handsome young man and everyone in the room (except for Molly) seemed to recognize him at once. The close up shot of the young man's face pulled back to show the entire person. He was sitting in an armchair with his legs crossed at the ankles and stretched out comfortably in front of him. He wore faded blue jeans, a medium gray button down shirt, a navy blue tie and a sport coat that matched the color of the tie. On his feet he wore comfortable and very worn leisure shoes but no socks. He seemed to be completely at ease. He was obviously quite comfortable with his clothes and appeared to be just as comfortable with himself. He exuded an aura of confidence and sincerity with just a hint of playfulness around his light brown eyes. In Molly's mind she had already labeled those eyes as the most incredibly attractive eyes she had ever seen. If she had still had the dish of ice cream in her hand, it would have ended up on the floor by now. The person on the screen started to speak.

"Good morning everyone. My name is Dylan Quick. I hope you all are enjoying the food spread we provided for you today. We here at HIS are very glad that you have decided to join us today and I think that we have a very exciting day planned for you. Let me rephrase that if I may. I don't think that we have an exciting day planned for you, I am absolutely one hundred percent certain that we do.

This will be an incredible day for all of us. Those of you that have been invited to see what we are revealing to the public today are going to be astounded. Those of us who work here are extremely excited to show you and the rest of the world what we have done. Also, to be honest, we are just plain tired of trying to keep this thing a secret any longer."

There were a few polite chuckles and the crowd in meeting room A murmured among themselves for a second or two.

Dylan Quick continued. "What you are about to see and hear has been top secret for quite awhile, but no longer. Today is the day we tell the world what we have done, and we have invited all of you to see and hear first hand what our latest project is all about. But first, let's get right to the important stuff shall we?"

The crowd buzzed with expectation and Dylan went right on. "Around here the most important news of the day is --"

He smiled and let his words hang in mid air for a count of ten before continuing on. "To determine who the baking competition winner will be!"

Everyone in the room had been holding their collective breaths without even being aware of it. Together as one they all let out a sigh. Laughter followed and the noise level in the room rose quickly.

Suddenly everyone realized that Dylan Quick was speaking again. "Every year the judging of these contests gets harder and harder to handle.

Although I must say that both Reid and myself consider this to be the best day of the year."

More laughter followed and Dylan chuckled at his own humor. "Seriously, some of our employees are in the wrong line of work. Instead of working here, some of them should open up a bakery or something. If you have been able to sample some of the items in that room, I know you will agree with me. It sure looks like Garth Perry agrees."

The crowd noise increased again as people asked things like: "Who in the world is Garth Perry?" or "Where is Garth?" or "What is he talking about?" or "How would Dylan know if Garth agrees or not?"

Finally someone in the back of the room laughed and said, "Hey Garth, he's talking about you, ya big slug."

Everyone turned to stare in the direction of where the man who had spoken was both looking and pointing. The crowd in that part of the room stepped back so that everyone else had a great view of Garth Perry standing at one of the tables. Garth froze in place as he realized that he had just been called out by Dylan Quick. Everyone could see that he was in possession of not just one plate, but two plates. He was balancing both plates on the inside of his left forearm while he wielded a fork that he held in his right hand. On one plate the crowd could see a fairly large pile of banana pudding that seemed to be heaped on top of two or three cream filled eclairs. On the other plate was a stack of four cookies, two crackers smothered in homemade cheese dip and what appeared to be the remains of something purple. The entire crowd roared with laughter. A live shot of Garth appeared on the video wall. Garth turned bright red but stood his ground and said, "Man, this stuff is incredible!"

The crowd laughed even louder and watched as Garth made a big show of taking a very large bite of banana pudding. As the laughter subsided Dylan Quick resumed talking and his image replaced Garth's on the wall.

"Yes I can see all of you but don't worry, I haven't been spying on most of you, just Garth." More laughter reverberated throughout the room as Dylan Quick continued talking, "And soon I want you to see me too. However we do have some unfinished business to attend to, right?" The crowd murmured their agreement and approval as Dylan continued.

"Reid and I have done our best to judge the food items and we have come to the conclusion that we just can't pick one winner. So this year there will be a tie for first place and each winner will get a couple of days at the condo out on the Outer Banks, courtesy of our own Reid Corder. Now, here's Reid with the announcement of our winners. By the way, this is being broadcast all over our campus to all employees so if you hear some far off shout for joy, no worries, that will just be our winners telling everyone how they feel. OK, here's Reid."

As Dylan finished speaking another man, much older than Dylan walked into view on the video wall and stood next to Dylan. Dylan stood up next to the older man, who Molly assumed was Reid Corder and said, "OK Reid, ya want to tell everyone the good news?"

Reid Corder smiled and without missing a beat said, "Sure, the good news is that I am full of the best food I've ever eaten."

Everyone in meeting room A laughed along with Dylan and Reid. "But I guess you meant for me to announce this year's winners right?"

Dylan nodded for Reid to continue, which he did. "So as Dylan just told you this is a really difficult job, but someone's gotta do it and Dylan and I are always up to the task. This year it was just simply too close to have only one winner and so we will have, as Dylan just said, two winners."

Everyone in the room cheered and Molly thought that she could even imagine all of the other HIS employees spread out over the five building campus cheering as well. She found herself hoping that Dr. Goldberg, whoever he was, would be one of the winners. She had never tasted creamier ice cream before and raspberry had always been one of her favorite flavors.

Reid Corder was speaking once more. "And now," he said with a flourish. "The winners are . . ." he paused and looked over at Dylan before continuing. "Do we have a drum roll or anything?"

Dylan laughed and said, "No but if you don't hurry up some of our employees are going to come in here and drum on your head."

Reid laughed and said, "Oh, well I really would not care for that at all so let's continue. The two winners are, Danielle Ramseur for something absolutely out of this world that she calls triple chocolate - double cream custard. For all of you in meeting room A, I suggest that you try to see if there is any left and try some. Just incredible." He was interrupted by the voice of a middle aged lady in a red dress standing by one of the tables on the wall near Molly.

"Sorry!" she called out as she pointed to a very large but obviously very empty serving bowl. "All gone."

"Oh that is too bad," said Reid. "I was hoping to get by there for one more taste of that custard. But we do have one more winner. She makes this for us from time to time and I always hate it when I find out that I was away or at a meeting or something on a day that she brought some in. But I had some this morning and Dylan and I both agree that this is the best she has ever done, even though I think she has won this contest once or twice previously. She calls it Blackberry Excitement and that is exactly what it is. Our second winner today is Ms. Stella Barnes."

Once again there was cheering throughout the HIS campus. Reid waited for things to quiet down again and said, "Now here's Dylan again with a few instructions for the next stop on today's schedule."

"Thanks Reid," Dylan said. "Maybe we should just pay Stella, Danielle and a few others to quit their jobs and just bring in baked goods for the rest of us."

Reid laughed and said, "Not a bad idea. Not a bad idea at all." He walked off out of the screen shot and left Dylan standing alone looking out into meeting room A.

Dylan waited a few seconds for the crowd to settle and then began to talk. "That was a lot of fun and I really enjoyed myself this morning. But we have a whole day ahead of us and I really think that you will not only enjoy what you are about to see but I think you will be amazed as well. There will be more to eat later on, but right now I'm going to ask you all to follow the green lit pathway. That path will guide you to your next stop."

As he finished speaking the lights in the room were lowered even more until it was almost pitch black. Just as the crowd in meeting room A was starting to get a little antsy, they all became aware that soft green lights had come on and were beginning to glow all along the baseboards of the room and all along the top of the room where each of the walls met the ceiling. There was easily enough light now to see clearly. Dylan's image was gone from the wall screen but his voice came through loud and crystal clear.

"No rushing. We have plenty of time. Just follow the blinking lights. I'll see you all in just a few minutes."

Molly did not see any blinking lights and was just about to ask the person standing next to her about that when suddenly there was a rise in the noise level in the room. It was coming from the corner of the room to her far right. She looked that way and could see that the food tables from that area had been removed. She guessed that someone had done that while Reid Corder and Dylan Quick were announcing the bake off winners. In that corner, one section of the wall was sliding open to reveal a hallway. The opening to the hallway was about ten or twelve feet wide. The baseboards and wall tops were lit up with the same green lights that meeting room A was lined with. As the wall completed it's opening up process, the lights lining the hallway behind the wall began to blink. The lights blinked in unison and were also blinking in a pattern; on for three seconds and off for one second. As the people in meeting room A began to file into the hallway, lights further down the hallway began to come on and blink in the same pattern, leading them all further down the hall. A voice just behind her and off to her left a foot or two said, "Pretty cool right?"

It was Garth. Molly smiled at him and said, "It is cool. Almost as cool as that scene you played out in there."

Garth looked embarrassed and Molly continued. "I'm not really sure I want to be seen with you right now. People might think I haven't eaten in days either."

Garth looked a little hurt so Molly quickly said, "Oh Garth I'm sorry. I was just kidding and I guess I really don't know you well enough to make jokes like that. I'm sorry."

Garth laughed and said, "No problem kid. My skin is thicker than that. Besides, I deserved it."

He lowered his voice and looked around to see if anyone else was listening. When he determined that they were not he said, "But that pudding was soooo good!!!" They both laughed and continued following both the crowd and the blinking green lights.

Molly turned to Garth and said, "I didn't realize that you and this Dylan Quick guy were such good buddies."

"Oh, we're not. I've met him a time or two but only for a few minutes and the last time was like five years ago or something like that."

"Well he sure seemed to know you."

"I don't know him well but let me tell you something that I do know about him. The word genius does not even begin to tell his story. It doesn't surprise me at all that he could meet me briefly years ago and then recall who I am like he did in there. No, this guy is special in a lot of ways, so no I'm not surprised at all. Not at all!"

Chapter 7

The blinking lights lead the crowd on for another two minutes or so. Finally they found themselves entering a large room. It was easily three or four times the size of meeting room A.

The end of the room where they entered was empty except for several tables in one corner. On the tables were chilled bottles of water, soft drinks and fruit juices. At the other end of the room a small temporary stage or dais had been set up. It was only about eighteen inches off the floor and measured about twenty feet wide by ten feet deep. The dais held one regular sized folding table and four chairs that were set just behind the table. Molly could see that the seats were made of the latest model of comform. She remembered then that HIS had patented comform years ago. Originally it had something to do with the space program. She recalled that originally comform had been specifically designed and created for use by the astronauts, technicians and researchers who lived on board the third and fourth orbiting space stations. They were the two stations that permanently orbited the moon. It had been top secret at the time but now many people had comform furniture in their vehicles, homes, offices or just about any other place. Molly herself had a chair in her apartment made of comform. It was one of the first commercial generation style of comform chair and had quite a few years on it now. That was all that she could afford. She loved that chair and the way the material molded around her body each time she sat in it. The chairs in this room however were from a much more recent style. She didn't recall ever seeing these particular types before and she guessed that they had not even been made available to the public yet. Each one must have cost a small fortune. She looked around and took in the rest of the room. In front of and facing the dais were many other chairs. Her eyes widened as she realized that each one was made of the new style of comform and the only thought that came to her mind just then was, "impressive."

There were sixty four chairs that were arranged in four different groups. Each group had sixteen chairs. The chairs were lined up in four rows with four chairs per row. Each group was separated from the others by aisles that were about eight or nine feet wide. On the outside aisles, between the outside most chair and the wall of the room, there stood a pole next to each group. Each pole was about two inches in diameter and about six feet tall. Each one was anchored in some kind of small square box that held the pole upright. At the top of each pole was a sign, approximately twenty inches wide by ten inches high. Each sign was of a different color. Molly realized that the signs were the same four colors as the name badges that had been handed out earlier. The signs also had words on them. The orange sign had the word History written on it. The word that was written on the maroon sign was Scientific, the light green sign had Technology written on it and the navy blue sign was labeled Media. Molly and others in the crowd quickly deduced that they were to sit in the chairs that were under the signs with their color and group name on it. If someone was standing on the stage and looking out to the groups of chairs, the navy blue media group was closest to the stage on the right. The orange history group was closest to the stage on the left, the light green technology group was behind Molly's media group in the back on the right and the maroon scientific group was in the back, on the left behind the history group.

Molly and Garth made their way over toward the chairs designated as being in the media group. On the way, Garth introduced Molly to two other people that he knew. One of them worked for a publishing firm. The other person Garth introduced her to was from the technology group. Garth told Molly that this person whose name was Stan (Molly didn't quite catch his last name) worked for the State of North Carolina as one of their top IT troubleshooters.

As everyone in the crowd reached their assigned groups they were all met individually by very young but very professional looking HIS employees.

"Hi Molly, welcome," said a young man as he reached to shake Molly's hand. She could see him reading her name plate. "I'm Douglas. I work in the PR department here. Nice to have you with us."

Molly smiled and told him that she was very happy to have been invited.

"Well we are absolutely delighted that you could join us today. We only invited a select number of visitors to be here. I think you're going to like what you see today. Now let's see," he said while holding his hand up to his chin. He proceeded to rub his chin as he pretended to be thinking. "Ah yes. Molly Mahan. Born in New Jersey, 27 years old, history major from a small school in West Virginia; West Virginia Wesleyan College I think, right?" He didn't wait for her to respond but continued. "Got a dog at home named Pepper, you're employed by writing a scroll that you own with your business partner. A portion of that scroll site deals with some sort of religious information and how history has been shaped by religion along with many other topics. Your hobbies are studying history, running, reading and traveling. I know that you have placed quite high in some of those running races. Coming in third at one of them I think. How'd I do?"

Molly knew that he had memorized some sort of file about her and let just a touch of indignation show through for a second.

"Ya'll spied on me?"

Douglas smiled and said, "Sort of but not really."

"And what does that mean?" Molly wasn't really angry, she was just messing with this guy a little bit.

"Before we sent invitations out we had to vet everyone to see who they were. We wanted a cross section of representation to come to this meeting today so instead of just inviting all of the old usual suspects," he said as he motioned with his head towards Garth who was looking the other way at the time. "We wanted to get some new blood in here for the event today. Your name came up in a computer search so we invited you. But before we did that, myself and several other people had to know a little bit about you."

"Why?"

"Well, as you will see later today there is some pretty serious stuff that is going to be rolled out and we wanted to know just who we were dealing with. You know, as in could you be trusted, or did you have some sort of axe to grind with HIS or were you someone who would try to see what might be in it for yourself in some way. That kind of thing. If you will think back to your invitation you will remember seeing a disclaimer that gave us the permission to dig into your background a bit. You signed it and sent it back along with all the other paperwork. Remember that?"

Molly wanted to be angry but she couldn't. For one thing she did recall signing that permission form. She remembered laughing to herself that her life was so boring that they would probably uninvite her once they found out just who she really was. Or perhaps her invitation was a mistake. Besides, she couldn't really get angry at Douglas. This wasn't his fault, it was hers and he was not in her face about any of this, he was actually being very polite and was just reminding her of some things that she should have remembered earlier.

"Yes of course I remember that. I was just a little surprised that you knew all of that stuff off the top of your head. And let's keep the age thing just between the two of us shall we?"

"You got it, no worries. So who is watching Pepper today?"

Molly smiled as she said, "My friend Emily's watching her for a few days until I can get back."

"Well I'm sure she is in good hands."

Douglas continued to greet the members of the media group one by one as they approached their assigned area. He had definitely done his homework and he knew a few tidbits of information about each person in the group. It made some of them feel a little like they were under a microscope. Molly fell into that category but it made others feel as though they were special and Molly had to admit that she felt that she was in that category also.

Everyone in the crowd eventually reached their designated group. Most were standing and chatting to other acquaintances that they already knew. Some were introducing themselves to others in their groups they did not know. This same thing was happening in the media group as well and Molly had already met several people whom she had heard of but had never met before. She was keenly aware that she and her small scroll site were not even in the same league as these people were in. These were power people in the media business and she was awestruck within seconds once she found out who some of them were. She was also stunned to find out that not only did many of them already know Garth, but that he seemed to be one of the bigwigs among the other bigwigs. And then it hit her. She had not paid a lot of attention to his name when they first met. She had been too busy trying to find her way to the correct building on campus. Garth Perry not only worked for WCRS in Charlotte, he also owned it. And if she remembered correctly, he also owned stations in Atlanta, Miami and Memphis as well. His family had cornered the market on media in the Southeast part of the United States years ago and he was "The Man" as far as anything to do with the media in that part of the country. No wonder Dylan had known who Garth was back in the food room. And no wonder Garth had not seemed overly embarrassed. He fit in perfectly here.

Molly thought, "What am I doing here? I am in way over my head with all of this, well whatever this is."

She didn't have too much time to worry about it because the crowd on the other side of the room was buzzing excitedly. She looked that way and saw that Reid Corder, Dylan Quick and two other people were filing into the room and heading for the dais.

All four of them climbed up on the stage but even before they had taken their seats, Reid Corder walked to the front of the dais and began speaking to the crowd assembled below.

"Well good morning again and welcome to HIS. We are so pleased to have you join us today. We are especially excited about the specific reason that we invited you all here. However, we will get to that in a moment. Please, please sit down, make yourselves comfortable. Actually you don't have to make yourself comfortable because your chair is about to do that for you." He chuckled as did everyone else in the room. Then there could be heard various ooohhhs and aaahhhs from several people in each group as they settled into the new comform chairs. He continued, "These chairs are just out of our Beta test mode. They are not being sold yet to the general public but we are going to be giving these to you at the end of the day. More ooohhhs and aaahhhs were heard across the room. Everyone realized what this meant and the excitement grew quickly. Molly was too stunned to react except to to think to herself that the chair that she was sitting in, that was now enfolding itself around the contours of her body, probably cost more than her annual income. Her next thought was to wonder how she was going to get it home and her third thought was, "Oh man does this feel good."

Her chair had begun a gentle massage all along her back and all down both the front and back of her legs. Just a slight hint of warmth radiated from the entire chair.

Reid was speaking again and he took her second worry away quickly. "Don't worry, we have your home addresses. If you can get it in your vehicle and want to take it home today, go right ahead. We'll have some people help you with that when the day is done. But if you can't get it home with you today we'll take care of that too and have it shipped out by the end of the week. No charge, our treat."

Everyone, including Molly, cheered and applauded exuberantly for a few seconds.

Reid continued, "Now the chairs have been functioning and attending to your needs like they are programmed to since you sat down and I'm sure you would all like for that to continue for the rest of the day. But I'm sorry, we can't allow that. If we did, you would all be asleep in less than ten minutes and we have a lot to show you today. In fact, our agenda today will astound you much more than any chair ever could. If you will reach down with your right hand, just under the seat you will feel a small raised icon. Please press down on that for about three seconds. This will accomplish two things. First of all it will imprint into the memory of your individual chair your specific fingerprint so that from now on, you and only you, will be able to operate that chair. Secondly it will also, for now, put the chair's individualized settings into pause mode. This way you will all be able to actually pay attention to our announcements coming up in just a short time."

He looked out over the audience to make sure that everyone was following his instructions.

"C'mon Garth, I see you pretending to reach for that icon. C'mon now. You'll be the first one asleep."

Laughter could be heard all around the room and Garth called back good naturedly. "Forget the rest of the day, I'm gonna take my chair home right now!"

Everyone in the room laughed harder at that and even Reid and the others on the stage laughed with him. It was all polite fun and games. Garth seemed very comfortable with the good natured teasing and that put everyone else in a relaxed mood as well.

Through the laughter Molly whispered to Garth who was sitting in the chair next to hers, "Why didn't you tell me you were such a big deal here? I feel like I am so far out of my depth."

For about the tenth time that morning she wondered to herself, "What in the world am I doing here?"

As the laughter died out, Reid Corder continued to address the group. "OK, we have been telling you all morning about the great things that we were going to show you. And we weren't talking about the chairs either. So now it's time to get to the main event. First let me introduce you to the other people up here on this stage. Over at the far end of the stage is Dr. Andrew Lamacelli. Dr. Lamacelli is the head of our Artificial Intelligence Development team and his role in this project has been huge, as you will see later on. Next to Dr. Lamacelli is Dr. Grace Ormond. Grace is our VP in charge of Scientific Technology and she and her team have also played an incredibly important role in the project as well. Virtually everything that we have needed in order to complete this project has had to be invented and/or designed from scratch. Well over two hundred and fifty patents for new technology and equipment have been awarded to teams led by Doctors Lamacelli and Ormond over the last five or six years alone."

Reid paused as the crowd applauded politely and then he continued speaking. "Yes you should be impressed. I know that I am. But the project never would have left the ground if it had not been for the vision, the foresight and the dreams of one man. That man is why we are here today and --"

The remainder of what he had planned to say was interrupted when Dylan Quick stood up and pulled Reid back away from the front of the stage where he had been standing.

Dylan laughed a small embarrassed chuckle and said, "Alright, alright already. Thank you for the intro Reid but I thought that we had agreed that we were not going to stand up here and talk about me this morning."

Reid smiled, pointed casually at Dylan and said, "Ladies and Gentlemen, our President and CEO, Dr. Dylan Quick."

The crowd started to applaud but Dylan motioned for everyone to quiet down. It was obvious to Molly that he was uncomfortable in this sort of spotlight. She couldn't help but notice the difference between Dylan and Reid. It was apparent to her that Reid loved the spotlight and if Dylan had not pulled him back, he might have gone on talking for a long time. But Molly got the impression that Dylan Quick had just the opposite nature. It seemed to her that even though he was the number one honcho in this company, he would probably rather see just about anyone else get some kudos than receive them for himself. As he began to speak, she knew she was right.

"Thanks Reid and thanks to all of you for coming today. As you all can see we have invited you here because you have some sort of focus, passion, knowledge or information in one or more of four different sectors. Those sectors are technology, science, history and the media. The reason for that is very simple. We are going to ask for volunteers from each group to be a part of the project we are about to unveil."

Even before he got to the end of that last sentence virtually every person in the room had his or her hand up. In fact in the entire group of sixty plus people in the crowd, only six had not raised their hands. Molly was one of those six.

"Whoa, whoa, slow down a little," Dylan continued. "We'll get to the volunteers later. And remember, you don't even know what it is you are volunteering for yet. So let me tell you about that and why you are all here today. Let me describe for you what we here at HIS have done. In a few minutes you will be using the word miracle to describe what you are about to hear and see."

Molly thought to herself, "I doubt that." But she smiled politely and applauded along with everyone else.

Dylan held up his hands and motioned for the crowd to be quiet and then went on speaking,

"We are going to be here a while so get up and get something to drink at the tables in the back of the room whenever you want to. Or get up and stretch, walk around a bit or whatever when you need to. We want this presentation to be informal and relaxed but please hold all of your questions until the very end because this is going to take quite a while to explain."

A few people in the crowd got up to go get a drink but Dylan did not wait for them to return to their seats, instead he started right in with the presentation.

"As I begin, I want each of you to think about one thing. If you had a time machine, but it could only be used once, where would you choose to go?"

He let that sink in a little and then continued. "Several years before my father passed away, I approached him about a ridiculously crazy, way out in right field, kind of idea. As some of you already know, at that time my job was to do just that; to try to think about the unthinkable and then find a way to make it possible. It is not easy to try to imagine the unimaginable. It's hard to try and come up with ideas in science or technology that no one has thought of yet. Well those were pretty tall orders. I did however have my own think tank that I could run my way with an almost unlimited budget. I loved it.

And as I was saying, I had come up with an idea and took it to my father to discuss. My idea was to build a time machine. Yep, you heard me correctly, a time machine. Dad said right away that the idea of a time machine was not new and that many people had written stories about time travel. Some of those stories go back many years, way back into the 1800's. Well he was about to throw me out of his office when I explained to him a little further with a bit more detail thrown in about what I wanted to do. I told him that I didn't just want to dream about it and I didn't want to write about it and I didn't want to make a video about it. I actually wanted to do it. I remember he looked at me for a long time without saying anything. He put his hand on my shoulder as he walked me to the door of his office and told me that time travel would always be fiction because in reality, it was not possible. I left his office and started walking slowly down the hall to go back to my lab. I can tell you all, I was pretty discouraged. I had walked down the hall about ten feet or so when he called to me. I stopped in my tracks and then turned slowly around. I just knew he was going to say something about me wasting time and money or something like that. But instead he surprised me. I will never forget what he said to me that day. We looked at each other for a second or two and then he said, "Let me know when it's ready!"

The crowd murmured loudly. Molly sat stunned and thought to herself, "Am I really about to hear what I think I'm about to hear?"

Garth leaned forward in his comform chair and Molly realized that she was leaning forward as well. She glanced quickly around and noticed that everyone else in the room was also on the edge of their seats. Dylan Quick had everyone's attention.

Everyone knew what was coming next and they instinctively realized that they were all about to become either a part of history, or a part of the world's biggest prank.

Dylan waited a dramatic moment or two and then said in a voice that was just above a whisper, "Well dad, we did it. It's ready."

Chapter 8

The room erupted into chaos. Everyone in the room was standing, yelling, laughing and talking all at once. Everyone that is except for Molly. Molly sat still in her seat trying to take in those momentous words. Garth reached down and grabbed her hand. He had a huge smile on his face.

Molly looked up at him and said, "Do you think it's true? Do you think they really did that? Could that even be possible?"

"I don't know," Garth replied. "But I've known some of these people for a long time and if anyone could do something like that, these are the guys that could do it?"

Dylan was holding his hands over his head and shouting for quiet. A few people in the media group had run to the back of the room and were attempting to exit the room. They wanted to be the reporters who had the first scoop of this announcement.

Dylan called to them first. "Come on back and sit down. You won't be allowed to leave just yet. I understand that all of you in the media section want to be the first to report this but you will all have to wait a while longer before you can do that."

Eventually order returned to the room and everyone found their way back to their seats.

Dylan was talking again. "Yes it's true. We've built a functioning time machine. My dad did not live long enough to see the finished project but you'll see it. You'll see it today. We accomplished something that most people would say is impossible but I'm here to tell you, we did it and it is here on our campus as we speak. Just be patient a little longer but don't worry, you're all going to get to see it. However, first let me tell you a little bit about it. Remember back a few minutes ago when I asked you to think about where you would take your one use only time machine? Well we have been thinking about that as well and we are all going to try to answer that question together.

Our time machine goes by the name of GeoHistoric, Lamanicity Altered, Spatial, Synchonisity". Dylan laughed and said, "Yes that is quite a mouthful so we just call it GLASS for short." He stretched out his left hand and pointed to Dr Lamacelli who was sitting at the table just behind where Dylan was standing near the front of the dais.

"Yes I know what some of you are thinking, that there is no such word as Lamanicity. There didn't used to be a word like that, but there is now. You recall that we introduced Dr. Lamacelli to you earlier? Well he is directly responsible for this invention and the very technology that made it all possible. Several years ago Dr. Lamacelli and I were deeply involved with trying to solve the puzzle that would make time travel possible. Dr. Lamacelli created something he called Lamanicity. It is pretty technically involved and we will get all of the pertinent info and statistics to you later on describing what it is and how it works and all of that. But for now let me just try and describe it this way. Lamanicity locates creases in both time and space, and also splices them together so that they are no longer separate units, but can act as one instead. These creases, or pathways can then be followed by an object, so that the object appears at the precise coordinates and at the specific time designated by whoever is using the GLASS at that time. In other words, we can send an object back to any location we want and have it appear in any minute, year, month and date that we specify. Pretty cool huh?"

For a moment there was just a stunned silence throughout the room. Dylan had asked everyone in the room to hold their questions until after he had completed his presentation but in the lull, Garth Perry spoke up.

"Dylan you said an object could go through this pathway, or whatever it is. What about a person?"

"Garth I did ask everyone to hold their questions til the end. But, I realize that everyone here must be asking themselves that same question so I'll answer it and then we will move on. The answer is . . . we aren't sure yet. We have tried GLASS using objects and we have tried it using living beings. But we have not tried it yet using a human. We think that it can be done with a human, in fact we are probably ninety nine point nine percent certain that we can do it because we have had success with our other tests. We see no problem with sending humans back in time successfully. But of course until we actually do send a living person through, we just won't have that one hundred percent figure that we all want. Now I realize that you all have about a million or so more questions, but so we won't get too bogged down here, I suggest we move forward. I think that many of your questions will be answered as we work our way through the day. At the end of our presentation, if some of you still have questions we will of course leave some time for you to ask those later."

Dylan then explained to the crowd of invitees that a breakthrough in the necessary technology had occurred some years back. Dr. Lamacelli had been working on some math equations that they had all hoped would help with the specifications for one of their new generation Specific Sentient Spatial Scopes. The Specific Sentient Spatial Scope (or S-4) was a device that HIS had developed several years earlier. The S-4 had been developed out of technology that was used initially to improve upon the old geosynchology that in turn had been developed from obsolete GPS technology. It was at that time that Dr. Lamacelli had stumbled upon, and accidently discovered the creases that existed in both space and time. Following that discovery he and his team developed all of the software, and nano hardware that was necessary to access the creases. Though other people in the science and technology groups were nodding excitedly, Molly was completely lost within seconds. She tried to pay attention but really had no idea what Dylan was talking about. She decided that she would hold onto the fact that HIS had declared only a few minutes ago that they had created a time machine and that apparently they had not yet tried to send a human through their machine. Other than that she was hopelessly lost as the presentation became more and more technical. After what seemed like an hour her ears perked up when she heard Dylan say to the crowd, "OK, I can see the glazed over look that some of you have on your faces so I suggest that we take a break. We will not be answering questions at this point either so forget about that. Find a restroom, get something to drink and stretch your legs a bit. We'll resume here in about fifteen minutes."

The conversations at the drink tables were loud and excited. Molly wished that she had a credit for every time she heard the words, "Can you believe this?" or "Do you think this can be for real?" She had asked herself those same questions several times already this morning. At other conferences and meetings she had been to, there were always several people who came back to the meeting late from break time. This morning, not one single person was late coming back from break. In fact everyone was back in their seats after just ten minutes instead of the allotted fifteen. Everyone was anxious to hear and see what would come next.

Dylan, Reid, Dr. Ormond and Dr. Lamacelli entered the room and walked to the stage. As they climbed up onto the dais the room got as quiet as a tomb. No one wanted to miss a single word. Dylan walked to the front of the stage and said, "Wow. I guess I really know how to quiet a crowd down huh? You'd think that I had told everyone that we had invented a time machine or something right?"

Everyone laughed politely and then Dylan was speaking again. "We're going to get into some of the technical and scientific specifics now so bear with us. Most of the info will be released to you later on in printed form or sent to your allcomms but for now Dr. Ormond and Dr. Lamacelli will tell us all how in the world they pulled this off. I was there so I already know all of this, but I want you to hear it in their own words because they and the other professionals who work with them are all really incredible people to work with and this whole thing is nothing less than a miracle of the highest order."

Molly thought again that even though this would be a world changing invention, it was still not a miracle of the highest order. Jesus' birth, His resurrection from the dead and God's incredible plan of salvation; now those were miracles. But she knew what Dylan meant so she held her tongue and remained silent.

Dr. Ormond spoke first, something about the gadget that did such and such and the theory about bending time and melding space into it and blah, blah, blah.

Molly wanted to be interested in what she was hearing but found her mind wandering in several different directions. This part of the talk was just too technically involved and she had no clue what Dr. Ormond was describing. Finally after about forty five minutes she realized that everyone in the room except for her was clapping. She glanced up at the stage and saw that Dr. Ormond had finished speaking and was heading back to her seat. Dylan Quick was nowhere to be seen and Reid Corder was up and talking again. Molly realized that he was announcing that it would now be Dr. Lamacelli's turn to talk. She applauded politely like everyone else but as Dr. Lamacelli walked up to the front of the stage, Molly knew that she just could not sit through another talk of forty five minutes, or possibly longer, of the kind of technical jargon that she knew was coming. She got out of her seat, scooted out toward the isle near the wall and headed back to the drink tables. She found her favorite soft drink, took a long swig and then leaned back against the wall with her eyes closed. For about the thousandth time she thought, "What am I doing here? I don't belong here. I am so far out of my comfort zone. I can understand the people over there in the technology and science groups understanding what is being described here but it even looks as if most people in the history and media groups understand this stuff too. How is that possible? I am really like a fish out of water here."

As Molly was deep in her thoughts, a voice came from just in front of her and a little to her left.

"Pretty boring huh? Looks like you would rather watch paint dry than to listen to this stuff right?"

Molly smiled. The voice was low and gentle and all she wanted to do was to keep leaning against the wall and maybe listen to this soothing voice coming from someone who was also most likely the only other person in the room who was as lost in the topics at hand as she was. However she knew that it was impolite to ignore someone who was talking to you so she smiled a little more, and slowly opened her eyes. She had planned on responding to whoever this nice sounding man was but all she could say was, "Oh! Oh no!"

Standing in front of her was Dylan Quick. He smiled warmly at her and said, "I came over here to see if you still had a pulse or if we had killed you with boredom. You look a little out of it."

In the background Molly could hear Dr. Lamacelli as he droned on. He was saying something about nano bits, or nano bots or maybe it was nano lots. She couldn't really tell. All she could do at the moment was stare straight into the eyes of Dylan Quick. She wanted to stay there forever. But she knew that she had been busted. She thought he might ask her to leave.

How could anyone be bored by being present when the most amazing invention since the wheel or the soft taco had just been announced.

She jolted upright away from the wall. "Oh, I am so sorry. I, I, I really didn't get bored, I just sort of don't understand anything they are saying. I am so sorry."

He continued smiling at her for a few seconds but when he didn't say anything she held her soft drink out to him and said, "I should probably leave now. Do you want this back?"

She cringed at what she had just said. "Are you kidding me?" she asked herself. "I'm face to face with one of the smartest people on planet Earth who also happens to be one of the wealthiest people on the planet and he is obviously one of the most handsome men I have ever met in my life and oh, by the way, he is single. And what do I say to him? I ask him if he wants my soft drink back. AGGGHHH."

While Molly was thinking these thoughts to herself, Dylan was chuckling. Not an unkind chuckle, just the kind you use when something amuses you but you can't laugh too loudly. He was also thinking thoughts to himself as he read her name badge. "Molly. Molly Mahan. Has a nice ring to it and she's really pretty. Not the drop dead beautiful kind that usually throw themselves at me when introduced. Just down to earth, everyday pretty."

He held out his hand and said, "Hi I'm Dylan. And I think we can afford to allow you to keep the soda. HIS didn't have as great a year last year financially as some we've had in the past, but I think we are a long way off from having to recycle used soft drinks."

Molly relaxed and introduced herself properly. They made small talk for a few minutes and she apologized about a dozen more times until finally Dylan said, "Look, if you apologize even one more time, I really am going to have to take that soda away from you."

Molly laughed and said, "OK, sorry."

When she realized that she had apologized again, her eyes opened wide and she covered her mouth with her hand. Dylan laughed again. He reached out and playfully took the soda from her hand. He gave her a playful look and said, "Look, I warned you. I clearly explained the consequences to you, now you'll just have to be thirsty the rest of the day."

They each laughed again but stopped abruptly as they both became aware that somebody was calling Dylan's name. They turned and looked toward the other side of the room where the dais was set up. Every single person had turned in their chairs and were staring back at them. Dr. Lamacelli had apparently finished his talk and had returned to his seat. Dylan held up his hands in a shrug.

"Well," Reid said with dripping sarcasm. "I know that we have only been talking about the invention of the world's first time machine, and I have no doubt that your conversation is so very much more important than that. But if you have a few minutes the rest of us would all like to continue with the presentation. That is if you can break yourself away from Miss, eh . . . Miss?"

"Mahan. Molly Mahan." Dylan said.

Reid continued and said with a healthy dose of more scorn and sarcasm, "Yes, of course, Ms. Mahan."

As he spoke Reid looked at Molly with a stare that might stop a charging Rhinoceros cold in its tracks.

Dylan quickly covered the distance from where he and Molly stood and the stage. He bounded up onto it and said to the group.

"I'm really sorry. That was rude, and entirely my fault. I cornered Ms. Mahan with a few questions about her work and kept her from listening to Dr. Lamacelli describe his project, even though she seems to be quite interested in it. I apologize again to Dr. Lamacelli, Ms. Mahan and everyone else here today. My bad. But now let's move on and I think you will agree that what's next is going to be really exciting."

For the next hour Dylan wowed the crowd by telling them that when he had used the word volunteer earlier, he really meant what he said. HIS was going to offer to a few chosen volunteers the opportunity to work with the HIS team for the next month or so as they got ready to attempt the first human use of the creases discovered by Dr. Lamacelli. All but a handful of people in the room put their hands up to volunteer but again, Molly was one of those who did not raise her hand. Dylan announced that they would be choosing volunteers later. He went on to explain a little more about GLASS, what it could do and what it could not do; what it was and what it was not.

He spent a lot of time explaining how it came to be. It seems that once Dylan had formulated the initial idea, the next step had been to go out and locate the best experts they could find to be hired by HIS to work on the project. HIS had hired the best scientists on Earth in a long list of technical fields. The list was impressive and included areas of expertise such as astronomy, biology, synthetic drip mathematics, nuclear cone splicing, both quantum and nano physics, artificial intelligence, geography, internal medicine, history and even theorists in fields that were really not accepted areas of science at all. These ancillary fields of study included space time travel, the theory of de-relativity, gravitational exceptionality, inner earth reverse splicing as well as geo-spatial swarms and secondary mass dwellings. Molly understood what only a few of those fields of study and research were actually about. But she did have to admit that the lists were impressive.

Next Dylan explained a little bit more about how Dr. Lamacelli came up with his theory regarding creases in space. According to Dylan, once the team had figured out how to identify some of the creases that existed in space, it was only a short leap to connect them in some way to similar creases in time. Once again, Molly told herself that she was in way over her head. She realized that no matter how many different ways someone might try to explain to her how there could be actual creases in either time or space, she was never going to be able to understand it. The closest she came to any sort of understanding of these topics was when Dylan used the word pathways instead of creases while he was explaining. She could almost picture some sort of tunnel or path that someone could travel on or travel through. She knew that it was much more complex than that, but those mind pictures helped her understand that traveling through time and space might be possible using a path or roadway of some sort. At the very least she understood that these people here at HIS believed it to be possible.

Dylan then explained the tremendous amount of power that it took to make this time machine or GLASS or whatever it was work. He told the crowd that the very first time they tried to use it they had to shut the entire campus down for almost a week because using the machines needed to power GLASS had caused a power outage not only on the campus, but for a half mile radius around the campus. This had caused a huge delay because HIS had then been forced to build their own power grid giving the campus a differential of electric power that was rated at about six or seven times the amount of power that they had previously had. Following that they had rebuilt or added to their amount of power twice more because they still needed more and more power for GLASS to operate. He explained that to this day, power, not monetary issues, was their number one concern. They thought that GLASS was safe, they just were not sure how to get enough juice into the system to make it work. In fact, their next trial run would require so much power that they might not be able to use GLASS again for perhaps another year or more. That was one of the reasons that the invitations had gone out to all of these guests. The guest invitees could witness GLASS at work and relay that info to the general public in case they were not able to duplicate the trial for a long time.

Dylan next explained the steps they took to begin actual trial runs. The first trials did not go well and were in fact complete failures. But with each failure they gained a tremendous amount of information and each trial brought them closer and closer to success.

The first seven trials were officially listed in the failure category but with trial number eight, they were able to send a simple object back in time successfully. At least they thought it was a success. The object was never able to be retrieved back at the HIS labs. The employees all still laughed about what people in the year fifteen hundred would have thought of a ping pong ball suddenly appearing in their midst. The GLASS team had chosen a ping pong ball because of its size and weight. During the next few trials they had used a twenty five pound free weight that had been borrowed from the silver recreational building. The weight had exploded in dramatic fashion causing extensive damage to GLASS and the lab. The team had also attempted to use a three foot long wooden plank, a trumpet and a vase full of flowers. Those objects, along with a bicycle, an old hardback dictionary and the desk chair from the office of Reid Corder (donated without his knowledge of course) were now on a list of objects lost during the experimentation stages of the failed trials.

The ping pong ball was not on that list because the team had evidence that they had in fact sent the ball back in time. No one said much about the fact that they never did get the ball back, but trial number eight was categorized as a success. As the number of trials increased, so too did the confidence of everyone involved except for the employees in the accounting office who nearly had daily heart failure while trying to find ways to pay for what they called "that madness" that had taken over the rose building where the GLASS lab was located. Finally, just a year and a half ago, GLASS was able to send and bring back an object. The object used during that trial was a small plastic replica of the statue of liberty. Ten minutes after the statue arrived back in the lab, it melted down into a puddle of molten plastic and then disappeared altogether. The team could have cared less about the final result of the statue. They celebrated the fact that they had done what they set out to. They all believed that they would figure out what went wrong at the very end later.

Since that time the team had tried to send objects back that could possibly record their efforts. They sent comms, old fashioned cameras, recorders, and even a pencil and paper in the hopes that someone back in the other time might write something down and send it back.

All of those efforts failed. But the team continued to learn from both their mistakes as well as their successes. Ten months ago the team decided that the improvements they had made to GLASS made it ready for a living being. Several were sent through and retrieved. The first living being that was sent back and retrieved was a worm, appropriately named, Worm. The second living being was a mouse named Bud, the third was a cat named Chaser and the fourth animal was a Beagle named Sonyador. The most recent test sent back two large animals together. They were a Golden Retriever named Ruby and a Labrador Retriever named Holly. All of those six animals had been brought back successfully unharmed. Worm and Bud were now deceased but were enshrined in the HIS hall of fame in glass display cases. Chaser was pretty old now and never chased anything these days. She lived comfortably in celebrity fashion in the green building. Sonyador had been adopted by a local orphanage and she was loved by all of the children who lived there. Ruby had also been adopted. One of the HIS employees and her family had taken her in as a family member and she lived now at their house about fifteen miles from the HIS campus. Holly had arrived on campus one day about two years ago as a stray. Employees in the green building had adopted her and she lived in quiet royalty now in that building. Chaser and Holly never really did get along with one another but now in their old age they had both seemed to mellow a bit and each of them seemed to understand that the two of them were in a very special club. A club which at this time contained just the two of them as well as both Sonyador and Ruby as members. They were the only four living members of the "I Am A Time Traveler" club.

Dylan told the group that the time had come to attempt the sending of a human back into time and that one of them would soon be involved with the next startling step that would add more members into the time traveler club. It was the intention of HIS to send humans through the GLASS to join Chaser, Sonyador, Ruby and Holly as certified club members.

Chapter 9

Dylan called for a lunch break and as he did, Molly heard and saw tables of food being brought into the room. Lunch was not a huge deal, just sandwiches and salads but she was quite content with any kind of free meal. As she stood in line to grab her boxed lunch she became aware of Garth standing behind her. She turned to him and asked, "What do you think?"

Garth smiled a mischievous smile and replied, "I think you have a new boyfriend."

Molly tried to play the shocked/surprised card and said, "What? What are you talking about? That is not what I was asking you about."

"Oh c'mon. You know very well what, or should I say who, I'm talking about."

Molly gave him a questioning look that was supposed to say I have no idea what you mean but Garth cut her off before she could say anything.

"I saw you earlier over there all cuddled up with Dylan. Can't say I blame you though. He has more money than several third world countries added together. He's a pretty nice guy and I believe that most women would find him easy to look at. Am I right?"

"You sir are a chauvinist and you most certainly are not right. I don't even know the man. He and I were just getting drinks at the same time and that is all there is to it."

"If you say so," Garth said with a smirk.

"I do say so. And mind your own business."

Molly tried to sound mad but the truth was that she just could not find it in her to be mad with Garth. He was too likeable. She was embarrassed maybe, but not mad.

Lunch flew by and suddenly they were being called back to their seats. Molly noticed immediately that Dylan as not on the dais. She was surprised to find that she felt a little disappointed but then shrugged that off and thought that she understood perfectly that a man like that must have a million and one things to attend to. She tried to concentrate on the proceedings at hand. Reid Corder was getting ready to address the group once again.

"Well, now that we have the boring stuff out of the way like, oh I don't know, the invention of time travel ..." he paused as he let laughter ripple throughout the group and then continued. "We can get down to some really exciting stuff. Earlier we heard Dylan explain that we are ready to go live with human transport through time by way of our GLASS system. But what he didn't tell you was that we think we have a way for at least one of you to travel with us."

The crowd exploded in a frenzy of noise as people yelled, called out to Reid, to each other, or tried to talk over each other. Corder let the excitement die down and then said, "Remember we said earlier that we would be giving each of you an opportunity to volunteer for something? Well now's your chance."

After the crowd settled down, at least enough for him to be heard by everyone, he explained that each of the four groups, media, history, technology and science, could elect three people from among themselves to represent their group. From those three people, one would be selected to be a finalist for a chance to travel through time. Finally, from among those four finalists, one from each of the four groups, one volunteer would be selected to go through time on the next GLASS run.

Again the room exploded in excitement as almost everyone tried to talk at the same time. Reid explained that each group would now meet by themselves to elect three people to represent their group. As he finished speaking, Douglas appeared, seemingly out of thin air, in the aisle next to the media group. He explained that he would take them to a nearby room where they could begin the discussion about their group selections. He lead the whole group out of the meeting room and down the hall just a short distance and then stopped in the hallway. "Here we are," he announced as he motioned for everyone to enter a room on the left hand side of the hallway. The room was plenty big enough for the entire media group and there were chairs for everyone. However, no one chose to sit except for Molly. She sat off to one side of the room while everyone else talked and no one listened. Each person in the room tried to explain in their loudest voice why they believed that they should be chosen to be one of the volunteers. Molly was both amused and horrified at the sight of each of these professionals making fools of themselves She suddenly realized that Douglas had appeared by her side.

"Not interested?" he asked. Molly explained that she was not interested at all and that she also was most likely the least qualified person in the entire building to become a time traveler. She would be content with reporting on the whole affair and would be fine with whoever the group selected. Douglas smiled but said nothing. Suddenly Molly became aware that another person in the group was looking at her curiously. As she caught Molly's eye, she walked over to where Molly sat. A few minutes earlier Douglas had explained the voting rules. It seems that one of the rules was that each person in the group would get to cast two votes if they wanted or they could just simply cast one vote.

"Hi," the other group member said. "I'm Katy. Katy Counsel. I work for one of the comm media giants out of Dallas Texas."

Molly stood up and introduced herself. Katy Counsel continued. "Looks like you're pretty bored with all this. Don't you want to be the volunteer to be included on the next GLASS run? Sure looks like everyone else would give their right arm to go."

When Molly explained that she did not really want to go on the GLASS run, Katy smiled and said to Molly, "Boy do I have a proposition for you."

Katy explained that the group was going to have to vote on three members of the group soon. She told Molly that everyone in the room was, no doubt, going to vote only for themselves. That meant that everyone would have one vote each and everyone would be tied with everyone else. However, the rules allowed for each group member to vote for up to two people. Katy thought that no one would do that and use only one vote to vote for themselves.

"Yeah I guess you're right," Molly said. "Sure looks like that is exactly what is about to happen."

Katy lowered her voice and said in a whisper. "Yep I think so. Unless of course you cast a vote for me and I vote for you and then we both vote for ourselves." Molly looked dumbfounded for a second and said, "Well I can vote for you if you want me to, no problem. But why in the world would I want you to vote for me when I don't want to be included?"

"Because we need to elect three people out of this group. You and I will end up being two of those people. You can then express your wish to bow politely out of the contest and that will just leave me and one other person. I think I will have a pretty good chance at that point if it is going to come down to me and one other clown from this group. Deal?"

Before Molly could answer Douglas was calling the group to order. He got everyone under control and then called for the vote. Molly had a funny feeling about this arrangement with Katy. She couldn't help feeling that she was rushing into this a bit fast but Katy was looking at her and Katy seemed to really want to go on the next GLASS run. "Besides," Molly thought. "Why should I care who goes or who doesn't. Just as long as it isn't me."

When the voting began Molly voted just as Katy had suggested. Katy's plan worked like a charm and both she and Molly were elected to be among the three volunteers from the media group.

Douglas had sat in a corner monitoring the proceedings as the group voted but as the voting wound down he called the group back to order.

"I've got the vote tally right here and I think this group has a great trio to represent the world's media. I think that you have done a terrific job of electing good representatives. Our volunteers from the media group will be Katy Counsel, Garth Perry and Molly Mahan. Congrats to each of you. Now, let's get back to the meeting room. I've been on my allcomm with both Reid and Dylan and it seems that we might be behind the other groups by a minute or two. No worries, but let's get back over there quickly and rejoin the others."

As they filed back into the meeting room Reid was already up on the stage and speaking to the other groups. As he saw them enter the room he stopped short and addressed them sarcastically, "Well, if it isn't our long lost sheep of the media group. Please, take a seat and join those of us who managed to make it back on time."

Everyone in the group found their seats while scowling at Reid. When they were all seated he continued speaking.

"Now. Each group has selected three representatives right? OK then. From among these twelve people we will find a way to end up with just one person. That person will have the opportunity to go on the next GLASS run. This volunteer will be able to report on all that is occurring here before, during and after the GLASS run in a personal and completely subjective manner. His or her report will not be as an employee of HIS but as someone who will be entirely free to see things their own way. Through their eyes everyone will see this project for what it is, a gift to the world of incalculable value."

Molly couldn't help but roll her eyes. She looked around and saw that even Dylan Quick had a look on his face that said he thought Reid was laying it on a little thick.

Dylan jumped up and said, "Wow Reid. That was just great. No pressure on our volunteers now huh?" Everyone laughed and Dylan went on to introduce the three volunteers from each group. When all twelve had been identified and introduced, Dylan told everyone that it was now time to try to narrow the twelve people down to just one. He started off by reminding everyone of the regulations that HIS had laid out in the letter of invitation.

"I am certain that all of you read that fifteen page invitation thoroughly from front to back. Am I right?" Everyone in the room laughed politely because everyone knew that almost no one had read the whole thing. Most of the invitees had only read far enough into it to understand that they were being invited to an extraordinary event and had not read a word further than that.

"I know," he continued. "It was really exciting stuff and most of you came just for the free food, right Garth?" Everyone laughed at Garth's expense but he played right along, just as Dylan knew he would.

"That is exactly right Dylan. But the next time you have a party like this one, you are going to have to find someone else to bake a cobbler for you."

Dylan looked a little confused and said, "Oh really? And why is that?"

"Because that stuff was great. I'm going to find whoever made that and marry her later today!"

Dylan let the laughter die down on it's own and then addressed the invitees again. "Seriously, included in that invitation letter there were a few pages of relevant facts and figures. There was also a page about regulations and qualifications for the person who would end up going on the next GLASS run with us. We have also mentioned a few of those qualifications today during our morning sessions. I'm going to release the rest of you so that you can get back to your lives. For those of you in the media group we have a room set up so that you can run over there and file your reports. I understand that you will want to do that as soon as you can. In just a minute you will go with the young lady standing in the back of the room."

Everyone turned and looked toward the rear of the meeting room. There they saw a young woman standing next to the exit door. She had light brown hair and was wearing a green and yellow plaid skirt. She smiled in a friendly manner and waved to the crowd.

"She will escort you to that room and give you any assistance you may need with comms of any type you need in order to file your reports. If you will just wait until we are done here she will guide you out to --"

Before Dylan could finish speaking the entire media group, minus the three chosen volunteers from that group, jumped up in unison and made a mad dash for the back of the room. Working in the media field they naturally all wanted to be the first person to file a report on exactly what was happening here at HIS. None of them wanted to be "scooped" by any of the others.

Once the media folks had left the room and order was restored Dylan continued, "Wow, those media types seemed really anxious to leave. Hope it wasn't something I said." The members of the remaining three groups laughed as Dylan went on. "Well we will just make sure that we have their comform chairs sent to them and we will get on with things here. Everyone else here except for our twelve volunteers is free to leave at this time as well. Just make sure you stay out of the way of any of those media types or you might get trampled to death. You are also welcome to stay here as long as you wish today. I know that many of you in our history, technology and science groups are, like most of us here at HIS, just naturally curious about almost anything. We have another room set up in the next building over, that's the gold building. In that room we have exhibits set up that will explain a lot of the science and technical specs that went into creating GLASS. We also have someone waiting in that room for you who will explain all about how our ideas became theories and how those theories became proven fact and how those facts were finally turned into physical reality. You will be able to see how we can actually do exactly what we say we can do. Later in the day, as I promised earlier, you will get a brief tour through the lab and you will actually get a chance to see GLASS for yourselves. Oh, and your chairs will be sent to you as well. I think they should get to you in a week or so. Thank you so much for coming today.

Now, for the remaining twelve volunteers, if you would be so kind as to follow me, we will begin our task of whittling the group of twelve people down to just one."

Chapter 10

Dylan lead the group of twelve volunteers down a long hallway to another smaller room. As they entered the room Molly could see that next to the doorway was a small plaque that said CONFERENCE ROOM D. There were several people already seated at a table in the room. She recognized Reid Corder, Andrew Lamacelli and Grace Ormond but not the others. As soon as they were all seated Dylan began with the introductions of the HIS team. He began with four people who had entered the room behind Molly. They were the four group assistants from the earlier meeting. She recognized Douglas of course and as she caught his eye he gave her a thumbs up sign. Dylan introduced the four group assistants and then went on to introduce the other HIS employees in the room. They were Rachel Parks, Director of Personnel for HIS, Dane Howe, a Physician who headed up the medical team here at HIS, Dr. Hunter Germain, the resident Historian at HIS and Dr. Jarrett Kove who was introduced as some sort of technical support wizard. Dylan also introduced the twelve volunteers. He then explained that the first order of business was to narrow down the twelve volunteers until only one was left. Molly felt relieved because she thought this would be easy. All she had to do was to tell the group that she no longer wanted to be included and then mention that she thought that Katy Counsel would be a good candidate to go on the GLASS run. But before she could say anything, Dylan jumped right in and told everyone that HIS Personnel Director, Rachel Parks would be facilitating this meeting.

Without missing a beat, Rachel started reading off the qualifications that would be needed for the person who would be going on the next run. She made sure that everyone understood that she was reading directly from the list of qualifications that had been sent to everyone in the invitation packet. Molly vaguely remembered reading through the list but she had to admit that she really had not spent much time on that part of the invite letter. She guessed correctly that none of the other invitees had either. Ten of the other volunteers looked very uneasy at the thought of possibly being disqualified. Garth looked like he could care less and Molly was very relaxed, knowing that she was going to remove her name from the list at the earliest possible moment.

Rachel Parks started off with a zinger of a qualification. The person selected would have to be single. In one moment she had eliminated six of the twelve volunteers. The six involved (one of whom was Katy from the media group) all protested loudly until Reid held his hand up. He read again from the list of qualifications and reminded each of the six that they had received the letter. He also reminded everyone that regardless of whether or not they had actually read the list, they had stated in writing that they had read it thoroughly and understood everything that they had read. He asked each of the six in turn if they recalled signing the statement and returning it to HIS along with their RSVP for today's product rollout. When all of them admitted that they had signed the statement he produced copies of their signed documents and asked them each to verify their signatures. All six did so.

Molly felt like she had been knocked out. She was stunned by what had just occurred over the last few minutes. Her first thought was, "Wait. What just happened?" But her second thought was that all would be well. Garth was still in the group of the six remaining volunteers. He was well known to Dylan Quick and many of the others here and on top of that, he represented the media group. He was probably a shoo-in to get the nomination to go on the run. She felt him looking over at her and when she glanced back she saw him wink at her. She felt relief like she had never felt before. All would be well. Garth had just signaled to her that he was going to go on the run and that she had nothing to worry about. She relaxed both inwardly and outwardly and then sighed a long, extremely loud exhale. Everyone stopped and looked at her. Dylan looked concerned and said, "Molly? Are you OK?"

"Yes. I'm eh, I'm fine. Sorry about that."

The six people who had just been eliminated left the room and a moment later Rachel Parks continued the meeting. She explained to the group that whoever was selected, along with one extra back up person, would have to remain here at HIS for at least one month and possibly up to two months. They would have to train for the GLASS run and get up to speed with the other team members here at HIS. There were several apartments on campus over in the silver building. These were normally used to house visiting dignitaries or visiting scientists but for now, they would house the volunteer who would be making the run and also house the back-up person as well. Of the six remaining people, three raised their hands almost immediately and explained why it would be impossible for them to remain here for that long period of time. There was one person from the history group who had a parent who was in ill health and was apparently the primary caregiver for that parent. Another of the three explained that only a month ago he had started his own Information Technology company and to remain away from his newly formed company for that length of time would most certainly be the end of that infant company. The third volunteer with her hand raised explained that she was to get married in just three weeks.

Molly felt another steep rise in her panic level but once again she looked over at Garth. He smiled at her and gave her a very slight subtle nod of his head and she knew again that all would be well.

"OK," she thought. "I should just go ahead and take myself out of the game in a minute or so. I've got to time it just right but I think that this should end up being fine. Garth is going to take this slot to go on the run and so if I stay just a bit longer I will be able to use this extra info in my next scroll. This really could be a win/win situation for me."

Rachel Parks told those three volunteers that HIS appreciated their interest in the GLASS project but they were excused to return to their lives outside of HIS. All three of them seemed disappointed but they also seemed to accept the fact that their outside commitments were higher up on their priority lists. Each of the three expressed their gratitude toward all of the HIS officials for being included and then left together.

Once those three volunteers had left the room, Rachel Parks stated the next qualification that the remaining volunteers needed to meet in order to go on the next GLASS run.

That qualification was medical health. She explained to the three of them that they would be required to partake in a thorough medical exam. Out of the corner of her eye she suddenly saw Garth slump ever so slightly in his chair as if all the wind had been taken out of him. Even before Ms. Parks had finished describing the medical exam to be taken, Garth raised his hand for her to stop and then cleared his throat.

"No need to continue my dear, I know where I stand on this issue. I would have very much loved to go on the next GLASS run, and I completely understand the requirement of the medical exam. In fact, I agree that there does need to be such an exam. It certainly makes sense that the people going on the GLASS run will need to be in top physical condition. After all, who really knows the strain on the human body just going through one or more of those Lamacelli Creases. And who knows what we might encounter once we have arrived at the site. The need for good physical conditioning at the designated site might be necessary. I hope you will forgive me when I use the word we for those who will be making the run, but I can see now that I will not be a part of this group. I had so hoped that I would be one of those going. But ... no, I won't be."

As everyone started to speak at once he held his hand up again.

"No. I will most certainly be with you in spirit, but I will most certainly not be with you in the flesh. Several months ago I was diagnosed with some difficulties in my heart. Seems as though one of the valves is not behaving as it should. This has caused some palpitations to occur. At first they just appeared every now and then. But over the last two months they have increased rapidly and now I experience these palpitations several times a day for long periods of time. Two weeks ago my Cardiologist told me that surgery is needed in order for me to avoid the heart attack that is lurking in my future. Just a few days ago I scheduled surgery to be done next Thursday morning."

The room was silent for a few seconds and then everyone began telling Garth how sorry they were and that they hoped all the best for him. Molly also expressed her sorrow and told him that she would be praying for him everyday. As the others continued to express their feelings with Garth, Molly suddenly had another thought. "Oh no. This means that I am one of the last two finalists. I'm going to either be the person to be scheduled to go on the run or I'm going to be the backup person. Either way, I don't want to be here, I don't deserve to be here and I need to tell everyone right now how I feel about it."

But once again before she could get the words out of her mouth, Garth began verbalizing his farewells to the rest of the group. As he shook Molly's hand and said good-bye, he also looked around at the other group members and said, "I know that Molly is going to do great! Just great!"

Molly was stunned and had no reply except to say, "Eh, thanks Garth. I just know that you are going to come out of surgery in terrific shape."

He smiled at her and walked through the doorway and out of the meeting room.

Reid Corder called the meeting back to order and Molly thought that she finally saw her chance to get out of the mess she was in. Before anyone else could speak, Molly blurted out a question. "Can I just say one thing about all of this?"

Reid looked a little annoyed and answered her quickly. "Yes of course you can, but would you mind holding on to that thought for later? We are running a bit behind schedule and we still have a lot to cover today. Now the first order of business right now is to decide which of you will be scheduled to make the next run and which of you will be the backup. Congratulations to you both, you are about to make history."

"But --" Molly said.

Reid continued speaking right over what Molly was trying to say. "I say that to both of you because the backup needs to be just as ready to go at a moment's notice as our number one person. Now if you will both stay right here, the rest of us are going to excuse ourselves for a little while. Our HR department has prepared dossiers on everyone who was invited today and we are going to discuss each of you in depth."

"But --" Molly tried again.

Once more Reid plowed straight ahead with what he was saying. "Though I don't anticipate that we will be discussing you in any derogatory manner, it seems best that you not be present. We'll be back as soon as we can. I've arranged for some refreshments to be brought in here in a few minutes and we will have some of our staff stay to keep you company while the rest of us are deliberating."

With that, Reid, Dylan and the rest of the HIS employees left meeting room D and headed off to meet in Reid's office which happened to be fairly close by.

Back in meeting room D, Molly quickly began to slide into a somewhat depressed state of mind. The other volunteer, a middle aged man from the technology group named Trevor, was very excited and was trying to talk to Molly about what a great opportunity this was and how thrilling it would be to go on the next run. Molly tried hard to be polite and to engage in the conversation but all she could think about were a million thoughts that seemed centered around three main themes.

1 - "How did this happen?"
2 - "What am I doing here?"
3 - "I hope that Garth will be OK and recover fully from his surgery so that I can strangle him with my bare hands."

While Molly and Trevor were talking, the HIS employees were down the hall deep in discussion about the all important step of deciding who the volunteer to go on the GLASS run would be and who the backup person would be.

At first almost everyone in the group seemed to favor Trevor to be the one to go on the run with Molly as backup. Reid had made it clear from the first few seconds of the discussion that Molly appeared to be, "One of those religious types," and therefore completely unqualified to be part of the project at all. If she must be a part of GLASS in any capacity, he insisted that she should be relegated to the back up position. Almost everyone agreed immediately and the vote was almost done in less than a minute. But at the last moment Dr. Lamacelli, of all people, spoke up and said, "Let's not be too hasty here. I myself am certainly no Christian, but there may be more here than meets the eye. My parents grew up in Italy before they came to the U.S. about sixty years ago. My mother was a strong believer and went to church every single week for as long as I can recall. Even though people who claim to be Christians are looked down upon today, that has not always been the case. There was a time when this country was the guardian of the Christian church and a large percentage of Americans were of the Christian faith."

Reid practically yelled across the table, "What's that got to do with anything? That is ancient history. That's like saying that most people on Earth centuries ago believed the world was flat. The world grew in knowledge and now we know that it is not flat. Most people used to believe that there was a God. OK, so what? The world has grown in knowledge some more and now we know that there is not a God. It's just as simple as that. There is no God and people who still believe that are just crazy. She shouldn't even have been invited here. She brings nothing to the table at all. GLASS is about science, not fantasy. Dylan, what do you say?"

Dylan felt all eyes on him and thought carefully about what his answer should be. After a few moments he finally said, "Well, she is pretty cute."

Everyone laughed and the tension fell away for just a minute.

"OK, OK," Reid said as the room settled down a bit. "Despite what our fearless leader thinks of Ms. Mahan's physical appearance, is there really any doubt that we should pick Trevor over Molly? I mean seriously?"

Everyone was quiet for a second or two and then Douglas spoke up. "You know, I have been studying these dossiers on each of them. It is obvious that Trevor brings a lot of tech savvy knowledge to the project. However we already have some of the best tech people on Earth working on this project. Do we really need another one?"

Reid answered, "Well at least he brings something to the table. What does this Molly person bring to the project that would be of any use to us at all?"

Douglas had his answer ready, "Well first of course is her media presence. Yes, admittedly it is a small, out of the mainstream scroll, but when the world hears that Molly Mahan has made the first GLASS run by a human, her scroll site is going to be front page news and her name will be known throughout the world."

That argument took Reid off balance for a moment and Douglas continued, "I also see in her dossier that her minor in college was history. She attended a small school by the name of West Virginia Wesleyan and graduated in the top fifty of her class. She majored in journalism and minored in history. She has authored and published two books about history topics. The first one was a book about the Roman empire and its influence socially as well as militarily on the world in the first and second centuries. Her next book seems to be about the impact of the founder of the Christian Church, Jesus Christ, on world rulers during that same time period. Oh and look here, she once wrote a three part biography series about, well would you look at this; it was written about the one and only Dr. Abigail Nicole. Anyone here ever heard of her? Hmmmm, imagine that?"

Again there was silence for a moment or two and then everybody started talking at once. The tide had turned in Molly's favor when one of the other group assistants spoke up. His name was Andrew Ball. He had been the assistant for the technology group earlier in the day and he too had been looking over the dossiers carefully. "As much as I would prefer to promote someone from the technology group, I think that I need to point this fact out to the group. I'm looking in Trevor's file here and I can see that he's had a bit of a boo boo in his past. Nothing really recent, but it says here that he was once charged with disorderly conduct in some sort of minor offense. It was back in his college days I believe and no doubt was just some sort of nonsense that college students get into all the time. No jail time served but still, this might be something that we want to stay away from."

Dylan practically jumped out of his seat. "Are you kidding me? We absolutely need to keep stuff like that out of here. We have always had a squeaky clean reputation and I don't think we want to mess around with something like that. I say we avoid that like the plague. How did he get in the mix anyway? I thought we vetted all of the people we invited long before the invitations went out. How did this happen?" As he said this last sentence he looked directly over at Rachel.

Rachel froze for a few moments and then finally managed to respond. "I, um, well we in HR did check all of them out of course. But there were so many of them that the last few we did, we sort of cut a few corners. No big deal, just to save some time as we were getting closer to the date the invitations were going to be sent out. I, uh, guess he must have been one of those last few."

Once again silence ruled the room but this time the silence was so thick it could almost be cut with a knife. Dylan finally broke off his stare at Rachel and then broke the silence as well.

"Let's vote."

Reid stood up to speak, "No Dylan. We should never vote while we are in such an emotionally charged state. We are all a little frustrated by all of this. Let's just cool our jets and think things through and then vote later on."

Dylan let Reid finish and then said, "I appreciate what you are saying Reid, but I think we have enough info on both Trevor and Molly. Let's go ahead and vote. Right now!"

CHAPTER 11

In meeting room D, Molly was still trying to wrap her head around the events of the morning. She tried to eat some of the food that had been provided for Trevor and herself but found that she was not even the least bit hungry.

Next she tried to distract herself from her present situation by outlining in her head the article that she would write for her scroll site. She wondered if anyone would even believe it. She was after all, having a lot of difficulty believing it herself.

Molly could tell that it was apparent to Trevor that he was to be the chosen one and that he would be the volunteer invited to go on the next GLASS run. He chatted incessantly, even though he could tell that Molly's thoughts were elsewhere. Trevor talked about a wide range of topics. He droned on and on about his expertise in technology. He spoke about his ability to rub elbows with the most intelligent scientists working for HIS and how he could match up with them, step for step when it came to scientific breakthroughs. He claimed to have intricate knowledge of time travel theories and stated that his theories could help some of the GLASS project technicians understand their mission a little more clearly. Trevor even floated the idea that he might be a good candidate to head up the GLASS project and, in effect, become Dylan Quick's right hand man.

Molly of course was thinking of other things. At first she tried hard to listen to Trevor's ideas. She really was interested in trying to be polite to him and she actually did want to understand what he was trying to say. However as his ideas strayed increasingly away from reality, she found her thoughts drifting farther and farther away from what he was saying.

Molly soon found herself concentrating less on what Trevor was saying and more and more on thoughts regarding her particular situation. Most of those thoughts were centered on how she could make sure that she would be the backup. Again she wondered how she had managed to get herself this deep into a hole of her own digging. How in the world had it ever come to this point? As the morning wore on she dreamed up scheme after scheme that might assist her in getting out of the mess she was in.

She thought she might be able to tell the group that she was a leper. Or that she was a spy from some foreign nation and was really here to steal the secrets of the GLASS project. At one point she actually thought about telling the group that she was Mary Mahan, Molly's evil twin, here on an undercover mission to undermine the GLASS project by selling all of its deepest secrets to a national tabloid. Things got so strange that during one very bizarre moment she thought of telling the whole group that she was, in reality, working for the CIA and was under direct orders from the President of the United States to shut the entire project down due to national security issues. It was about at that point that she found herself admitting to herself that perhaps the ideas that Trevor was coming up with were not so weird and outlandish after all. The ideas and scenarios that she had thought up were just as strange and off base as his.

As she schemed she also prayed but the prayers that she directed at God were prayers that He was most likely getting a kick out of, instead of taking seriously. She prayed, "God, can you give me pneumonia? Like really quickly?"

Another prayer was, "OK God let's make a deal. If you get me out of this I promise I will go on a date with that guy my mom wants me to go out with. You know that guy, what's his name? The guy with just the one top tooth and maybe five or six left on the bottom? Yea that guy. I'll do it. I'll do anything. Just get me out of here!"

Molly waited anxiously for a few seconds and tried to tune her senses to some sort of response from God while Trevor droned on in the background. When God continued to be silent, Molly spoke to Him again, but this time with an edge of frustration. "Father I'm really trying to understand what is going on here and what my place in all of this might be. And I do realize that silence is a form of communication that you choose to use at certain times. But you have to know that for those of us down here, the silence is extremely frustrating. I'm not trying to be a jerk about this and I am certainly not trying to second guess you about anything. But the silence not only frustrates me, it also makes me scared and I'm scared right now. Plus I don't understand. I don't understand why I'm here, I don't understand about time travel, I don't understand what you have planned for me here or anything else. I am totally lost and I feel like I'm on my own because I have not heard from you about what it is you want me to do or say. On top of all of that I am confused about almost everything that is going on here today, starting with this Dylan guy. He is so far out of my league. But the way I ran into him and talked to him over by the food table earlier, well that was just a weird moment. What is going on with that? Was that your doing? If so that probably scares me and confuses me more than just about anything else going on around here today. I would really like to hear from you about all of this. I feel like I'm in the center of a tornado with events swirling all around me. I'm frustrated, confused and scared because I can control literally none of these events."

Immediately Molly felt the presence of God flow through and around her and she knew at once that what she had just said to God was the whole point. She recognized that she needed to stop trying to control events and simply allow God to take over.

Just as Molly finished praying, Dylan walked into meeting room D with the rest of the team following close behind. Molly said another quick prayer, "OK God, please just get me out of here. I have always heard that you answer every prayer. Well now is the time. Please let Dylan say anything other than that I am their number one choice for the GLASS run."

Dylan looked solemnly around the room and then said, "Molly is our number one choice for the GLASS run."

Molly slumped in her chair, shot her eyes skyward and then silently said to God, "Oh c'mon! Really?"

CHAPTER 12

The team talked together for an hour or so. Trevor and Molly were asked for a list of items that they needed from their apartments. Dylan told them that HIS would take care of all the necessary arrangements for them both to live on the HIS campus until the next GLASS run could be completed. Trevor and Molly expressed concern about that and asked if they were in fact prisoners of HIS. Dylan assured them that they were not. He explained that there were security matters as well as privacy matters to consider but in no way were they to see themselves as prisoners. He reminded them that the other members of the media group had left hours ago and that by now what HIS was claiming to do with its GLASS project was worldwide news. He assured them that if they were to leave the campus now they would not have even one minute of privacy for the next few months. Molly wondered again for the millionth time how she had gotten herself into this mess. She rolled her eyes skyward and spoke to God silently once again. "I know that I am supposed to thank you for everything Father so thanks, I guess. This is just absolutely terrific."

Immediately she was apologetic for the sarcastic tone she had just used with her creator. She was about to continue her prayer when she realized that Dylan was addressing the whole group again.

"OK gang, we've been at this for quite a while now. Let's go ahead and take another break. Then we'll get back together again later this evening. We have a lot to do but I am so excited about this and I know that you all are as well. I'll catch up with you all later. I'm heading down to my office. UNC played Clemson last night and I didn't get a chance to watch the game. I'm going to go check it out on my allcomm."

With that he left and the others drifted off to various parts of the complex. Molly found herself in the cafeteria. After she got her meal she looked around and saw Dr. Ormond at a table off to the side. No one else was at that table so Molly took a chance and wandered in that direction. She stood next to the table that Dr. Ormond was seated at, hesitated for just a second or two and then sat down across from Dr. Grace Ormond.

"I hope I'm not disturbing you. I really don't know many of the people who work here yet so I thought I would come over. If that's OK with you?"

"Oh you most certainly are not disturbing me. Please sit down. We can get to know each other a bit better. Now why don't you start by telling me about your home life. You know, like where you are from and --"

Grace Ormond stopped speaking in mid sentence as she noticed Molly had become unusually quiet and still. Molly's head was bowed slightly and inclined downward toward her food. Dr. Ormond could see Molly's lips moving slightly.

After a few moments Molly looked back up at Dr. Ormond and smiled, "I'm sorry. What were you saying?"

"Um, eh, were you, eh, just talking to your food?"

"What?"

"Well I saw you with your head bent down to your food and I thought I saw your lips moving a little. Do you often talk to your food that way?"

Molly laughed, "Oh my no. I wasn't talking to the food. I was talking to God."

Dr. Ormond looked blankly at Molly for a minute and then asked, "Why?"

"Well He provides everything for us. Even if we are not aware of it sometimes, He provides for us. For example, He gives me the ability to work. That allows me to earn money, and with that money I am able to purchase food. So therefore God has given me this food and I was just thanking him for that."

Dr. Ormond just sat and stared at Molly for a long moment and then quietly said, "Extraordinary. How very extraordinary."

Neither said any more about it for the remainder of their lunch time. After what seemed just a few short minutes, Rachel Parks suddenly appeared next to their table. She informed them that the group was getting ready to get together again and that they should all go down to Dylan's office and meet there. Molly did not know where Dylan's office was located but Dr. Ormond did so they walked together. Along the way, Dr. Ormond asked Molly if God ever responded and spoke back to her. Molly answered in the affirmative, that God did indeed answer her. She explained that God never spoke in words like humans used but rather spoke to her through her daily Bible reading, scenes of nature, conversations with other Christians, certain specific circumstances that Molly found herself in (like right now) and a variety of other methods of communication. She told Dr. Ormond that it was rather difficult to explain, but yes, God always responded in some way. Molly went one step further and said that there were times when God's voice could be barely sensed, just a hint of a whisper coming through her thoughts. Some Christians described this as just a subtle, still, small voice reaching through from the far corners of their consciousness.

Dr. Ormond looked at Molly as if Molly had just sprouted wings. That look told Molly that Dr. Ormond thought that she must be living entirely in some other alternate universe. Molly sighed inwardly. She had seen that look many times when she had tried to tell people about God.

At that point they both got very quiet, each intent on their own thoughts as they approached Dylan's office. Just as they reached the door to the office Dr. Ormond looked at Molly and said, "Extraordinary. Absolutely extraordinary."

They were the last of the group to arrive. The group included, Dylan, Reid, Dr. Ormond, Dr. Lamacelli, Hunter Germain, Trevor and herself. Molly thought she would try to break the ice a little bit and said to Dylan, "So how was the game, did your team win?"

"Oh I only got to watch the first half. I didn't have time to watch the whole game. I'll finish watching later. Clemson was up thirty eight to thirty four but their leading scorer is in foul trouble so I'm hopeful the Tar Heels will pull this out."

Molly looked at him with a quizzical look and asked, "What's a Tar Heel?"

Dylan stared at her as if she had just arrived from another planet. The look was similar to the one that Dr. Ormond had given her just a few minutes earlier. He started to respond to her question with a smart alec answer but thought better of it.

"I guess you're not from around here huh? It's kind of a long story but you see, way back in the day . . ."

Reid loudly and rudely cleared his throat and said in a huff. "Could we just get on with the issues at hand please?"

Dylan gave Reid a cold look but then turned and addressed the entire group, "Well I suppose Reid is right so I guess we should get back to it. Our next order of business today will be to discuss the target of our next GLASS run. Reid is going to facilitate this for us. Reid, go ahead."

"OK thanks Dylan. As was mentioned earlier, GLASS takes a tremendous amount of power to run. During our past runs we have managed to cause power failures almost every single time we've made a run. As the project got further along and got bigger and more powerful, it of course needed more and more power. Today there just does not exist enough power on Earth to do what we need to do in order to make these runs. However, the good news is that we put our minds to the task and we have figured out how to solve that problem. To put it simply we needed to discover or invent a new power supply. We did both of those things and there really is nothing simple about it at all. We won't take time right now to get into that, we'll discuss that later. I only mentioned it because even with our new power source, we will only have enough juice to make one GLASS run right now. Following this next run it will most likely be quite some time before we can make another. We estimate that after this next run it could be a full year or possibly even longer before we will be ready to make another run. And that brings us to our current discussion. It is absolutely crucial that we decide on the absolute best target, or location for the next run. In other words, we need to decide where we are going to go. Remember, we won't get a second chance for quite a long time.

Now, I have had our resident historian, Hunter Germain prepare a short list of possible targets for us. From that list, we must decide which location to target."

With that he gave a short nod to Hunter who was seated two seats down to Molly's right. Hunter took a second to organize several papers he had on the table before him and then began to address the group.

"As you can probably guess, there are literally thousands of places that we could choose to go visit. The trick is this, we need to pick a target location that will be worth the expense of the GLASS run as well as pick a place that will prove to the world that GLASS actually works. Having said that, there are still far too many places available to us, and we need to decide on just one. As Reid just said he has asked me to come up with a few possibilities. Each of these targets will immediately command worldwide attention. At the same time they will benefit the entire world by answering questions that people have had for years about these locations and the circumstances surrounding them. You will see what I mean in a moment when I present the list. All of these are world famous occurrences and each of them also has many questions regarding them. We know from history that they did indeed happen. What we don't know is exactly how they happened. History itself is only a fair record keeper. In all but the last few hundred years, there have been no actual recordings of historical occurrences. Today we have allcomms. Going back in time we know that there were things like cell phones, old time videos, movies and sound recordings. They are old fashioned to us but are really not what we would call ancient. Prior to that of course there were only written recordings and going back further than that, there were only verbal records. So we want to pick a time and a location that we can go back to visit and prove to the world that that particular occurrence in history really did happen and give the world the details of how it happened. We will do this by actually being there to witness the occurrence and by taking plenty of vid/comm and holo/comm recordings while we are there."

He stopped for a moment for a dramatic pause. Molly could tell that he was enjoying his moment in the sun and she couldn't blame him. The subject matter that they were discussing was, until today, only talked about in terms of Science Fiction. But these people, with herself included, were actually preparing to attempt it. Science Fiction was becoming reality and she was right in the middle of it. She said a quick prayer before Hunter could continue. "God is this you? Is this your doing? I hope so because this stuff is really blowing my mind and I understand only a very small portion of what we are talking about here. If this is no fluke, if you really do want me here, please let me know what you want me to do or say. I don't see how I can possibly help here because I hardly even know what this group is talking about. Show me how I can help these people see you in some way."

Hunter was passing out papers to each member of the group and speaking again. "Molly and Trevor, you should know that you are not late to this party. Everyone here is seeing this list for the first time. With the exception of me of course. Everyone please look it over carefully and then we will discuss each possible target in turn. They are in no particular order. I did that on purpose so that no one would feel like I had put them in the order of my priority list. So take just a minute to check these sites out."

The room was as quiet as a tomb. Molly read the target sites on the prepared list. She was surprised to see that there were only five.

The signing of the Declaration of Independence
Adolf Hitler's suicide
The signing of the Magna Carta
Napoleon's defeat at Waterloo
The first flight by the Wright Brothers

After about two minutes Hunter continued. "I know that all of you probably have a favorite time and place you would choose to visit if you could. We can of course discuss those possibilities in addition to these. This list is not set in stone and it is not all inclusive. I put this list together mainly to get us started although I think that each of these could be excellent targets that we could use for our purpose. Anyone want to jump in first?"

Reid was the first one to speak up. "Well right away I think I see my favorite. I vote right now for taking GLASS to witness the signing of the Declaration of Independence."

Dr. Ormond agreed almost immediately but Dr. lamacelli disagreed at almost the same time. When Reid asked him why he disagreed, he reminded everyone that they were all Americans and so they naturally thought that things that happened in America were the most important in the world. He reminded everyone that the rest of the world did not see things that way. He in turn was reminded by Dylan that Dr. Lamacelli himself was an American. Dr. Lamacelli replied that even though he was an American, he still thought of himself as Italian. Trevor voiced the opinion that the Declaration of Independence could be considered a world wide event due to the fact that the world had changed so dramatically after the United States had become an independent nation and soon after that, a world power.

The discussion shifted when Dr. Ormond asked why Hitler's suicide was on the list. Hunter explained that is was a world wide event and that there were many questions surrounding that event. Many people believed that Hitler had not actually killed himself but only pretended to do so. Dr. Ormond countered that argument by stating that even if that were true, it was not a world wide game changing event. She further stated that she could not see that it was important enough to use their one precious GLASS run to go to some musty, stinky old bunker.

After about a two hour discussion, Hunter could see that they were at a stalemate.

"Why don't we take a short break? You know, kind of stretch our legs a bit, maybe get some refreshments? We need to step away from this for a little while and clear our heads."

Everyone agreed that a break was needed. Molly stepped outside and headed immediately for the paved path that encircled the lake. As she walked she could hear footsteps coming up behind her. She moved over to the right side of the path to let the oncoming person pass her but the footsteps stopped right behind her. Her first thought was of safety but she could see right away that there were at least seven or eight other HIS employees walking at different places along the path ahead of her, all of whom could see her easily. It was also in the middle of the day, so her fear passed by almost immediately.

"Sorry. Didn't mean to startle you," Dylan's voice came to her over her left shoulder. She turned to face him as he continued talking. "Just thought you might like some company."

"Oh sure," she said. "That would be great."

They strolled in silence for a few seconds and then Dylan said, "I don't know about you but I was really glad Hunter called for a break when he did. That was some really deep stuff we were into back there. Pretty big difference between Ben Franklin and Adolf Hitler huh?"

Molly chuckled, "Yeah, guess so. I was thinking that maybe we should go with something like the first flight made by the Wright brothers. That would be pretty cool I think."

"Yeah maybe we should. That's not a bad idea. Happened here in North Carolina too so that might be a bonus for those of us who live here."

They walked along the path chatting about the target site discussion but also about other things. Dylan asked Molly about her earlier life and her scroll site and she in turn asked him what it was like to grow up in a rich and famous family. They chatted easily with each other and were so engrossed in the conversation that they did not see Reid until he spoke to them from just four feet away.

"Hello? Earth to Dylan, Earth to Molly. We've been waiting for you two to get back to the meeting."

"Oh, sorry," Dylan said. "Guess time just got away from us a little bit."

"Yeah," Reid replied sarcastically. "I guess you could say that. We've watched you two circle this lake about five or six times."

Both Dylan and Molly were stunned. They realized that if that were true they must have been walking for about an hour.

Both of them apologized several times as they followed Reid back to the meeting but behind his back they giggled, smiled and winked at each other as if they were in middle school.

They arrived back at Dylan's office to find everyone else waiting. Hunter jumped right in.

"Alright, now that we are all here let's get right into it. When we left off we were--"

Suddenly Molly, who had not said a word in the earlier part of the meeting, blurted out the word, "Jerusalem!"

Hunter stopped in mid sentence and stared at Molly with a confused look on his face. Molly put her hand over her mouth and wondered why she had said that. She had certainly not planned to say that and really had no idea why she had said Jerusalem at all. She looked around the room and saw that Hunter was not the only one staring at her. Every person in the room was looking at her. All of them looked too stunned to say anything until finally Dylan spoke.

"What?"

"Eh, sorry," Molly replied sheepishly. "I'm so sorry, I don't really know why I said that. It just sort of exploded out. Sorry."

Still no one spoke for another long moment until Dr. Lamacelli spoke up.

"Well you must have had some reason to shout out like that. What about Jerusalem? Are you trying to suggest that you want us to consider going there with GLASS?"

For a long uncomfortable moment no one spoke. Finally, in the briefest of moments Molly realized why she had said that.

"Yes," she said. "Jerusalem."

"Well," Reid said. "For goodness sake what about Jerusalem. What in the world are you trying to say?"

"Jerusalem," Molly said again with more confidence. "We should make the next GLASS run to Jerusalem. We should go back to the year thirty three and witness the crucifixion and resurrection of our Lord Jesus Christ."

If the silence in the room previously had been quiet, the silence that now followed Molly's statement was twice as deep and ten times as heavy. For a full minute not one person even seemed to breathe, let alone speak. But as if on cue, everyone in the room except Molly started speaking, yelling, gesturing, banging their fists on the table and stamping their feet. The noise was so loud that two HIS employees who were walking down the hall outside of Dylan's office actually came into the room uninvited just to see if everything was OK.

Finally Hunter started to wave his arms to try to get some order back in the room. As the noise level began to get back to a level where the group members could actually hear each other, he started to talk. "OK, OK. Let's just all calm down. Molly's proposal is a bit out of order but she--"

Reid jumped to his feet and shouted Hunter down. "Oh for Pete's sake Hunter stop. Just stop talking! You're out of order, Molly's out of order, this whole outrageous meeting is out of order." He looked around the room but then looked directly at Dylan and began to address him as if they were the only two people in the room. "I'm laying this at your doorstep Dylan. You had this crazy idea of inviting non HIS people in here to be part of this. I counseled you not to do that. I even begged you not to do that. We should have kept this to ourselves here at HIS where we are all working on science. You remember science don't you Dylan? It's what we do here and people like Molly just simply do not belong in this environment. It was a mistake to bring her here in the first place and now look at what this grand experiment has become. It's a farce, or it soon will be unless we get her out of here and get back to our mission. And while we're at it we would be wise to remember that our mission is based on science, not imagination. We need serious people here doing serious work and not just some nutcase bringing up suggestions about going into fantasy land. Yes Jerusalem is a real place but Jesus is not a real person. He never was. Hey I've got an idea, while we're at it why not go see if we can take GLASS to be there on the day that Frosty the Snowman speaks his first words like in that old Christmas song kids sing."

"Yes," Molly said. "A Christmas song. Sung at a time of year when we all should remember who and what that Holiday is really about. It's about the Christ! It's about Jesus! He did live! He did die and yes, He was resurrected from the dead and He still lives today!"

Reid shot back quickly. "You are out of your mind. We are not using this machine to go chase some make believe nursery story. Molly you are no longer wanted here. You should leave! Now!"

Molly was about to explode into tears but Dylan jumped up and took two steps until he was standing between Molly and Reid.

"You're out of line Reid," Dylan said. "Molly stays."

Reid looked surprised but recovered quickly and replied, "You're crazy too. If you think that I am going to stand by and watch this company be flushed down the toilet just because you have a romantic interest in some crazy person you had better think again."

The shouting started all over again. Finally Hunter got control of the meeting and called for another break. This time he told the group to return in an hour but also cautioned them to not talk to anyone else on the team. He wanted them to think it out for themselves and then bring their ideas back to the group. One by one each team member stormed out of Dylan's office. Molly was the last to leave and she headed at once for the outside walking path. She got about halfway around the path and then collapsed onto a wooden bench that was located under a large Maple tree. She put her head in her hands and cried for at least ten minutes.

"God, where are you? Is this what you want? I thought I could feel you urging me to bring Jerusalem up and so I did. But this meeting has turned into a total disaster. These people all think I am a complete lunatic. And I am beginning to think that they might be right. I thought you had my back. Are you even here?"

While Molly was struggling internally, Reid was in his office. He had poured himself a glass of his favorite brandy and sat sulking at his desk. He started to call the HR department to inform them that the services of

Molly Mahan were no longer needed and that he wanted someone from security to escort her out of the building and off of the campus when he was interrupted by a knock on his office door.

"Not now!" He shouted, but it was too late. The door opened and Dr. Ormond walked in. Without being asked she walked over to his desk and sat down in one of the chairs facing his desk.

Reid canceled his comm call and said, "What are you doing here? Didn't you hear Hunter? We're not supposed to be talking to each other during this break. Or maybe it just doesn't matter much anymore."

"Oh I heard him," Dr. Ormond said. "But I assure you, it matters a great deal."

Reid looked at Dr. Ormond and saw that she had a slight smile on her face along with a dark gleam in her eyes. Reid stared at her for a second and then said, "You know something don't you? What is it?"

Dr. Ormond laughed and said, "Yes indeed I do know something. I know a great deal that I think you will be interested in. I came in here to make your day. This meeting that we just had? You know the one you labeled a disaster? I think it is really a gift, and I think once you hear me out, you'll agree."

Reid glared at her for a moment or two and then said, "Ya know what I think? I think you're crazy too. If you think that --"

Dr. Ormond held her hand up to stop him and then softly said, "Reid, I'm on your side. Just hear me out."

Dr. Ormond then proceeded to tell Reid all about the conversation that she and Molly had had during their lunch break. She told Reid how Molly actually believed in God. She told him how Molly talked to God (or talked to someone or something) every day. She told him how Molly believed that God talked back to her in a variety of ways. When she finished Reid could only shake his head and say, "She really is nuts. How did this happen? We've got to support Trevor as our number one guy and we have got to get Molly off of this campus. She's a danger, she's a menace and she just does not fit in here. She simply is in the wrong place."

Dr. Ormond smiled and waited for Reid to calm down and then said, "Oh no my friend. She is in exactly the right place. She is just where we need her to be."

Reid looked up slowly. "You really are out of your mind. Everybody around here has gone crazy. Surely you don't believe all of that Christian nonsense about Jesus and resurrection and all of that do you?"

"No I don't. And that is why she is in just the right place, at just the right time."

Reid looked confused so Dr. Ormond continued. "Let me explain my plan and I think that you will see that when this is done, you and I are going to be the most famous people in the world. We talked earlier about proving to the world once and for all the facts surrounding what actually took place at the signing of the Declaration of Independence right?"

Reid nodded.

"And we also talked about sending the next GLASS run to a time, place and to a circumstance or situation that the whole world would be interested in and not just Americans right?"

Again Reid nodded.

"Well what if we did send GLASS back to Jerusalem? What if the mission of the next GLASS run was to try and find Jesus and witness His death and resurrection?

However what if there was nothing there to be found. No Jesus, no crucifixion, no resurrection. What if we went back there and found ... nothing. We would end up --"

Reid jumped to his feet. He interrupted Grace Ormond and finished her sentence for her.

"We would end up disproving the entire case for Christianity and therefore also prove that not only was Jesus a fake, but in the process we would end up proving that God is non existent as well. Our whole world would be changed forever, and for the better I might add. Science would rule and religion would be destroyed. We would be the winners and we would end up being heros to the entire world."

Chapter 13

The group got back together as planned. This time Molly made sure she was the last to enter Dylan's office. She looked around the room and saw that no one could (or would) meet her eyes. She was able to take that from most of the group members but she was really hurt that Dylan seemed to be siding with the other group members and not her. On a professional level she could actually understand that. After all, he was a scientist and the originator of the idea that had eventually become the GLASS project. But what really hurt her was that he had not called Reid off when he had been yelling at her and calling her names. Well if she was honest about it she had to admit that he had done exactly that. However she was still a little hurt that Dylan had not gone a bit farther when sticking up for her. It seemed to her that Dylan was still thinking of the project first and of her second. But then again, what could she really expect him to do. Reid was someone Dylan had known his whole life and he and Molly had met just a few hours ago. "Oh well," she thought. "It was a mistake to come here in the first place. I thought I had a handle on what I thought God's plan was for me here. Guess not."

Hunter cleared his throat and Molly could tell that the meeting was about to get under way again. But before he could say anything Molly spoke up.

"Before we begin I have something to say to all of you. You have all been so nice to include me in this project that I can't begin to thank you enough for your hospitality. I have enjoyed my time here today, but I think we all know that it is time for me to leave. I don't understand very much of what is going on here and I really am like a fish out of water. I thought that I had a good idea with the suggestion about Jerusalem, but I can see that the rest of you don't agree. So for the good of this team, I think that I should step down and Trevor should go on the GLASS run."

For a brief moment no one said anything. Reid looked like he was about to say something but before he could, Trevor stood and spoke up. "Well Molly, thank you for saying that. We all know it must have been hard to say those things but I think you are right and I think that I can be a very important part of the team. So I accept and--"

"Oh why don't you put a cork in it?" Reid asked Trevor harshly. He stared at Trevor until he sat down and then addressed Molly specifically. "I appreciate you saying the things that you just did Molly, but I believe that you are being a bit hasty."

Everyone in the group except for Dr. Ormond was stunned by what Reid had just said. He continued. "Yes I realize that earlier I came across as a bit gruff and I apologize for the language and the words that I used. Over the last hour I have thought about the things that I said but mostly I have thought through your suggestion of taking the next GLASS run to Jerusalem. I am still not sure at all about this Jesus person you speak of, but I think that this project is larger in scope than just me and what I think. This project has relevance across the globe and maybe the world does have a right to see once and for all just what this religion thing is all about. The best place to do that would of course be in Jerusalem. I most certainly do not think that you are crazy. I respect your religious beliefs and I think that there may be some merit to your plan to make Jerusalem the target for our next GLASS run. I suggest that without delay we vote right here and right now on making Jerusalem the focal point of our next run. Hunter will you please conduct the vote?"

Molly, who did not really know Reid Corder well at all was overjoyed and thought that perhaps she had misjudged him. Reid had always been like a father to Dylan and so he knew Reid better than anyone else. He was happy too about Reid's little speech. However his thoughts about Reid were opposite from Molly's. Dylan knew that when Reid talked nice like that, everyone had better watch out. Dylan knew better than anyone else that Reid was the master of alternative agendas. Dylan thought that something might be burning in Reid's kitchen and Molly and everyone else needed to be careful about what Reid might be about to dish out.

It took Hunter two or three seconds to pick his chin up from off of the floor but he finally managed to get himself under control. He called for a vote and without any further discussion Jerusalem was decided upon as the target for the next GLASS run.

Everyone in the room had spent a lot of energy during the day and Dylan could see that they were all exhausted. He called the HR department and had Becca Knight come to his office. Once she arrived he asked her to escort both Trevor and Molly to their rooms. Becca guided the two of them to their guest suites in the silver building. As they were about to begin the walk across campus to the silver building, she handed them an itinerary for the next day. It was loaded with tours, meetings and training sessions all throughout the day. She also handed them a dark blue notebook about an inch and a half thick. Molly thumbed through hers quickly. Inside were page after page of instructions, descriptions and diagrams about things that she could only wonder about. She sighed and looked up at Becca who smiled thinly and said. "Yep, you guessed it, homework. Each day's assignment is clearly labeled. We are not putting this on allcomms because if some of this got off campus and into the wrong hands, the whole project could be ruined. Enjoy!"

With that she led Trevor to his apartment and Molly to hers. It was only about five o'clock in the afternoon so Molly thought that she would get settled in and start reading the assignment for the next day. At least she could get started on that before she went to get something to eat.

About two hours later she put the notebook down and rubbed her eyes and then her temples. She knew that she had been reading for two solid hours and she also knew that she remembered almost nothing at all about what she had read. Much of it had been very scientifically oriented. She started off toward the cafeteria thinking the whole time that all she could hope for was that when the time came for her to push a button or two that somebody would tell her which button to push and when to push it. She didn't think she could handle much more than that.

Suddenly the Spirit moved within her and she stopped in mid stride. She realized that she had not spoken to God since Reid's incredible turnaround back in Dylan's office.

"Father in Heaven," she prayed out loud. "I don't care who hears me now. You are obviously in control of what is going on around here and even though I have no idea what is happening around me, I know that you do. In fact I can see now that you are orchestrating this entire thing. I still don't know what you want me to do, but I want you to know that whatever it is, I'm going to try to discern your plan and carry my part of it out as best I can. Amen."

"Amen." Came a voice from inside of a doorway that she was standing next to.

Molly was startled and almost jumped out of her shoes.

"Who's there?" she asked.

"Sorry," Dylan said as he walked out of the room. "Didn't mean to scare you."

"Oh, you didn't. Much."

"Sorry about that. I was just catching up on some things I needed to do."

"Why don't you use your own office instead of stalking and spying on innocent people as they are on their way to get something to eat?"

Dylan had been smiling until now but he could tell that Molly was a little angry. He wiped the smile off of his face and responded. "Oh, look I really wasn't stalking you. I truly was in here working. No one has been assigned to this office in several years so I come in here sometimes just to get a bit of alone time so that I can work distraction free for awhile. Know what I mean?"

Molly did not say anything back to him but just continued to give him the evil eye.

"Look I can explain," he stammered. "And if you are angry that I overheard you praying, I'm sorry. I wasn't trying to eavesdrop but you were talking, I mean praying out loud, just outside my door and . . . look I really don't care about all of that stuff so no worries. You want to pray, go ahead and pray."

Still Molly did not say anything and Dylan was becoming a little bit confused and a little bit frustrated.

"What?" was all Dylan could think to say.

Now Molly unloaded on him. "It's not the praying and it's not the stalking and it's not scaring me half to death."

"What then?"

"You didn't back me up earlier today when Reid was yelling at me and saying some not so nice things about me."

Dylan slumped a little and leaned against the wall. "Yeah, you're right. I knew while he was yelling at you that it wasn't right. I knew I should have said something more than I did to get him off of your back but I just froze. Didn't know what to say. Look I'm really sorry about that."

Dylan had to beg for forgiveness several more times before he finally saw the beginnings of a small smile on Molly's face.

He spread his arms wide out to the side and asked, "Forgiven?"

"For now, I guess."

"Good. Looks like you're heading down to the cafeteria. I'd better join you if you don't mind. I know which foods are safe for human consumption and which should be avoided at all costs. You know we have several items down there that we sometimes use for fuel for GLASS."

Molly was confused for a second and then looked up at Him. He was trying hard to hide a smile. She saw that he was teasing her so she punched him lightly on the shoulder as they made their way down to the cafeteria.

Chapter 14

The next day and the days that followed were a blur to Molly. She tried hard to keep up with her reading assignments but most of what she read was far beyond her scope of understanding. Dylan seemed to realize this and each day at mealtimes or at breaks, Dylan and Molly could usually be found together. They both said that getting together so often like that was only to get Molly up to speed as quickly as possible on the things she needed to know in order to make the GLASS run. However, most of the other HIS employees who saw them together saw things a little differently. Everyone could tell that there was more to it than just the GLASS technology that they were talking about when they were together.

Most of the HIS team seemed indifferent to this budding relationship but there were a few employees who were more than a little upset by Dylan's relationship with Molly. Molly sensed that the small group of disgruntled employees was growing and she somehow thought that Reid might be behind that in some way. But she had no proof of anything like that so she kept her mouth shut and just tried to concentrate on learning more about GLASS and what her part of the project was. She hoped that things would just work themselves out.

On the third day the team of HIS employees who had been assigned to go to her off campus apartment and get her personal things arrived back on campus. She had drawn up a list of items that she wanted brought from her apartment so that she could have them with her while she was staying at HIS. As she unpacked the items they had brought she was absolutely delighted to see that everything she had asked for had been delivered. On her first day at HIS she had made arrangements for her dog Pepper to be cared for by her co-worker Emily so she had no worries about that even though she missed Pepper a lot. After her personal items arrived she felt a little bit more at home and actually seemed to be feeling like she was in a pretty good place as far as her mental and physical health was concerned.

But then as her first week came to a close, things took a turn for the worse. The daily itinerary showed that this day would be the first time that she and Trevor were scheduled to see GLASS. They both had asked Dylan and Reid several times when they would get an opportunity to see GLASS but each time they had asked, they were told that the time to see GLASS up close would come later and that they were not yet ready for that step to be taken. Now however it seemed as if the time was at hand and Molly felt excited as she dressed. She re-read the itinerary and felt a sudden cold stab of horror run throughout her body. How had she missed seeing this the first time she had read through the itinerary. There on the schedule, right after breakfast was a two hour period of time when she would be tested orally on her knowledge of all she had learned about GLASS up to that point. Molly fell back on her bed and put her hands up to her head.

"What will I do?" she thought. "I know virtually nothing about GLASS. I barely even know how to spell GLASS let alone understand how it works!" She was ready for a long and intense self pity party when her allcomm notified her of a call. She saw that it was Dylan and thought, "He's the last person on Earth I need to see or talk to right now." She ignored the call and went back to her misery. Over the next ten minutes Dylan called her five times. She ignored all five calls. Finally he seemed to get the message that she did not want to speak with him and he stopped calling.

She glanced at her allcomm and saw that it was just about time to go. Just then there was a knock on her door. She thought at once that someone had been sent to fetch her to make sure she showed up for the test so that they could all see how much she did not understand. Trevor would be promoted to her position right away and she would be left with, what? Nothing? Well maybe that was just the way it should have been in the first place.

"I've known all along," she said to herself. "I'm really am not good enough to be here so I have no complaint. It's just that over the last few days I was starting to think that maybe I really could belong here. Maybe I did have something to offer."

Another knock on the door (this one louder than the first) brought her back from her musings. She sighed, walked across the room and opened the door.

Dylan stood there with a covered plate of something that smelled fantastic. He smiled at her, bowed low to the ground and said, "Breakfast in bed for m'lady."

Molly thought again that whatever was under that cover smelled delicious. She started to smile back but then realized that she was still in her night clothes which consisted of a tee shirt (torn in two or three places) and a pair of gym shorts that used to be dark green but were so old and faded that they appeared now to be a sort of mottled color that defied description.

A look of horror quickly spread across her face. She screamed at Dylan, "Get out!!! You can't see me like this!" She then slammed the door squarely in his face. On the other side of the door she heard the plate fall, heard Dylan groan and then heard him slump to the floor. At first she didn't care but then thought that he might have been hurt somehow. She yanked the door open expecting to have to give first aid and call for help. Instead she put her hand to her mouth and tried (unsuccessfully) to stifle a laugh. There sat the great Dylan Quick in the middle of the hallway. On his right shoulder were the remains of what she thought might be scrambled eggs. A piece of bacon hung from his right ear and his left wrist and hand were covered with grits. His pants were soaking wet from the coffee that had only a moment earlier been inside the pot that was now laying several feet away on its side against the far wall.

They looked at each other without speaking for a minute. Then Molly reached down and grabbed the piece of bacon that had now fallen onto Dylan's shoulder among the remains of the eggs. She hesitated a moment and held it out with a mischievous grin and then popped the bacon into her mouth.

"AAAGGHHHHH!" Dylan moaned. "That's gross! That is really disgusting!"

Molly looked thoughtful for a second and then replied, "No, not really. It's really pretty good. Crispy, just the way I like it."

She watched his eyes grow huge and then she laughed until her stomach muscles hurt.

"Nice shorts," Dylan said.

Instantly Molly stopped laughing and turned beet red. Now it was Dylan's turn to laugh.

Molly glared at him. "That's not funny."

"Yes. Actually it is."

They both looked at each other for a few seconds and then both started laughing even harder than before.

Dylan told Molly that he would be back in half and hour and walked off down the hall toward someplace where he could get a quick shower and get cleaned up a bit. Molly took advantage of that time to take a shower herself and put some decent clothes on.

Soon Dylan was back. He explained that each evening he was sent the next day's itinerary to approve. When he saw what was planned, he had canceled the morning test. In fact he had canceled all future tests as well. He did not tell Molly that he suspected that Reid might be behind the oral tests regarding GLASS knowledge. Instead he explained to Molly that there had not been time to re-write the itineraries so Molly had received the original with the test still listed. There had also not been enough time to put anything new in that time slot so everyone had free time for almost the whole morning.

"Good," Molly stated. "You can help me study."

"Study what? I just told you that there aren't going to be any more tests."

"I know but I still don't know a thing about GLASS or what it is or how it works or anything at all. I really am excited about it and I really do want to know all about it but most of this is just way over my head."

"Don't worry about it. You are being trained for exactly what you need to know and do. Don't worry about all that other stuff. Look, if it makes you feel any better, there are people here who are far smarter than me. They know GLASS backward and forward in much more detail than I ever will, and I'm the guy who invented it. Everyone here has a job to do, you included. You need to know your job and when to do it. Then we need to trust everyone else to do the same thing. Besides, if there is something I can help explain just ask me. Forget about all of those stupid tests."

"Well, there is one thing that I have been thinking about and trying to understand, but I just can't get my head around it."

"OK, what is it?"

"Well," Molly said. "Let's talk about that in a minute. There is something I must do first."

"What's that?" Dylan asked.

"I need to pray. Will you pray with me?"

Dylan looked very uncomfortable and somewhat scared. "I, uh, well you see, ummm, well."

Molly laughed and said, "No worries. I can see you're not exactly comfortable with that. Tell you what. I'll pray and you sit and listen."

Now it was Dylan's turn to wonder what he had gotten himself into. He nodded as Molly closed her eyes and began to speak out loud to her creator.

"Dear Lord, I am so sorry to let you down so much. Just earlier this morning you had things all worked out for me about getting out of those tests, but all I could do was worry and whine about them. I have done nothing this whole week except cry about this or that. I've spent a lot of time thinking about how pitiful I feel and about how messed up everything seems to be. But all the while you have done nothing except time and time again prove how powerful you are and that you have this whole thing under control. You are incredibly good to me and I have such a hard time trusting you. I am so sorry and I can only pray that you will help me with my lack of faith and help me to trust you more.

Also please help my friend Dylan to know that you are real and that you care about him. He is a man of science but please let him come to realize that you invented science and that you only want a close personal relationship with him. Help him understand that his relationship with science is actually designed to go hand in hand with his relationship with you. Amen!

Oh, I almost forgot, please let Dylan know that he still smells a little bit like bacon and that maybe he should take a little more time in the shower before coming to call on a young lady next time."

Dylan's eyes flew open to see that Molly's eyes were already open and that they were crinkled up at the corners as she grinned from ear to ear. She burst out laughing as she saw a look of horror spread across Dylan's face.

"You can't say stuff like that! I may not know much about God," Dylan yelled. "But I know enough to know that you're not supposed to kid around and make jokes like that with Him. You're going to get it!"

Molly laughed even harder but finally managed to say, "Oh right. Where did you hear that?"

"Listen I'm not criticizing your religious beliefs but everyone knows that if you mess with God like you just did, then BAM, you get zapped with lightning or something and get turned into a crispy critter."

This time Molly laughed so hard that she thought she would wet her pants. When she could finally speak again she had a question for Dylan.

"You don't believe in God?"

Dylan shook his head slowly and said, "I'm sorry Molly, I don't."

"Well if you don't believe in God, why would you believe that people could get zapped. Who, exactly is going to do the zapping?"

Dylan was stunned by the question but even more shocked to realize that he did not have a good answer for it. He tried to change the subject to more familiar ground.

"You thanked God for working things out for you and getting rid of the tests. God didn't do that Molly, I did."

He sat back smugly with his arms folded over his chest.

Molly looked him in the eye, leaned forward slightly and quietly said, "You sure about that?"

Chapter 15

Lunch went by quickly and Dylan could keep his mind on just two things. The first was that Molly really had looked terrific in that tee shirt and shorts and the second was trying to figure out what she meant about her reference to God working things out and not him. Of course it had been him that had worked things out. God really had nothing to do with it. That is what he, as a scientist did, work things out. It had been all him. Right? Or was it? Perhaps there really was something else to it and if that were true, what was that something else? He didn't have time to ask her more about it because the sessions after lunch came fast and furious. He attended the first session after the lunch break just because he wanted to. Trevor and Molly were about to get a crash course on the power source used by GLASS. He knew all about it but he thought he might show up anyway just in case he was needed there for something. He was confident of the abilities of the rest of the staff and he knew the chances of him being needed were very slim. However he still tried to convince himself that his knowledge might come in handy at that session. In any event, Molly was going to be there.

The after lunch session was to be held in meeting room D and Molly was late as usual but finally burst into the room full of apologies.

A young lady was talking quietly with Trevor. Dylan was there and several other people as well.

The lady who had been talking with Trevor saw Molly enter the room and stood up to address the group.

"OK, now that we are all here we can begin. My name is Dr. Melanie Towns and I am head of the Design and Engineering Department here at

HIS. It really will not matter very much to the two of you," she said as she looked directly at Molly and then at Trevor. "But we are going to go over some of the basics of the how GLASS is powered. Not really sure when you might need this info but just in case you do, you will at least have some of the basics down.

Remember, right now there are about forty or fifty reporters camped outside of our campus, all trying to find information about GLASS. We have done a pretty good job of controlling that but once this is all done, you two are going to be in high demand for interviews. Like it or not, that is just the way it is going to be. You won't need to know all the heavy science, but you should know something about it. Now then, let's get started.

You already have been told that GLASS uses a tremendous amount of power to operate. Hardly any other system on Earth uses as much power as we do. There are some government projects of course that use a lot of power, even more than us. But in the private sector, we are pretty sure that we are way above anyone else regarding the amount of power that we require. In fact we use so much power here that it is, at times, in short supply. You know that the next GLASS run will utilize so much power that it will be quite some time after that before we will be able to make another run. So, where do we get enough power to do what we need to do here? In the beginning we used simple electricity. But we soon out distanced the amount of electricity that we had and when we went on a few runs, we caused power blackouts all around this region. I think that you have been told that previously but I want you to understand just how much power we are talking about. There was more than one occasion where blackouts occurred from Greensboro all the way over through Durham. Even then we still did not have enough power to run GLASS.

We next explored nuclear and hydrogen power but never did get too far into those. The government started snooping around to see what we were up to and we realized quickly that those power sources were going to end up being non starters for our purposes anyway. Yet even with those types of power, we were going to come up short of what we needed. GLASS was growing very rapidly at that point and we all knew that what we needed did not exist. So, as we have done many times here, we set to work trying to figure out just what to do about that. We knew that we needed to either discover or invent some completely new type of power source. Not really the type of thing people, companies, agencies or even governments do everyday right? But that is exactly what we did."

She stopped for a moment to let those words sink into the thought process of both Trevor and Molly. Trevor was excited and was thinking that he was really going to love this. Molly was depressed and was thinking that she was going to have to spend the next few hours being completely lost once again.

Dr. Towns continued. "We first put together a team as a sort of think tank. I was the chairperson of that team. It was our job to dream up some ideas that might work for us. It took some time but finally, we did. The team came up with a theory about where we might be able to find these vast amounts of power we were looking for. Next we designed some experiments that could prove, or disprove, our theory. Once those theory issues worked out and became fact, we took the whole thing to my Design and Engineering Department. There we were able to design and build the mechanism by which we could obtain the power that we need for GLASS. We call the source of this power - HOOPS. That is an acronym for the Harvesting Of Open Particles System. Put the other way around it is a system for the finding, or gathering of the Open Particles we need. Now I am certain that you both are saying to yourselves, sounds great doc, but what in the world are you talking about?"

Molly had been thinking that exact thought as Dr. Towns continued. "There are a few questions that you need to be asking yourself at this point. In no particular order those questions should be:

1. What is an Open Particle?
2. Where are we to find these particles?

And lastly, how are we to go obtain, or harvest them?

Of course there are many, many more questions about Open Particles but we will leave those to the experts for the time being. We realized that if we could not find answers to these three basic questions, we might not have any need to investigate them any further as a source of possible power. So let's look a little closer at those three questions.

The first question was actually the hardest of the three. Remember, knowledge of these particles did not even exist prior to us investigating this possibility. We were really investigating something that had not yet been proven, at least not in the practical sense.

Science has known for many years that embedded deep within solar rays there are a variety of powerful substances, or particles. It has been common knowledge in scientific circles that they were there, we just didn't know what they were made of or how mankind could harness them. In fact it was pretty much unknown whether or not any of those particles could be helpful to the human race at all. So we spent a lot of time building machines that could be launched into the outer atmosphere to take a closer look at several of those particles. We made a lot of progress and found some that will no doubt be very useful to humans in the future, especially in the medical development fields. But in the process we also discovered one particle in particular that seemed to be exactly what we were looking for. The design of these particles resembles a door that is partially open and so we decided to call these particles, Open Particles.

The next question was about where and how to locate them. I've already answered that for you. They are located in ordinary, everyday sunbeams. These rays originate on the Sun and after travelling through space, eventually reach our Earth. We find the particles to be most plentiful in our thin upper atmosphere. We do not really know why just yet, but it seems that left unattended and undisturbed, they dissipate to some degree as they pass in and through the thicker parts of our atmosphere. We have found that in our lower atmosphere there are hardly any at all. However in the upper levels of our atmosphere we find them in huge numbers. They are in fact so plentiful that at this time their actual numbers are incalculable. We must capture them, or harvest them in the upper reaches of the atmosphere, before the particles begin to self destruct or fade away as they get closer to Earth. Hardly any survive to actually reach the surface of our planet. Again, we are not exactly sure why this happens, we just know that it does.

The third question was answered in a very simple manner. Our team had been stewing about how we were going to go get these particles and we were getting nowhere fast. Honestly we were stumped. At that particular time it seemed as if every department all across our campus was also struggling with the projects that they were working on. Every department had hit some sort of major roadblock at about the same time and morale here at HIS hit rock bottom. Dylan sensed this and decided on drastic action. He announced that we would have a few days of just sort of getting away from our projects. He hoped that getting away from our worries for a little while might help. So we had two full days of doing nothing that involved the projects we were working on. Instead of work we had games and team building sessions and things like that. HIS also scheduled a day for employees to bring our children to work. One of our employees who worked over in Accounting brought in her twelve year old son, Brendan I think was his name. She was showing him around the campus and happened to come by our department while some of us were discussing the problems we were having. We really weren't supposed to be doing that, but we were.

So this young man overheard us and quick as lightning asked me why, if we already had space vehicles and machines that had gone up into space and located these particles, could they not be tweaked or modified in some way so that they could collect the particles while they were up there. I was stunned by the simplicity of that question and in just a couple of weeks we had done just that. So now we have the capability to travel regularly into the upper atmosphere and harvest these particles.

The outcome is that we have all the power we will ever need. These particles, when treated correctly and combined with a few other simple man made hybrid substances, produce power in incredible amounts. Good, clean, reliable, easy to use and fairly inexpensive power.

We have not allowed any of this info to get out into the public but of course later on we will. That information will change humanity forever. As for our current needs, our power problems have dissolved completely. We still only have enough power to run GLASS once over the next year or so but that is due to the fact that we can only harvest so many Open Particles at a time right now. Later I am sure we will increase our capacity and then everyone's power problems will dissolve, along with our own."

Chapter 16

The next few days went fairly smoothly. Though Molly still struggled with understanding even the most basic of technical issues surrounding the GLASS project, she at least was beginning to feel more comfortable with her role at HIS. This was due in large part to her relationship with Dylan. Everyone at HIS could see that the two of them were attracted to each other and almost everyone saw that as a good thing. Reid Corder was not in that group. He still thought of Molly as a loose cannon on the team. He had known Dylan all of Dylan's life and thought of himself as not only Dylan's friend and coworker, but also as a sort of role model, mentor and even a protector figure of sorts for Dylan. In that role he definitely thought of Molly as a danger to Dylan. He was aware that they had been spending a great deal of time together and he assumed that during those moments, Molly was filling Dylan's head with a lot of religious nonsense about Jesus, and resurrection and ghosts living inside of a person and who knew what other craziness. He could also plainly see that lately Dylan had his mind much more on Molly Mahan than on the GLASS project. Reid was convinced that Dylan's infatuation with Molly was going to end up being detrimental to GLASS and HIS. He trusted Dylan because he knew that at heart, Dylan was a scientist. But he also knew that after all was said and done, Dylan was a young man who was falling for a pretty girl. He decided that it was his responsibility to "help" Dylan get out of this situation.

The knock on his office door startled him back to reality. Reid checked the time and realized that his visitor was exactly on time. He shouted for her to come in.

"You wanted to see me Reid?"

"Yes, Becca, come on in. Please sit down," he said indicating one of the chairs in front of his desk.

The two of them made small talk for just a minute and then Reid got right to the point.

"You know, Becca, things have been really stressful for those of us who have had to stay here overnight without going home for the last, oh what has it been now, almost three weeks I guess."

Becca stiffened instantly in her chair and said to herself, "Where is he going with this?"

Reid seemed to sense that she was uncomfortable so he quickened the pace of his conversation.

"Dylan seem OK to you?" His question had the desired effect of putting her off guard. She had not expected that.

"Um, Yeah I guess so. Why?"

"Well he seems to be stressed out a bit to me. There is a tremendous amount of pressure on all of us here but of all of the people involved with GLASS, he probably feels more stressed out than all of the rest of us put together. Wouldn't you agree?"

"Well, yes, I guess that makes sense."

"Yes it does and yes he is pretty stressed out. He needs some time off. Just to get away a bit and get his mind off of things. At the very least he needs someone to vent to now and then. He and I are pretty close, but I'm an old man. I think he needs someone to talk to closer to his own age. Someone he can relate too. Help get him through all of this stress and pressure."

Reid was quiet for a moment, letting his words sink in.

Becca sat back in her chair and crossed her arms. "Are you suggesting that . . ."

Reid recognized the defensive stance that Becca had adopted and cut her off in mid sentence.

"Oh please don't misunderstand me. I'm not suggesting anything. It's just that I've seen Dylan, well you know, sort of take a quick glance at you now and then in the hall, or in the cafeteria, or wherever. Nothing perverted or weird or anything like that. Oh my no! He is, if nothing else, a gentleman. I do get the feeling however that he really might just like to get to know you a bit better. That's all, just as a friend. And right now that young man can use a friend."

Becca thought about that for a minute and started to relax. "Well, maybe he does seem a little stressed out. But who could blame him, right? I mean there has to be a lot of pressure on him right now so I guess I can understand that."

"Sure, sure. Of course. And I think he needs a friend right now. Just someone to talk things through a little bit. Ya know?"

"Yeah, I guess so. But everybody seems to think he is getting pretty close to that Molly what's her name person. I'm sure he talks to her a lot."

"Well you're right, he does talk to her. But that's only because they are sort of forced to talk to each other, you know, about GLASS and all. I think that I can assure you that he has no interest in her as a person at all."

Reid could see Becca relax even more as she thought about all of this new information.

"Look," Reid continued. "I'm not really supposed to do this because those of us working closely on the GLASS project are not supposed to leave the campus. I know that you can leave every day, but the rest of us, including Dylan of course can't. I think that it might do him a world of good, just to get away a bit. Maybe just for a few hours."

Reid could tell that Becca was once again showing a little defensiveness so he quickly went on. "Listen, he loves basketball. His favorite team is playing tonight over in Chapel Hill. He has season tickets. He mentioned to me that he wished he could go to the game. Right now however he is not planning on attending the game but I think he should go. Just to get off campus for a few hours. But who wants to go to a game by themselves? Besides, I think he really has an interest in you. I mean just as friends of course."

Reid could see that the hook had been set.

"Well, I kinda like basketball too and Dylan does need to get away from all of this, I can see that. But are you sure he wouldn't rather have that girl go with him? I think he might. I'm not even sure that he knows I'm on the same planet with him, let alone in the same building."

"No, no. He needs to get away from Molly, from campus and from the whole project for a little while. All they ever do is talk about the project. Except of course when she is filling his head with all sorts of crazy ideas about God, and Jesus and maybe Voodoo for all I know. No Becca, he needs some time away from her. And I really do think that he would enjoy going to the game with you."

"Voodoo? Oh that's terrible!"

"Well, who knows what sort of crazy ideas she has been talking to him about? I know for a fact that she has some really bizarre ideas about that sort of stuff."

"Dylan is so nice," Becca said. "He probably thinks he needs to be polite to her and listen to all that junk."

"Yeah, you're right. He probably does."

"Well in that case count me in. He would never hurt a fly and there she is filling his head with all that stuff. I bet he does want to get away for awhile. But how can he get away from campus. After all, you and he were the ones to suggest that you all stay here on campus until the next run. How will we get him to the game?"

"You just leave that to me. Just leave everything to me."

Reid already knew exactly what he was going to do to put his plan in place. After the afternoon training sessions were completed Reid found Dylan alone in his office catching up on some paperwork.

"How's it going Dylan? What's new?"

"Ah, not much Reid. Got a lot of paperwork to take care of."

"You feeling OK? You look a little pale. Been eating OK? Sleeping alright?"

Dylan didn't answer but Reid knew that he had heard him.

"You know when we planned all of this we all knew that there would be a great deal of pressure on us all. Lots of stress. But I think we underestimated how much stress there would be. What do you think about getting everyone involved with the project a little down time. You know, sort of get everybody's batteries recharged. Sort of like we did a couple of years ago when we were all looking for our power source. Remember that? It did everyone a world of good to get away from their projects for a little while."

Now Dylan looked up. He could never remember Reid ever caring about anybody's best interest or overall health. He knew that Reid was good at what he did, but as far as caring about the people who worked here; well to Reid Corder they were all just cogs in the machine. There was a warning bell going off way back in Dylan's brain, but for the moment he ignored it. Reid's idea was just exactly what Dylan himself had been thinking about that very morning.

"What'd you have in mind?"

"Well for starters I had you in mind. I happen to know that UNC is playing the University of Virginia tonight and I also know that you would love to be there. Might be good to get away for a few hours. What do you think?"

"I think that's an awful idea. You're suggesting that I make everyone else stay on campus, and then I go off and go to a basketball game? We do need some down time for everyone, but not like that. Not me first. Forget about it."

Reid got up from the chair where he had planted himself and sighed. "Yeah I guess you're right. That probably wasn't the best idea she's had was it? And believe me, she has had some strange ones."

He laughed and headed for the door.

Dylan started to laugh too and then stopped short and said, "Wait a minute. You said she."

"Yeah? So?"

"Well who is the she you are talking about? Ya know, as in 'she who'?"

"Oh, I'm sorry. I guess I forgot to tell you. I overheard Molly talking with a couple other people in the cafeteria. It seems that she was also thinking about the same thing. She thinks that it would be a great idea if we just got everyone off of campus for some down time. She said that the down time we had built into our schedule here was just not enough. She wants to get off campus for a little while, you know, just to clear her head."

Dylan was all ears now and Reid thought that for the second time that day he had set a hook pretty well.

"Really? She said that?"

"Yep. I heard it myself. She even said that she was having a bad day and that if at all possible she would get off campus tonight if she could."

The warning bell inside Dylan's head went crazy and was now ringing very loudly but he was way beyond being able to either hear it or to think clearly. As far as Dylan was concerned at that particular time, the warning bell did not even exist.

He thought for a moment, then looked at Reid and said, "You think anyone would mind? I mean if I left campus for a little while. I really shouldn't be breaking my own rules but I have been under a lot of pressure lately. And we could arrange for maybe two or three people to go out every night or so?"

Reid laughed easily and put his hand on Dylan's shoulder.

"There was a lot in that last mouthful of yours to try to answer. But let me give it a shot. (1) No I do not think anyone will mind. I think that everyone will appreciate it. You know you're not the only one who is stressed. Everyone here is feeling the pressure. (2) You and I made those rules but we can also adjust them as we see fit. Besides, in your much younger days you were not exactly known as a keeper of the rules in many cases. Have you now become so stuck in the mud that you can't even bend a little rule here or there when it makes sense to do so? (3) As for letting everyone go off of campus now and then, I see that as a good thing and will most likely result in everybody jumping back into their work in much better spirits. Sort of give everyone a chance at a fresh start to carry us down to the finish line."

Dylan grinned like a school boy. He thought for a second and then said, "OK, Let's do it."

Suddenly the grin disappeared from Dylan's of his face. He looked up at Reid who was ready for this moment.

"You want to know how we are going to pull this off, right?"

Dylan nodded slowly.

"You go ahead and get ready. I'll make sure the young lady is ready as well and we'll get both of you to Chapel Hill in plenty of time for the game. Just leave the rest to me."

CHAPTER 17

Reid had one of the HIS employees by the name of Brian Grant meet Dylan on the far side of the campus, away from the main gate. Brian had worked in the HR department for over fifteen years and knew both Reid and Dylan well. Brian drove Dylan into Chapel Hill to one of Dylan's favorite eating establishments, a local grill by the name of The Blue Victory.

"Reid told me that you like the food at this place," Brian said. "I think he said you were supposed to meet someone here,"

"Yeah, the burgers here are unbelievable," Dylan said as they pulled up to the front of the eaterie. "I appreciate the lift. Thanks."

Brian dropped Dylan off at the curb.

As Dylan exited the car, he saw someone seated at one of the outside tables waving to him. He took a quick look around for Molly but when he saw that she was not there, he ambled over to the table where a young woman was still waving at him.

"Hi Dylan," Becca Knight said as Dylan approached.

"Oh, hey Becca," Dylan said apprehensively. "What brings you here? Are you alone?"

"Yes I am. Reid told me that you liked to come to this place sometimes and that you were going to be here tonight before going to the basketball game. He said that you had an extra ticket and that you and I could go to the game to get your mind off of work."

"Oh is that right? Reid told you that huh?" Dylan was beginning to smell a rat. "Well I was supposed to be meeting someone here this evening. I hope you don't mind."

Becca looked crushed as she began to realize that Reid had mislead her. She replied, "Oh. Well no I didn't know that. No worries though. I'm good to go here."

Dylan looked at her questioningly and said, "You sure?" He could tell by the look on her face that she was embarrassed. "I am going to have a little chat with Reid when I get back to campus." He thought to himself. But to Becca Knight he said, "Well look, this is obviously a little awkward for both of us. My friend isn't here yet so why don't I just sit here for a while until she arrives. How's that sound?"

Becca thought that sounded wonderful and she told Dylan that. She thanked him for being so understanding and kind and as she spoke to him she reached her hand out and placed it lightly on Dylan's forearm for just a few seconds. It was a simple gesture of friendship and gratitude.

Dylan patted her hand just for a moment as he said, "Sure, no problem."

Just at that exact moment another vehicle came to a halt on the other side of the street. The bistro was in full view of the occupants of that vehicle. They could not hear the conversation between Becca and Dylan but they could easily see what was going on, or rather what appeared to be going on.

While Dylan was being picked up and delivered to The Blue Victory, Reid had picked Molly up at another gate located at the other end of the campus. In fact, Dylan and Molly were waiting at the two service gates at the same time. However the gates were hidden from each other by several hundred yards of very thick shrubbery and a variety of trees. Reid had watched and waited until Dylan had been picked up by Brian and had then waited an additional five minutes before driving around and picking Molly up. He had everything planned to the minute. Truthfully he knew that his plan would fall apart pretty quickly and that Dylan, Becca and Molly might all figure out what he had done in a short period of time. He really didn't care about that. He had calculated that this little escapade would drive a small wedge between Molly and Dylan. Just enough for them to begin to see that they were not really well suited for each other. The stress that they were under would help to unravel their little relationship and the rest would take care of itself.

He knew Dylan and even though he really did not know Molly all that well he knew enough to say with confidence that Molly was going to destroy Dylan and all that he had worked for. He needed for them to separate. Then when this run to Jerusalem completely proved once and for all that Christianity was just a made up religion with no truth behind its beginnings at all, Molly would end up being a laughing stock in front of the entire world. He just couldn't let that happen to Dylan.

As Reid's car pulled up just across from the restaurant, Molly and Reid could clearly see Dylan and Becca. At that particular moment Dylan was leaning close to Becca. She had her hand on his arm and his hand was covering her hand in what looked for all the world to be a caressing manner.

"Oh my dear, I am so sorry," Reid said with conviction as he smiled to himself. "I had no idea he had a girlfriend. But now that I see this, I realize that I should have seen this coming long ago."

Molly looked stunned but managed to croak out a hoarse whisper. "What do you mean?"

"Well I should have known about this. In fact now that I think about it, I actually have known about it. Dylan has a lot of girlfriends, usually dating a couple at the same time. He has dated several young ladies at HIS in the past so I should have realized that Dylan and Becca were an item. I've seen them together quite often on breaks and such back at the campus."

Molly was silent for a moment and then said, "I thought you were setting this up so that he knew I was coming tonight?"

"Well I do indeed need to take blame for that. I regret to say that I didn't tell him that you would be joining him. I thought that it would be a nice surprise if you showed up unannounced. I am truly sorry."

Molly sat quietly for a few seconds watching Dylan and Becca.

"Yeah. Looks like quite the surprise alright," Molly said.

"I am so very sorry. Would you like me to go over there and . . ."

"Can we just go back to HIS now. I just want to go. I need to get away from here."

Reid pretended to protest a little more until Molly insisted.

"PLEASE! Can we just go?" She turned her face to the window of the vehicle so that Reid would not see the tears streaming down her cheeks. Reid pulled the car back into traffic and headed back in the direction of the HIS campus. He smiled to himself as he drove and thought. "Perfect! That was masterfully done if I do say so myself. Absolutely perfect."

Chapter 18

"I'm thinking of firing you. I want to be clear about that."

Dylan was furious and his face had turned a dark reddish color.

"You violated just about every trust issue I can think of. My own, Molly's and poor Becca's. She was hurt a lot, and for what? Just so you could try to manipulate my life and any other lives you choose too?

Reid had expected something like this but in his mind he believed that he had done the right thing. At some point all of this would blow over and things would go back to the way they were.

"Dylan I know that you can't see it right now but this was the right way to go. For you, for HIS and probably for Molly as well. She is a nice enough girl but she just does not belong in our world."

They argued about it for several days. In the meantime the whole project had to be put on hold. Dylan felt it necessary to give everyone involved some time off. He had had a night away from HIS and even though that evening had not turned out like he had thought it might, he realized that everyone else who was involved with the project should have a night off too. A lot of planning had to go into that so that not everyone would go out on the same night. They also now had a huge security nightmare on their hands.

Dylan finally hit on the idea of securing tickets to various events like concerts, movies, sporting events and things like that. It was decided that only four employees who were involved with GLASS would go at a time and would be joined (not escorted or accompanied) by two HIS security guards. The guards were there mostly to hold off reporters who might be following some of the employees. No one, including Dylan, was really overjoyed with the plan but it was the best they could do. The project slowed to a crawl. Dylan had met with Becca Knight and explained everything to her. He told her as much as he knew about what had happened. She told him that it was very embarrassing but that she understood that it wasn't his fault. She realized that they had all been set up.

Almost everyone at HIS felt compassion for Molly, Dylan and Becca and felt that Reid was the main villain in the whole sordid affair. The two people at HIS who felt otherwise were Reid and Dr. Ormond. They both truly believed that it would be shown in the end that Reid was a true hero, not a villain.

Molly was sort of an outlier. Her distrust and dislike of Reid Corder grew intensely for obvious reasons. But what really got everyone's attention was that she cut off almost all interaction with Dylan after that night. She understood what had happened, Dylan had explained things to her several times. But she just could not let go of the thought that when she first saw Dylan with Becca at the bistro, he seemed to be enjoying himself a little too much. She thought that she would never be able to forget the sight of Dylan holding Becca's hand. That forgive and forget stuff she had always heard about was a little harder to deal with when she was the one who was supposed to be doing the forgiving and forgetting. "I know that you are probably trying to teach me something here Lord," she thought. "But if you don't mind. I really do not care to discuss it. Even with you."

Molly knew in her heart that wasn't the way things worked. You didn't get to choose which things you wanted to deal with or not. But in this case she stubbornly held onto her disappointment like it was a long lost diamond. At one point she even found herself thinking to herself, "This is my misery and I'm going to hang on to it no matter what anyone else thinks about that. So there. It's just my lot in life right now to suffer through this and that's just exactly what I intend to do, suffer. That is all there is to it."

Finally after two weeks or so the training sessions got started again but it was no longer business as usual. Things around HIS had definitely changed for the worse. Morale was at an all time low. Dylan and Molly saw each other everyday but rarely spoke to each other. When they did, it was only because they needed to do so for whatever task they were working on.

During those times Dylan tried hard to strike up a conversation with

Molly about anything other than GLASS. However Molly could not get past her internal pain and personal embarrassment. She spoke to Dylan in short, to the point, sentences and refused to talk about any topic that was non GLASS related at all.

Still, the project was moving forward. It was moving slowly, but some progress was being made every day. The incident at The Blue Victory Grill and the days that followed had not stopped the project, but they had definitely managed to slow the pace down dramatically. In fact the timetable for the next GLASS run had to be pushed back several weeks.

Reid was frustrated with that and he tried to push people a little harder to complete their tasks within the original time frame. That only seemed to make things worse.

At the end of the fourth week following the debacle at The Blue Victory, Dylan called a meeting of all HIS employees. A lot of people were excused from attending because a company like HIS could never really be shut down completely. There were things that needed to be attended to every second of every day. Those employees who were crucial to the ongoing work of HIS were excused from the meeting but that still left about seventy percent of all HIS employees who were able to attend. Dylan had not announced what the purpose of the meeting was and no one had been able to find out prior to the meeting.

The meeting was held in the largest meeting room that HIS had but even so the room was packed way past capacity. If a Fire Marshall had arrived while that meeting was going on, he or she would have been extremely unhappy.

At the appointed time Dylan walked into the room. This time there was no dais or stage set up so Dylan climbed up on a chair. He did not have to ask for quiet because as soon as he had entered the meeting space, the room had become deathly silent.

He stood quietly for a moment looking out over the crowd. He hoped that along with the other HIS employees that Reid, Becca and Molly would all be in attendance. He noticed Reid right away standing by himself in a far corner and he finally saw Becca standing off to one side of the room. He searched for a long moment but could not locate Molly. He sighed out loud and then began to explain to everyone why he had assembled them all here.

"I'm thinking seriously of resigning."

The uproar caused by that statement went on for several minutes and finally Dylan had to call for quiet. Then he began to explain his reasons for thinking about that decision.

"I know that sounded very dramatic and all, but I really mean it. The project that we are all focused on could very well be the most important project ever in the history of mankind. Again that sounds melodramatic, but it actually could be just that. If not the most important, it most certainly would have to rank in the top two or three or so of all time."

He waited for that to sink in and then went on. "Without laying blame on anyone, I have come to realize that I am no longer the person to lead this project."

Again there was a complete uproar in the room and again he had to call for order.

"I know that in the past we have done great things together but there is just too much at stake here right now. We all know that all things must come to an end sooner or later, and I think that my time as President and CEO here has come to that point. Because of recent events and circumstances, my leadership abilities have been greatly diminished.

This project must go forward. It must be completed. And that probably will not happen with me at the helm. In addition to that, I have managed to hurt the one person on this planet who I love the most. I was careless with the feelings of other people as well and I realize that this was just simply wrong. I feel that it is now time for me to--"

"Wait," a small voice called out from the back of the room. "You love me? Are you talking about me? Did you just say that you love me? Cause I love you too!"

The room seemed to become even more quiet as everyone looked first toward the back of the room and then turned in unison to look toward Dylan.

Dylan squinted toward the rear of the meeting room. "Molly is that you? Yes! Yes I love you and I know that I have hurt you and I am so very sorry about that. I've been trying to talk to you this past week and to try to see how I can make it up to you. I wanted to tell you how much I love you, but you just didn't seem interested in talking to me."

Molly's voice again came from the back of the room. "Yeah, that's because I am being a big baby. I thought I needed to make you pay for what you did to me by giving you the silent treatment. But I know deep down that it really wasn't you. I want you to love me. I want you to love me so much. I really do want that because I love you too. But I was hurt and I was scared and, oh I don't know; I was just a jerk."

Now the crowd in the room started to part so that Molly could move toward the front of the room. At the same time, Dylan jumped off of the chair and started to make his way toward her. They met in roughly the middle of the room and hugged for a full minute. HIS employees throughout the room exploded with cheers and well wishes. Dylan pulled himself slowly away from Molly and held her at arm's length. He gazed into her eyes for a second, smiled and asked, "You love me?"

He did not wait for her to answer him. Instead he placed his lips on hers and pulled her into a very long, warm and gentle kiss.

The HIS employees cheered and yelled even louder. The cheering was so loud that people working down the hall heard the noise. Indeed the noise reached such a high decibel level that it could almost have been heard in the other buildings on campus as well. But Molly and Dylan were preoccupied and never heard a thing.

As the cheering resounded throughout the building, Reid slid out of the meeting room unnoticed and headed for his office. Once there he locked the door and then opened his top left desk drawer. From the drawer he removed a bottle of Scotch and poured himself a drink. He took a large gulp and then sat back in his chair. He sipped his drink a little slower and said to himself, "Not over yet my friends. Oh no, this is not over by a long shot."

CHAPTER 19

Later that evening Reid was still in his office, still drinking Scotch and still muttering to himself. Dylan poked his head into Reid's office and greeted him pleasantly. "Hey Reid. Burning the midnight oil I see."

Reid froze with the glass of Scotch halfway up to his mouth. He stared back at Dylan and asked, "Am I fired?"

"No Reid you're not. At least not right now. Everyone here has to put their collective feet down hard on the accelerator and move this project forward. That includes you. We need to get this thing done. Everyone needs to dig down deep and finish this project. After this is all over, then we'll see where we are with everything."

Reid sat quietly for a minute and then looked over at Dylan and said, "OK. I'm in. And, I really am sorry."

"Like I said, we'll talk about it all when this is over. Good night Reid."

Dylan left Reid's office and Reid resumed drinking and grumbling. Just as Reid took another swig, Dylan's head reappeared in the doorway of Reid's office. Reid was so startled that he spilled half of his drink onto his desk top, with some of it dripping down into his lap.

"Oh and by the way Reid. I'm not stepping down. Just for your information, I'm still the President and CEO of HIS. Just so we're clear. See ya tomorrow."

Over in her room Molly was on cloud nine. She had just finished praying and telling God how amazed she continued to be each time He did something incredible. It seemed to Molly that the incredibleness was occurring almost minute by minute. Now she was reading the itinerary for the next day and she could see that a majority of the day would be spent in the GLASS lab. She and Trevor had asked Dylan almost daily if they could get to see the actual GLASS apparatus. However time and time again they had been put off. Now it looked like their time had arrived. According to tomorrow's itinerary it seemed apparent to Molly that she would finally get to see GLASS up close for the first time.

About mid morning of the next day Molly and Dylan walked together from the silver building over to the rose colored building where the GLASS lab was located. As they entered, a security guard checked both of their ID badges. Molly looked at Dylan with a questioning look and he answered by saying that they were all pretty security conscious around here, especially in that particular building and even he had to show his security ID every time he entered the building.

Their ID's were checked once as they entered the building and then again as they were about to enter the lab. Just past the second security check there were two changing rooms, one on either side of the hallway. The one on the left was marked "Men's Changing Area: Clean Room Entrance."

Directly across the hall there was another area marked in similar fashion except that of course that room was marked as the "Women's Changing Area: Clean Room Entrance."

Molly could not help notice that the doors did not appear to be actual doors. It looked for all the world to her like someone had just painted a two inch wide line on the wall that approximated the size and shape of a door. There was even a doorknob painted on the wall in the proper place where a doorknob should be.

She stared at the doorway that was painted on the wall for a few seconds and then looked at Dylan and said, "Ummm, how do I get in? I mean what am I supposed to do here? This is not really a door."

Dylan tried to pretend that he was confused by her remarks and said, "What are you talking about? Of course it's a door."

Molly looked at him for a moment and responded. "No, it isn't. It's just a place where a door should be, but instead of a real door, somebody just painted the outline of a door on the wall here."

Dylan knew that he was showing off a bit but he just couldn't help himself. "What's the matter with you? It is obviously a door. Anyone can see that. And in answer to your question about how you will get in, you are supposed to walk through it, just like you would with any other door. Like this."

As he finished talking he stepped toward the door marked as Men's Changing Area. An opening appeared in the wall inside of the painted outlines of the door. Molly's jaw dropped as she saw the opening appear. She was shocked to see that the opening did not open like a regular door. This one opened like no other door that she had ever seen. The door spiraled open like an eye pupil opening up. A small dot of an opening appeared about waist high in the precise middle to the painted outline. It spread outward from that point like a wave until the entire painted door outline was open. It made no sound as it opened and the entire opening process only took about two seconds. The wall where the opening occurred just simply seemed to disappear. After Molly recovered she stuck her head in the opening. There was no place that she could see where the wall (or door) had recessed into. She checked both sides and the top and bottom as well but there was nothing to see. The wall inside of the painted lines was just gone. She pulled her head back out of the doorway and stood in the center of the hall looking at Dylan

"How did you do that?" She asked.

Dylan replied, "Nothing to it. I did it like this." As he spoke he stepped out of the doorway and rejoined Molly in the hall. As he did, the wall closed behind him in exactly the opposite manner from the way it opened. The wall just seemed to start reappearing from all angles inside the painted lines. It began appearing first at the lines outlining the door and then closed toward the middle so that the last part of the wall that remained open was in the middle of the painted lines. In just a fraction of time, the door (or wall opening) had closed. It had closed just the same way that it had opened, except in reverse.

Molly was speechless. Dylan laughed a little and said, "Pretty cool huh?"

Molly just continued to stare so Dylan continued.

"Look, if you really do want to see the GLASS lab, you need to first go on into the changing area. The GLASS lab is a clean or sterile area so we have to get rid of all of these clothes. In your changing area you'll find a locker with your name on it. Leave your clothes there. Then walk to the wall where the lines are painted in dark green, outlining another door. It will look pretty much like these doors do and it will open in the same way as you walk up to it. No magic words are necessary, the door will know when you get close enough and it will open automatically. Once you're through and the door closes behind you, you will find that you are in a very small room, maybe five feet wide by six or seven feet long. You can move around if you want to or you can just stand still. The walls of that room will start to glow a kind of burnt orange color and there will be a high pitched whistle. You'll see and hear both of those for about ten seconds. You won't feel any pain at all. In fact you won't feel anything. All of us carry bacteria on every inch of our bodies. We have bacteria on our skin, our hair, our nails and every other body part as well. Even though you will have felt nothing, the bacteria that you carry on you will have been destroyed. I'm not exactly sure if the bacteria will feel any pain but I know that you won't. In front of you, you will see the painted outline of yet another door. When the glow fades away and you can no longer hear the whistle, you will hear a woman's computerized voice telling you that it is OK to walk forward. That's TERRI's voice, the voice of our AI, the Artificial Intelligence in our computer system. TERRI stands for Technical Elaborative Relationally Realistic Intelligence and she is present everywhere in the lab. In fact, from today onward TERRI will be present with you all over campus. Always remember, TERRI knows everything. Just step toward the outlined door that is in front of you when she tells you to do so and it will open and let you enter yet another room. In that room you will find another locker, pretty much like the first one. This one will have a jumpsuit hanging on a hook. It will be a light gray color and will have your name embroidered on it. Don't worry, it's your size and if you are worried about fashion, forget about it. Everyone in the lab wears the exact same type of jumpsuit. The only difference in jumpsuits is their color. Computer technicians wear red jumpsuits, the science guys wear green, the Open Particle power experts wear black and there are several other colors that people in there are wearing according to what they do. You get the picture right? Those of us going on the run will be wearing gray, but all of the jumpsuits look identical except for the color. All set?"

Molly was fighting hard to not become too overwhelmed. She nodded and said, "Well, this place never ceases to amaze me. New discoveries around every corner I guess." She paused to gather her thoughts and then said, "By the way, I'm glad to see that there are both women's and men's changing areas. I remember seeing old vids and allcomm records of the olden days. Did you know that for a while people tried to have just one uni-gender bathroom for everyone to use? Man, what were they thinking?"

"Yeah, I've seen some of those old videos too. I don't know what that was all about. Interchangeable genders of some kind or maybe they were trying to make everyone be just the same as everyone else. I don't know. I think things were really weird back in those days. Can you imagine, gender neutral bathrooms and stuff like that?"

They both laughed for a minute and then Molly shrugged and said, "Well, here goes."

She walked toward the wall and sure enough, just as she got within two feet of the wall, it opened again like a human eye pupil opening and then it shut behind her.

Dylan waited for just a second and then walked into the changing area designated for men.

CHAPTER 20

Molly emerged from the women's changing area and stared into the huge lab in front of her. The doors that she had gone through still amazed her, but nothing amazed her like what she was seeing before her now. As she stood gazing into the room trying to take it all in, her thoughts were interrupted by Dylan's voice close beside her.

"Pretty incredible right? I still feel insignificant when I come in here, and I'm usually here every day."

He knew that she must be overwhelmed by what she was seeing so he allowed her to try to gather her thoughts as much as she could.

They were standing just inside the room and Molly could see the entire lab unfolding in front of her. There were a few things she recognized but she could only guess at the purpose of most of the items in the lab. She thought for a second that this must be how some Science Fiction writers would envision a lab in some future time. That thought was made even more impactful as she realized that this was no Science Fiction novel. This was real. These people had invented a time machine and she was standing in the same room with it. Dylan's voice brought her out of her musings. She looked at him and said, "Hummm? Were you talking to me?"

"Yes. I said that we can have a look around later but there are a few people I want you to meet first."

He walked with her over to a group of about ten people who were standing about thirty feet over to their left. As they approached the group, Molly realized that she must look to them like a deer caught in a car's headlights. A strange thought occurred to her, that a saying like that had survived through the years even though it had been a long time since vehicles had actually had real headlights.

Dylan was already introducing her to the others standing in the group. She knew a few of them already. Reid, Dr. Ormond, Trevor and Dr. Lamacelli were all standing in the group. Molly immediately recognized one other person in the group. They had never met, but Molly recognized her anyway. She was the final person in the group introduced to her by Dylan.

"Yes, I already know who Dr. Nichole is," Molly said. "And I am very excited to be included in this project with such a well known person."

Reid rolled his eyes skyward and sarcastically blasted Molly. "Oh come on. You can't possibly know who this is," he said as he indicated Dr. Nichole with a nod of his head. "You're just trying to make it seem like you fit in around here again. I'll give you fifty credits if you can tell us anything more than just one or two bits of information about Dr. Nichole."

"But I do know. I know exactly who Dr. Nichole is and what she's done," she insisted. "I'm not generally a betting kind of person, but in this case I'll accept your challenge Reid. You're on! When I was in middle school, I had an assignment to do a scroll on someone who had been in the news around that particular time. It's kind of how I found out that I loved to scroll. And with my love of history and historic personalities, the assignment fit me like a glove. I chose Dr. Nichole for my assignment. I probably can't recall everything I learned, but let me give it a shot. Dr. Abigail Nichole. Born and raised in Perth Australia. At age fourteen entered M.I.T. and graduated with a bachelor's degree in Pseudo Solidarity Physics when you were still about sixteen I think. From there you went on to do graduate work at the University of Helsinki in Finland and got a PhD. there in just one year. I think your degree there was in some kind of engineering; seems like it was Advanced Biometric Engineering or something like that. After you received your degree there I know you went back to MIT and graduated with double majors. One in Astro-Engineering and the other in Sub Zero Mathematics. I have no clue what any of those degrees are, I just remember that you received them. When you graduated from MIT you were still only nineteen if I remember correctly. You were instrumental in the design of, and the building of, the world's second orbiting space colony known as Space Station Eden. I think Station Eden is the permanent home of over five hundred people.

Then came the project that you are most known for, the creation of the first permanent colony on the Moon. I remember that it seemed to take forever to build but it was finally inhabited about nine or ten years ago and has been going strong ever since as far as I know. It's purpose is to mine rare minerals that were discovered deep under the lunar surface. You were so important to that project that they named that colony after you; Nichole Station, although I think everyone today just calls it Nikki Town."

She turned to Reid and asked, "How'd I do?"

In answer he just scowled and told her that he would pay her later. Everyone else in the group laughed lightly as Reid's face turned three different shades of red.

Dr. Nichole looked hard at Molly for a few moments and then spoke directly to her.

"You know, hero worship is really not my thing. And if I thought that was what you were trying to do then we would be done right here and now. But I think you were honest about the scroll assignment you told us about. You made me feel pretty old, but I guess that is OK because in truth I am pretty old, at least compared to you."

Everyone laughed as the tension of the moment began to drift away.

"Besides, anybody who can put Reid Corder in his place like that is a friend of mine. C'mon, I'll give you the grand tour."

Reid sulked like a little boy as everyone else laughed again and the remainder of the tension dissipated entirely.

Dr. Nichole took Molly by the arm in a friendly gesture and led her away from the group. She turned and looked back over her shoulder and said, "You all just go on and do whatever it is you're doing. This dear girl and I need to discuss a few things. I'll show her around while we talk."

Dylan had wanted the privilege of showing the lab to Molly but Dr. Nichole was the senior scientist on the project and no one ever said no to her. She literally was a living legend. Technically, as CEO Dylan could have pulled rank, but even though he was disappointed, he was smart enough to let it alone.

Chapter 21

Dr. Nichole and Molly walked through the lab. Molly was introduced to other people in the lab working at things she could only wonder about. As they walked they chatted about a wide variety of topics.

"First of all, don't ever call me Dr. Nichole again. Abbie will be just fine. I don't really like all that fussiness with all of that Doctor nonsense. Everyone here calls me Abbie and I want you to call me Abbie as well. Sound like a plan?"

"Well Dr. Nichole, oh, I mean, ummmm, Abbie, that is really going to be hard for me to do. Everyone here is so smart and so well known in their respective fields; but you, you're one of the best known people on the planet. I have looked up to you and your work for a long time. In my mind you have always been Dr. Nichole and probably always will be."

"Listen. As I said, that formality stuff is a lot of nonsense most of the time. You call me Abbie just like everyone else. Starting right now, OK?"

"Well, sure, if you say so. But can I tell you something else?"

"Certainly, go right ahead."

"I just love your Australian accent. It is really cool."

Abbie just smiled and shook her head slowly as she spoke, "Well now, isn't that amazing. We are walking through the most astounding science lab the world has ever known with the world's most amazing machine not even fifty feet away from us, and you are interested in my accent. Well, that's an American for you."

They both laughed easily for a minute and then Molly got a little bit more serious.

"Abbie, will you show me the actual GLASS apparatus ? I can see what has to be it over against that far wall, but can you show it to me up close and tell me more about it?"

"Yes, I could. But I'm going to let Dylan do that. He's so proud of it, I will let him have the honor of showing it to you in detail."

Molly looked over at Abbie and said, "But I bet you actually built it right?"

"Yeah, I guess so but who cares. It really was a great team effort. I'm not really into all that who gets credit for what stuff and all of that. I've received enough credit for things and believe me, it's not all that big of a deal. Besides I know he really likes you and I think I will let him show GLASS to you as well as many of the other amazing things in this room. By the way, I heard what happened to you over in Chapel Hill. Some date huh? Please allow me to give you two quick pieces of advice:

1. Stay close to Dylan and get closer if you can. They don't come any better than him, he's the real deal.
2. Stay as far away from Reid Corder as possible and then try to get farther away if you can. He's the real deal too, but in a negative way.

Reid is a very brilliant man and I don't think that HIS would be where it is today without him. But deep down inside he is also a snake. He wants what's best for himself and he will go to great lengths to get those things. I have learned very quickly to never trust him. When he tells me something or gives me information of some kind, I make sure that I verify it from some other source. You need to be careful around him because he will not be careful around you. With Reid it is always about him first and HIS second. That's it, nothing else matters very much to him. Just be careful.

Dylan on the other hand is as nice a person as you will ever meet. He's brilliant too but he cares a great deal for other people and he is always looking for ways to improve working conditions around here, although they're already great. He is just an all around good guy.

OK, I've said my piece on those two guys and I apologize for preaching about them that way. Just wanted you to know how things seem around here from my perspective.

So now I've probably bored you to death. I realize you didn't come in here to hear me babble on about those two knuckleheads. I know that you must be really excited to get your first look at GLASS. But before I get you back over to Dylan, I need to ask you something personal if I may."

Molly was ready for some question about previous boyfriends, or about her scroll or something like that. Insead Abbie asked her a question that seemed to come out of thin air.

"I've heard that you are a Christian. What exactly does it mean to be a Christian?"

Chapter 22

Molly was taken completely off guard by Abbie's question. She looked at Abbie without saying anything. Abbie laughed easily in a non threatening way. She explained to Molly that the entire HIS staff had been pretty angry over the decision to take the next GLASS run to Jerusalem to look for Jesus. She further explained that everyone knew that it was because of Molly that the decision to go to Jerusalem had been approved. Almost everyone working at HIS were either scientists or science oriented in some way and as such almost all of them were exclusively non religious in nature. Though no one at HIS really liked Reid Corder all that well, they all felt pretty much as he had originally felt about using GLASS to try to prove something that they all felt was a fairytale. Almost everyone liked Molly as a person, but no one really understood what her faith meant to her.

Molly could tell that even though Abbie had used the word angry a minute ago, she really wasn't. Molly guessed correctly that it was not really in Abbie's nature to be angry but she was a little worried that just about the entire staff of HIS thought she was an idiot and a trouble maker. A creative and positive thought suddenly burst into her brain as she heard that subtle whisper of a voice explain to her that people once thought of Moses, John The Baptist and the early missionary Paul as troublemakers. Molly knew that she should be glad that she was in such good company but she also knew that she was in way over her head. In her personal relationship with God, Molly considered those men to be the rock stars of her faith. She was more of just a dumb rock and not really in their ball park. Abbie's voice brought her back to the current conversation.

"So don't get me wrong. I have always thought of myself as being open minded about things like this. But I'm sorry. I just don't buy it. I can't find it within myself to believe in this Jesus person as the one and only true son of God. I've just never seen any evidence of that."

Molly thought for a second and then responded. "You probably have actually seen a lot of evidence, you just didn't recognize it as such at the time."

Abbie stopped walking and stood facing Molly for a few moments. Finally she smiled and said, "Well there is certainly more to you than meets the eye isn't there? Maybe we can talk more about it later. For now though, I need to get you back over to Dylan so he can show you GLASS by himself. I know he is so proud of this whole project. Look at him over there, like a little boy who is waiting to show off his new toy."

Abbie and Molly walked over to where Dylan was pretending to be busy. They could both tell that he had been doing nothing really except watching them as they toured the lab. He had seen that Abbie purposely had not taken Molly over to GLASS on their brief tour of the lab and he was very excited to know that he would be the one to show GLASS to her. However, he pretended that he did not know that GLASS had not been part of the tour.

"Well, what did you think of GLASS up close?"

Abbie replied, "Oh come off it. We didn't go over there and you know it. I know that you would love to show Molly the actual working parts of GLASS so here you go, she's all yours."

They all laughed briefly knowing that Dylan was busted. His charade was exposed and they all knew it.

"Thanks Abbie. I owe you one."

"Oh you owe me more than one pal, but we can talk about that later."

Dylan took Molly's elbow and began to guide her over to the far wall where GLASS was set up. As he did he looked back over his shoulder to catch Abbie's eye. When he saw that he had made eye to eye contact with her he motioned slightly with a nod of his head toward Molly. His eyes asked Abbie the silent yet all important question, "So what do you think of her?"

Abbie understood the silent query. She smiled at Dylan and gave him a thumbs up sign. Dylan nodded that he had received her message and smiled back.

Concerning most things in his life, Dylan usually could care less if people approved or not. But if there was one person in the building whose approval he did seek out now and then, it was Dr. Abigail Nichole.

Dylan continued guiding Molly over to GLASS. As they got closer, Dylan said to Molly, "Well here she is. What do you think?"

Molly had no words to answer him. She just stared at GLASS trying to take it all in. Directly in front of her, against the far wall, were six large oblong objects Each of them were about eight feet tall and four and a half feet wide at their widest point. They were made of some substance that Molly could only guess at. The material they were made of appeared to be plastic or perhaps acrylic but as she looked more closely she could tell that neither of those was the material that had been used to create these things. From where they were standing, about twenty feet from the objects, she couldn't be sure what they were made of. She guessed correctly that the material was most likely something that the team here at HIS had invented just for this purpose.

The tall oblong items were tinted a deep gray color. Molly could see inside of them but the tinting was so dark that she could not make out many features or details on the inside.

"These are the tears," Dylan stated.

"Tears?"

"Yeah, doesn't the shape of them remind you of teardrops?"

As soon as the words were out of Dylan's mouth, Molly immediately saw the resemblance. They were indeed shaped exactly like human teardrops.

Dylan was speaking again. "One of the techs here gave them that nickname a year or so ago and it has just sort of stuck. They really do have actual scientific names that even I can't pronounce or remember sometimes, so everyone just refers to them as the tears. Simpler that way."

"Wha, what do they do? What are they for?"

"These are the actual time capsules that we will travel in."

He spread his arms wide and told Molly that this whole area and everything in the lab was the actual GLASS project. The capsules, or tears, were just the centerpiece of the whole unit. Molly asked if she could touch one of them and Dylan laughed as he walked over to one of the tears with Molly beside him.

"Of course you can touch them. After all, in just a few days you will be traveling in one of them."

He let that sink in for a few minutes as Molly ran her hand over the surface of the second tear from the left. She tried harder to look inside but still found it difficult to make out more than one or two items inside the tear. One object she could see a bit more clearly now was a large chair. She could tell that it was centered inside the tear with other objects and instruments situated around it but she was not able to see much more than that.

Dylan had her by the elbow again and was guiding her to the left. Located at a ninety degree angle to where the row of tears were, Molly and Dylan came to a raised booth of some sort. The booth or work station was about thirty feet long. It was encased in glass but this glass was clear so Molly could easily see inside. Dylan explained that this would be where some of the technicians would sit during the run. They would be monitoring a vast variety of things. Some of those were medically oriented functions like heart rate, blood pressure, respiratory rates and many other functions. Other people who would sit here would monitor things like the on board cameras and computers as well as the vast array of other components built into the tears. In addition to watching and checking those items there would be other techs here whose job it would be to monitor the crucial power supply. The amount of power that was fed into each tear was critical and had to be regulated and adjusted constantly during a run.

Dylan allowed Molly to get up into the monitoring area. It reminded Molly of the old time judging booths or reviewing stands that she had seen in old vids or comms. She could imagine one of these holding judges for parades or perhaps dignitaries viewing some sort of competition of one kind or another. The booth held two rows of comform seats with eight seats in each row. The second row was elevated above and behind the first row and was offset a little from the seats in the front row so that the people seated in the second row could easily see around the people seated in the first row. Every seat had a small console in front of it so that the person sitting in each seat could operate their own equipment easily without hindrance from anyone else. Molly could see that each of the seats had an unobstructed view of the tears.

Dylan went on to explain who would sit in each chair and what their specific job would be. Molly tried to be attentive to what he was explaining but realized quickly that the science aspects of it all were, as usual, way beyond her comprehension.

Next Dylan guided her over to another booth. This one was much smaller and was located directly across from the first booth they had toured. It too was at a ninety degree angle to the tears. The two monitoring booths faced each other with the tears located between them down at one end. This second booth was built in a similar fashion to the first booth. However, this booth was much smaller and could hold only four people at a time. Another difference was that there was no glass covering this booth, it was open aired to the room. She could also see clearly that whereas the other booth had small individualized consoles for each of the seats, this booth had one long console. All four seats in this booth faced that one console. It occurred to Molly that the four people working in this booth would be working together, probably as a very close knit team; a team that was comfortable with each other and used to working together. Looking closely at the console Molly could only guess at their work assignments or tasks. Dylan tried to explain what would be happening inside of this booth during the GLASS run but again Molly understood very little of it. She did manage to breathe a sigh of relief when Dylan told her that Abbie would be sitting in this booth during the run. Abbie's seat was to be the one on the far left of the booth, closest to the tears. Molly was pleased to hear that Abbie would have complete override responsibility of one hundred percent of the physical aspects of the tears themselves. If something had to be changed or adjusted or modified during the run, Abbie would be the decision maker for all of those things.

Molly tried to take in everything that Dylan was saying but mostly she just stood and stared at the intricate equipment in front of her. She had thought of the time machine as just one piece of equipment but she could now see that it was actually made up of several parts, only one of which was the piece of equipment that would take her back in time. As she continued to stare, she became aware that another group of people was approaching. She caught sight of them out of the corner of her eye and heard Dylan greet them. She turned to see Abbie, Reid, Dr. Lomacelli and

Trevor coming towards her. When they were all together Abbie spoke to Trevor and Molly.

"Well, there it is. Your ride back in time. We'll come back to it a little later and tomorrow you will actually get to go inside for the first time. We'll let your comform seats adjust to your bodies and we will begin to explain in a bit more detail some of the controls you will see inside the tears once you are in there. But for now, we still have work to do out here. I'm sure you have some questions and we also have some info to give to the two of you as well, so let's take a ten minute break and then meet over in that area over there."

As she finished speaking she turned and pointed to a corner of the room that was set up as a mini classroom. It had no actual walls like a real classroom would but there were about ten or twelve chairs set up in classroom style and someone had placed a comm screen next to one of the walls. The screen had been placed in hover mode and it hung in free space about two inches away from the wall. The bottom of the screen was about three feet off of the floor.

As the group began to break up, Molly looked at all of their faces. Trevor, who had taken his tour just a few minutes before Molly still had a stunned look on his face. Molly was pretty sure that her face had a similar expression on it. Doctors Nichole and Lamcelli looked like proud parents, Dylan had that little boy in the candy shop look. He looked so excited that Molly thought he might explode at any minute. Reid had the usual scowl on his face but when he saw that Molly was looking at him he suddenly grinned from ear to ear. Molly smiled back politely but looking at Reid caused her to suddenly think of how a fox in a chicken coop might look. She made sure that she put a little extra distance between herself and Reid as she walked over to the temporary classroom.

Chapter 23

There were twelve chairs set up in the corner classroom but it seemed that there were only eight participants invited to this session. In addition to the little group that had assembled briefly over near the tears a few minutes earlier, a few more people had joined the group. Those additions were Dr. Ormond, and two technicians who were introduced quickly to Trevor and Molly. Abbie explained that from now on, this was going to be the crew that trained together for the last few days prior to the run. She said that there would of course be other HIS employees coming into and out of sessions as need be, but from now on, this group was on the front line of the GLASS project. Next she addressed the group as a whole.

"Even though Molly and Trevor are obviously not as familiar with GLASS as the rest of us are, from now on we train together and go over information together as much as we can. Trevor and Molly, I am certain that you have many questions for the rest of us so let's start there and get some of those out of the way as quickly as we can."

Even before she stopped speaking Trevor shot his hand straight up in the air and blurted out. "How in the world does this thing work?"

Everyone but Trevor and Molly burst out laughing and started passing monetary credits around to one of the new techs who had joined the group. Molly and Trevor both looked questioningly around at all the other group members.

Molly finally said, "What's so funny. If he hadn't asked that question, I sure would have. What's goin on?"

At that the other group members with the exception of Trevor laughed even harder. Once the laughter had subsided, Andrew, the tech who had collected the money explained. "We all knew that the question Trevor just asked was going to be the first question asked, in one form or another, by one of you. We took bets on how quickly that question would come up. I bet on one second, and so I just became one hundred and fifty credits wealthier at the expense of my colleagues who bet that you two would wait a little while before asking that question."

He then turned to the others, bowed dramatically from the waist and said, "Thank you all very much. All contributions to my desperate personal cash flow situation are greatly appreciated."

After more laughter Abbie called the group back to order again. "OK. Now that the fun and games are out of the way let's get down to it shall we? We did anticipate that one of you would ask that question pretty early on in this session so let's talk a little bit about that. How exactly does GLASS work? There are three crucial portions of the equation regarding the workings of GLASS. Of course there are about a million other facets of GLASS, but for our purpose here today, we will limit our discussion to just three. Those three are:

1. Power
2. Guidance
3. Target Orientation

Without each of those three synchronized together in perfect coordination, GLASS simply does not work.

Let's take a look at the second component, Guidance and begin there if we may. How will we know where in time or space we have been, where we are at any one particular time and where we are going, right? We touched on this a few days ago but let's go through it again and dig down into a few more of the details. I am going to turn the session over now to Dr. Lamacelli. This is his baby and he knows more about this than anyone here."

With that she smiled at Dr. Lamacelli and took a seat next to Molly. Dr. Lamacelli stood up and faced the group as he began to speak.

"I think that I can explain this best by giving a small demonstration."

He held up a plain white piece of paper. It looked to Molly to be square, about twelve inches on all four sides.

"Let us pretend that this paper represents space. If I make a mark on the paper in this corner with an X like so, and make a similar mark in the diagonal opposite corner, like so, we can see that those marks represent two different and separate locations."

As he spoke he drew an X in the top left hand corner of the paper and then drew another X in the extreme lower right hand corner of the paper.

"We will say that this X in the top left corner is here in Greensboro and we will pretend that the X in the lower right hand corner represents a location somewhere near the center of Antarctica."

He paused a moment to let that sink in and then continued. "Obviously if we want to travel from Greensboro to Antarctica, we need to travel a great deal of distance to get from one to the other. This travel is not only represented in distance but also in the amount of time it would take us to travel that distance. Yes?"

After a short pause and nods from everyone in the class he continued speaking. "But what if we did not need to take a great deal of time to go that distance, what if we could get there a lot quicker than it would normally take us? And what if we could get there without traveling that great distance at all?"

He held the paper out to the group so that they could all see the two X's he had drawn in the corners. He then drew a line connecting the two X's.

"That line represents both the time and the distance that it would normally take for us to travel from Greensboro to Antarctica."

Again he waited for nods from everyone in the group indicating that they were following him and then jumped right back in to his explanation. "But, what if it were possible to bypass that line, and do this."

As he spoke he slowly rolled the paper so that the X in one corner approached the X in the other corner. When he had finished rolling the paper, the two X's had met with one lying on top of the other. He had curved the paper forming a sort of open ended tube with the top left hand corner (Greensboro) now touching the lower right hand corner (Antarctica).

"If this paper represents both time and space, we have now been able to curve both of them so that there is now no distance between our two destinations and we can see that it would take us no time to get from one to the other because the two X's are in fact, touching each other and are now situated in one and the same place, located together at exactly the same time."

Molly was getting used to her jaw dropping so when it hit the floor this time, she did not react at all. She glanced at Dylan and saw that he was smiling at her with that little kid in the candy store look again. She glanced toward Trevor and saw that his jaw was actually lower than her own. She thought to herself that what Dr. Lamacelli had just described was not possible. Or was it? She shook her head to clear the haze that had formed inside as she realized he was speaking again.

"Of course this theory did not start with me. It is not a new idea at all. Many people, going back many, many years have thought about this curved space idea and some have actually tried to find ways to make it function in the real world instead of just in theory. All have failed. They have failed simply because it is not possible to do what I have just demonstrated with this paper. It would be nice if time and space travel were just that simple. But unfortunately for us, that is not the case."

"I knew it," Molly thought. "Time travel isn't real after all."

Dr. Lamacelli was speaking again. "What I realized several years ago was that all of those scientists and researchers failed because of one simple fact. That fact is that space is not, after all, curved. When I came to this conclusion I realized that if space and time were not curved then they must, by process of elimination, be flat or linear. The next step was to develop a theory stating that perhaps we could travel through a linear time and space module in a manner something like the curved paper model I just demonstrated. But what would that look like? If we could not curve time or space to travel from one point to another, then perhaps it might be possible to "fold" time and space to get from one point to another. In other words, we cannot travel through time and space by traveling along a curved path because there is no curved path. However I began to wonder if it might be possible for us to locate and travel through some sort of a fold or a crease that might already exist in both time and space. Allow me another demonstration."

He held up the paper once more, the X's in the corners plainly visible. He began to fold the paper in half, and then in half again and then in half again. He was only able to fold the paper six times before it got too small and thick for his strength to fold it any more. By this time the paper measured only about and two inches per side. Molly could still see the two X's. They were not touching each other but they were obviously closer together than they were before Dr. Lamacelli had begun to fold the paper.

"I am sorry that I have not worked out in the gym more. My forearm and finger strength is not what it should be. These are all the folds my strength will allow me to make. Too many hours spent in a lab I guess."

Everyone in the group chuckled politely and then he continued his explanation. "But I hope that you can see what I am trying to demonstrate. If I did have more strength, more "power", if you will, and if I was able to fold this paper hundreds or even thousands of more times I would eventually be able to make enough folds so that the Greensboro X would be in contact with the Antarctica X. At that point they would in fact be in the same place at the same time.

Dylan reached over and carefully placed his open palm beneath Molly's jaw. He pushed up gently so that she closed her mouth. She looked over at him and he said, "If this wasn't a sterile room you'd be able to catch a lot of flies that way."

She continued staring at him and realized that he was just teasing her slightly. She also realized that her mouth had been open, again.

"Sorry," she said, "But can this be true? This folded space stuff?"

Dylan reached over and took her hand in his, "It is true. It's all fantastically true!"

Dr. Lamacelli was talking again. He looked directly at Dylan and Molly and said, "Now if I can have everyone's attention again please, we will continue. After our theory was developed, we began to experiment. At first we made little progress, but one by one the breakthroughs began to occur. Finally we were able to prove and to demonstrate the existence of these folds through both space and time. We found that they resembled creases rather than folds and once we were able to see those for what they truly were, we were then able to pinpoint exactly how we could travel through them. There are separate creases for space and other creases for time. It took us a while but we are now able to discern between the two. Also we can now pick and choose which creases we need to use to travel from one place to another and also to travel through time in a similar fashion. There is no direct route from Greensboro to Antarctica, but by choosing the correct creases, we can weave our way from here to there. Then by choosing the correct time creases we can simultaneously travel from here to there and arrive whenever we want to. It all comes down to choosing the correct creases for both space and time."

Before he could continue Abbie jumped up and addressed the group. "Well I can see from the expressions on Molly's and Trevor's faces that we have discussed enough mind blowing stuff for one session at least. It's just about time for lunch so let's meet back here at one fifteen this afternoon. I've got the afternoon session so I'll be leading you all through that. We now have a pretty good idea of what it will be like to actually travel through these creases. We think we can predict what it might look like and what it might feel like to travel through time and space.

Oh, by the way, in honor of our own Dr. Lamacelli who discovered these creases we have given them a very honorable and appropriate name. We call them, Lamacelli Creases. OK, I'll see ya after lunch and we'll get into more detail this afternoon."

Molly and Dylan ate lunch together as they did almost every day. They talked about their individual interests, hobbies, families and other life experiences. Molly tried to bring her Christian beliefs into the conversation but Dylan stopped her before she could really get started.

"Molly, please. Can we just not talk about that right now? I am really enjoying being with you, but I just don't believe in this Jesus the way that you do. I don't want to offend you and I know that your faith is important to you, but I just don't see things the way you do. Can we just stick to some of the things that we have talked about that aren't so controversial?"

Molly was hurt a bit but she was also smart enough to know that most of the things that she said about Jesus, God or Christianity in general were just going over his head. Sort of the way the science that he talked about usually went over her head.

"OK," she replied. "For now. But sooner or later you are going to have to let me tell you why I believe some of the things that I do. Here I am trying to listen to all of you scientists. I am lost beyond measure and I don't understand what ya'll are saying most of the time. It makes no sense to me. But I believe in all of you. I have faith that what you are telling me is true.

Well my faith is no different. To you it makes no sense. But you have to trust me that I am telling you the truth in the same way that I trust you when you are talking about all this scientific stuff that I don't understand. Then later you are going to have to trust Jesus, even at the point where you see no proof. Christianity is about many things and one of the most important is that it is about faith, not proof. I know that will be difficult for you, but that really is the bottom line."

"I know what faith is Molly. It's just that I have always had faith in things that I can prove with my senses."

"I know that. But I am going to try to get you to see without using your eyes. I'm going to try to get you to accept something without any tangible proof. I'm going to try to get you to understand that it was a creator that gave you those senses that you rely on so much."

Dylan sat still for a moment and looked at Molly with a blank expression on his face.

"I'll try. That is all I can promise right now. Is that enough for you?"

Molly knew that eventually it would not be enough for her. She took seriously the stand of not being unequally yoked and it broke her heart to think that she had fallen in love with someone who she might not ever be able to be with in a more serious relationship.

She gazed at Dylan for a long moment and then said, "Yes it is. For now it's enough. Let's just go with that for the moment."

He agreed and they walked together back toward the GLASS lab. Molly emerged through the door that she still thought of as "that magic door" and found Dylan already in the lab waiting for her.

She smiled to herself when he whispered, "I really do not understand Christianity. But I was serious when I told you that I would try. I will try."

Molly knew that his road would be difficult. To try to understand Jesus through the scientific methods that he would be likely to use would be a road filled with roadblocks. But then she smiled again as she heard (or sensed) that same still small voice quietly tell her.

"Might be a difficult road, but then again it might not be. Let's just see how it goes, shall we?"

Chapter 24

When they arrived in the little open corner classroom, everyone was there except Reid. Abbie started right in. "Reid already knows this stuff and he is off working on some other HIS business projects not associated with GLASS, so we will just go ahead and get started."

Molly smiled and thought how wonderful Abbie's Australian accent was. "I really do not understand a great deal of what she is saying," she thought to herself. "But I could stay here all day listening to her say it."

She kept that thought to herself as Abbie really started to pick up speed. "Now, let's talk about what it will feel like to go on the run. Remember that no human has ever actually gone on a run yet, so this will be the first. That means of course that we have no real eye witness account of what it will be like during the run. However we have sent a lot of data gathering equipment on previous runs so we have a pretty good idea, just not an exact idea. That make sense to everyone?"

Once she had received nods from everyone, she proceeded. "Those of you who will be traveling on the run will enter the tears about an hour or so before the scheduled run time. That way we can get up to speed on the medical situation for each of you as well as to thoroughly check out all of the systems that will be in play during the run. You will be wearing period appropriate outerwear. In fact most of the clothing is ready and we have a fitting scheduled for this evening after dinner. So you will be sitting in your individual tear, wearing clothing that we hope will allow you to fit in as much as possible when you arrive on site. We really believe that you will fit in rather well. We have colored contact lenses to change your eye color, we have hair dye to change the color of your hair, we have hair pieces and extensions and chemical products that will change the complexion and hue of your skin and so on. We think that all of this will allow you to look fairly similar to the other people around you. Underneath your outerwear you will be wearing skin suits designed specifically for you. These suits are made so that even you will have difficulty realizing that you are wearing them. They are transparent and they are quite thin, about the thickness of a human hair. They are designed to mold and shape to your body as you sit, walk, run or whatever. Really, you will not even be aware that they are there. But they are really important. They will keep you warm if it is cold and they will keep you cool if the temperatures are high. Your suit is designed for you only and it will adjust automatically to your personal comfort levels. The suits will also be connected to us here in the lab and will appear to us in hologram form. This will make it easy for our medical team to monitor blood pressure, heart rate and so on. All of this is built into your suit. Your suit is designed to begin at mid calf and fit up around your torso and shoulders rising about halfway up your neck. Sitting here I know that you are all thinking that it sounds very uncomfortable. Don't worry, it isn't. I've tried them on many times and you will too over the next few days. Trust me, you will not even know you have it on. One of the more useful items embedded in the suits is the translation system. The translator will instantly allow you to understand other people who are talking to you, if it comes to that. We have built into these suits several languages that you might come across although we believe that you will most likely come in contact with only a few. Those languages include, Aramaic, an early form of Hebrew, Greek, a pre-Latin dialect as well as several other languages that we believe could have been used in Jerusalem during the first century. The translator also will allow you to converse with other people. Let the other person speak first if at all possible. Then when you respond back to the other person who had first addressed you, that person will hear your voice in their own language. You just speak English as you normally would, the translator in your skin suit will do the rest."

Molly sat bolt upright in her chair and yelled, "Hey, that sounds just like that time in the book of Acts. You know, when the Holy Spirit came down on the disciples. Remember? They all ran out into the street and started talking to people in languages that the people in the crowd could understand. Remember?"

As she finished speaking she looked around at the other group members. They were all looking at her as if she had ten heads. It was then that she recalled who she was talking to. She remembered that the people in this group had little or no idea what she was talking about. Molly realized that they had probably never read the book of Acts. In fact, she thought, they most likely had never even heard of Acts.

They all continued to stare at her.

"Uh, I guess I must have left that off of my summer reading list last year," Dylan said uncomfortably.

Molly understood that he was trying to make a small joke. Not at her expense, but so she would not feel embarrassed. She wanted to hug him for trying to make the moment a little easier for her but all she really wanted to do was crawl through the floor. In the end it was Abbie and not Dylan who came to her rescue.

"Yes Molly, I agree. I've read Acts," she grinned at Molly and then winked as she went on. "In fact, unlike these other heathens here, I've read the whole Bible through and through."

Everyone in the group now took their gaze off of Molly and stared straight at Abbie.

"You're a Bible reader?" Dr. Ormond asked. "Are you telling us that you are one of those Born Again types?" She then quietly added under her breath, "Whatever that is?"

Abbie looked Dr. Ormond in the eye and said, "Yes, I have read the Bible and no I am not a Christian. But I try to respect those that are, like our Molly here. There is a lot of good material in the Bible and I think everyone could benefit from reading it now and then. I don't really agree with a lot of it, don't even understand most of it I guess. But I do try to respect others like Molly here who are believers. And by the way, all of us will be required to work our way through several study sessions using the Bible as a history book as well as a geography book in preparation for the run. These sessions will take place over the next few days and are designed to familiarize ourselves with the time period and place we are targeting on this run. We'll be counting on Molly to guide us through some of that. Now, if we can continue, let's move on."

Molly could have hugged her.

Abbie continued talking and Molly tried to listen closely. "Now then, there will be a countdown that will begin forty five minutes prior to the time of our run. Each tear has a clock built into the consoles within easy eye sight so that you will be able to follow the countdown. It will be audible as well. TERRI will be calling out the countdown numbers over the final two minutes as well as doing about a million and a half other tasks. Speaking of TERRI, I almost forgot that Molly and Trevor have not yet been formally introduced to her. TERRI, say hi to Molly and Trevor."

"Hi to Molly and Trevor," said a voice that seemed to come from the midst of the room itself.

Abbie laughed a little and asked TERRI, "Why did you say it like that?"

TERRI responded. "What? You told me to say hi to Molly and Trevor, so that is what I did."

TERRI chuckled a little bit in her computer voice and said, "That is an old joke from my archives. Did you enjoy it? I have been waiting a while to use that one."

"Oh yes, quite funny TERRI," Abbie said as she too laughed. "And you're correct, that is a very old joke."

"Yes," TERRI admitted. "An oldie but a goodie."

Though Dylan had already mentioned TERRI to Molly earlier, Abbie went on to explain that TERRI was the Artificial Intelligence in the lab. Basically she was the voice of the macro super computer that was involved with every single aspect for the GLASS project. Abbie further explained that TERRI had seen and heard everything that had been said and done in the GLASS lab, almost since day one. She told the group that TERRI would be on the run and would be able to communicate with each of the time travelers as well as with the group left behind in the lab at all times. Without TERRI, the project would be impossible and GLASS would not exist.

"Besides being a super smart computer," Molly whispered out loud. "TERRI sounds like a name that should belong to some really pretty lady, not just a machine. So I'm going with that."

The whisper was very low and so quiet that no one else in the room heard it. But TERRI heard it.

"Thank you Molly! I like your name too."

Molly blushed and smiled at the same time.

"So TERRI," Abbie continued. "Will be with us the whole time both here in the lab and on the run itself. Feel free to ask her for anything you need. She is quite well versed by now on the actual time period we are attempting to visit.

Now, as the countdown proceeds and we here in the lab are satisfied with what our instrumentation shows us, we will stop that countdown at the traditional ten second mark. At that time we will verify that each of you inside the tears are satisfied with what your instruments are indicating to you. Once we are set and are all agreed that everything in the tears matches up with what we are seeing in our lab monitoring stations, we will proceed with those last few seconds of the countdown. After we go under ten seconds, only TERRI, Dylan or myself can stop the run from proceeding. If there are any problems seen by anyone, they will have to alert one of us.

As the countdown proceeds under that ten second mark you will begin to see a mist like substance fill your tear. From outside here it will look like there is a dense copper colored fog inside each tear. But we know from comms that we have sent back on earlier runs that to those of you inside the tears, the mist will appear to be a sort of goldish color. As the countdown hits zero, you will not be able to see us, and we will not be able to see you inside the tears. You will however be able to see your console. Communications are all set as well for the most part but there will be a brief moment of about twelve seconds where you will be unable to hear us and we will be unable to hear you. Also during that time you will not be able to communicate with each other. This is the twelve second period of time it will take for you to travel down through the Lamacelli Creases to reach your destination. So during that brief amount of time, you will feel like you are pretty much alone. Just remember that your fellow time travelers will be very close to you and traveling through the creases with you. And of course TERRI will be out of communication with you as well during those few seconds.

You will see the mist that has filled your tear and the mist will feel just like any other mist, sort of cool and moist. For those twelve seconds you will feel as if you are falling. It will probably feel like an elevator that drops too fast. You will feel that you are in a free fall; falling and falling each moment, only to fall, yet again. Then, just when you think that it can't go on any longer, you'll feel that falling sensation stop just as suddenly as it began.

Those twelve seconds will most likely seem like an hour to you. Rest assured though, it really will be just a few seconds. The timepieces that are built into the comms on your consoles will tick the seconds off for you.

After twelve seconds the mist will quickly dissipate. That process will take roughly another five or six seconds. When the mist clears you will be in Jerusalem in the year thirty three. Even though you will be sitting in your tear during the entire countdown process, when you arrive at your destination, you will be standing and the tear will have disappeared from sight. You will be standing together in a group, maybe four or five feet away from each other.

Now remember, in old videos and pictures that we have seen, those people who designed stories about time travel had the actual time machine appear back in the other time. But we now know differently. The tears will transport you back in time and bring you back here again, but the tear itself will stay right here. Those of us who will be here in the lab will see the mist clear from inside the tear. At that point you will be gone and we will then be monitoring your journey while the tears stay here. When you are ready to leave, the same thing will happen in reverse. You will all go off somewhere in a small group, hopefully to a place where you can't be seen. The mist will appear around you and the falling sensation will begin again. We here in the lab will see the tears fill with the mist again and after a few seconds, you will all be back here sitting in your teardrop, good as new.

I will have the responsibility for bringing you all back here. I will be in communication with all of you so together we will work that out when the time comes and you are ready to return. In case of emergency TERRI has override capabilities. As a double back up plan in extreme emergencies, Dylan as the senior team member on site will be able to override both TERRI and myself and get everybody sent back here if and when he decides he needs to do that. I can't imagine it will come to that, but just in case of something strange happening, we have three levels of control for the return run to bring you back.

Now, let's talk just a bit about your appearance at the site. Some of you may have read a story about something that used to be called a carnival fun house. Perhaps you may have even seen an old video or comm where someone went into a fun house. In these fun houses there was usually some sort of room that was called a hall of mirrors. But the mirrors used there were not regular mirrors. Those mirrors were used to distort the outward appearance of a person in some way. Some of the mirrors made a person look squat and wide while other mirrors made that person look very tall and extremely thin.

In a similar way, your appearance will be distorted as well.

As you travel through the Lamacelli Creases, the dimensions around you will make changes to your appearance. We have been able to make adjustments for some of those changes, but not all. Now remember that it is not you who is changing so there is no pain and no risk of injury or anything like that to you. It is only your outward appearance that will change. Others in the time and place you are traveling to will be able to notice that you do not look quite like everyone else. Let me explain further.

Traveling through the creases will change the appearance of your dimensions. Time, in this case, is not the culprit, space is. The further you travel through space, the more dimensions you must travel through. The more dimensions you travel through, the more drastic the changes will appear to be. Not really in a negative way, just a changed appearance. I'm sorry but we just don't have the time to go through all of the scientific reasons that makes this so, please just let me tell you about the changes that you can expect to experience. Just as with the fun house mirrors, your bodies will not change, but the appearance of your bodies will change so that you will look different to others around you. If a person is standing directly in front of you or behind you, you will look perfectly normal to them. You will have height and width, just as you and I do now. What you will not have is depth. If that person decides to walk around to your side, they will see the depth of your body begin to shrink. As they get to a ninety degree angle, and are looking directly toward the side of your body, you will pretty much disappear to them as far as their vantage point is concerned. There will actually still be width to you, but it will probably be about the thickness of a piece of paper, so unless they are looking VERY carefully, it will really look to them like you have disappeared.

You are going back mainly just to be observers so this may not be a big deal at all. You can probably find vantage points from which to observe that will allow you to not call any attention to yourselves. If Molly is right, everyone at the scene we are sending you back to will have their attention on Jesus being crucified. If Molly is wrong, who knows what else might be going on at this site and we might pull you back early because in that case, we would have proven that there was no crucifixion, no resurrection and no need for anything else.

It will be best if you could find a location where you could stand in one place with no one to either side of you. However, you will have the ability to move around if you wish. You can walk, run, sit, jump, squat, bend or whatever else you would normally do."

Abbie stopped speaking, looked at each team member one by one and then said, "We have just four days left before the run. Let's make the best of those days. While we were at lunch I was informed that Rob Maxman, one of our guys in the Historography department needs to have a word with us all. Let's take a break for, oh let's say fifteen minutes. I'll go get him and see what's up. He was not scheduled to meet with us today so I hope all is OK. In any event we'll see what he has for us. See you all here after break."

Chapter 25

During the break Molly asked Dylan if he had heard anything about why this guy from Historography wanted to meet with them. Dylan said that he had not heard anything but admitted that it seemed sort of strange to be having unscheduled meetings like this so late in the game. He was obviously a little nervous about it so Molly let it pass.

As the team gathered back together following the break she could see Abbie and someone who she guessed was Rob Maxman in a heated and animated discussion. As they approached, Dylan asked Molly to wait for him near the chairs and he then walked over to join Abbie and Rob. They both spoke briefly to Dylan and then he too began to wave his arms around dramatically and Molly heard him sigh loudly a couple of times.

"Doesn't look good," she said out loud.

"No, it certainly does not," said a voice behind her.

She turned and saw Reid standing just a few feet behind her. He too had been looking at the group having the conversation or argument or whatever it was and he was wearing a worried look as well. Just then the conversation broke up and Abbie asked everyone to take their seats.

"Looks like we have come upon a fairly good sized problem," she said. "It seems to be pretty serious and in a worst case scenario we might not be going to Jerusalem after all."

Abbie sat down as she continued. "For those of you who have not met him yet, I would like to introduce you to Rob Maxman. Rob works in our Historography department. He's here to get us up to speed on the problem."

With that she waved at Rob to begin and he started off in a quiet but worried voice.

"Well, I don't really know where to begin. This is all kinda new to me too, so I'm just going to jump in here. We don't just have one problem, it looks like we have several problems that are sort of related to each other.

The day before yesterday one of our researchers in Historography first identified these problems. We have not come to you all sooner because at first we weren't exactly sure about these problems. Then later when we were sure, we tried to find some solutions. We think that we have done that, but again, we're just not sure. To make a long story short, we just can't be absolutely certain what year we need to be targeting for the run. It doesn't take a long time to enter the correct coordinates into GLASS, but we can't be sure if we have the correct coordinates or not, and we are not really sure how to fix that. We have located a lot of data that tells us with one hundred percent accuracy that there once lived a man named Jesus. What we don't have with any kind of accuracy is a date as to when he was born or a firm date of his death. It seems that when the calendar we use today was first created, it was indeed based on this Jesus fellow. But the people who created the calendar kinda made an educated guess at the year in which he was killed. Our current year could be off by perhaps ten or even twenty years from what we think it is. There is just no way to tell for sure. The next problem that we discovered is this; we have some pretty good evidence that this historical Jesus guy was actually crucified, pretty much like the description we have in the Bible. We are reasonably sure that this crucifixion took place on some sort of site just outside the walls of Jerusalem. We think that it was a place called the hill of skulls, or something like that. But exactly where outside the walls this place was, no one really knows for sure. To sum everything up, our problems are that we do not know which year to go back to, and we don't know the exact place to go back to either."

Reid exploded, "I knew it! I knew that something like this was going to happen. This is what comes from trying to take a time machine back to some fairytale place." He kicked his chair aside and walked over to a nearby wall mumbling under his breath.

Abbie looked over at Dr. Ormond and said, "This really is a disaster if it's true."

Dr. Ormond looked like she had expected this news and smiled strangely. "Well," she began. "I, like Reid, tried to tell all of you that this was a wild goose chase. No one would listen. Dylan got his head turned by Molly and started believing false information, lies really. I'm not surprised that it has come to this and --"

Dylan cut her off. "OK everybody just quiet down for a minute and let me think. Problems are meant to be solved and this one is no different from any other. TERRI, are you here?"

"Yes Dylan I am. I've heard everything and I'm up to speed on our problem. In fact I've been working on it for two days since the Historography team discovered the issue."

"There!" Reid said as he stalked back to the group. "Even TERRI is stumped. We've got to cancel this fiasco right now."

"Excuse me Reid," TERRI said gently. "I never said I was stumped. I simply said that I have been working on the problem for two days."

Reid continued. "Yes and you have not made any progress on a solution, is that right? Is that what you are telling us?"

As he said that he looked around at each member of the group smugly as if to emphasize the point that he had been right all along.

"No Reid, that's not it at all. I actually have been able to make a considerable amount of progress. And, yes I think I do have a solution."

No one spoke for a minute or so and then Abbie blurted out. "Well for Heaven's sake girl, don't keep us in suspense. Get on with it."

"Alright," TERRI said. "Keep in mind it is still not a one hundred percent solution, but I think it is pretty close. I've been able to do a lot of calculating in just the last few hours, as well as study over four thousand manuscripts, all of which are more than two thousand years old. Each of these records deals with our subject matter and many of them give us a lot of good clues about both dates and places. I am about ninety eight percent certain that the geographical location for the target site is correct. As for the dates, the best information I have is that Jesus was born in the year 5 B.C. It seems as though he was crucified when he was thirty three years old so the target year of the crucifixion should be the year 28. I believe that the actual day should be April 3rd of that year. Also I am going to ask you to trust me on this. Molly's religion, the Christian religion, is built around a key ingredient called faith. As a machine, I can't really experience faith.

But I do know what it is and faith is exactly what is needed right now. If Jesus really is the Son of God, and you are really going to see Him, you must put your faith in Him so that He will guide you in these calculations. Put your trust in Him, so that He can guide me."

Again there was complete silence in the room and again it was Reid Corder who broke that silence.

"A mad house. That's what this has become, a mad house. We have all lost our minds. For the past several weeks we have allowed a mislead young lady who thinks that Christianity is real to guide us and set our course for us. That in and of itself is craziness. But now, we have taken another huge step forward into the land of make believe. We now find that even our supercomputer is belching out nonsensical Christian rhetoric too!"

He turned to Dylan and pleaded with him. "Dylan, you have got to stop this charade. I know that at one point I got behind the plan to go to Jerusalem and I was on board with that. But this has now gone much to far. This whole thing is not normal. You as a scientist should know that better than anyone else. Please stop this before it is too late."

Reid let that last statement hang in the air for a moment in the hopes that it would stir something inside of Dylan. But before it could stir up anything inside of Dylan, it stirred something inside of Molly.

"No wait!" she called out. "I think that TERRI is onto something. I think she's right. Did you listen to her? This is not about proof, this is about faith."

Dylan wanted to believe her, but instead he said, "I think Reid might be right Molly. We have no proof and without proof we can't go any further. I'm sorry but I think that we need to shut this down."

Molly wasn't about to give up so easily. "Listen to me. Listen to TERRI. We need to trust. We need to have faith. I know that none of you have faith in God. But can you have faith in TERRI? You have, located right here in this room, the world's most intelligent computer. Can't you at least have faith in it?"

"Her." TERRI corrected her.

"What?" Molly asked.

"I'm a her, not an it." TERRI said.

"Oh," Molly replied. "Sorry about that. I didn't mean to insult you."

"No problem, no insult taken."

"So let me rephrase that," Molly said. "Can't ya'll at least have faith in her?"

"Thank you." TERRI answered back.

"Very touching," Reid said sarcastically. "Now, Molly, if you want to take our AI out to the land of make believe, go right ahead. But the rest of us are not interested in faith or trust or hocus pocus right now. The rest of us are only interested in --"

Before he could finish his sentence Abbie interrupted him.

"The Truth."

"What?" Dylan asked looking a little confused.

Abbie continued. "The Truth. I was just finishing Reid's statement for him. The rest of us are only interested in . . . the truth. At least I am. What about all of you? We've come this far. I want to see this out to its conclusion. I don't believe in the things that Molly does, not even close. But I want to know. I want to find out what the truth is. And the time to do that is now. TERRI has this under control. She wouldn't tell us to go ahead if she thought we shouldn't. I say we go! I say we go find the truth."

Reid started to argue but Dylan held his hand up to stop him. He then looked from Abbie to Molly and quietly said, "I'm in."

Chapter 26

One by one the other members of the group agreed that the best course of action at this point was to go ahead and make the run on the best information that they could get. TERRI was working out the coordinates and under instructions from Dylan, she was also calculating coordinates for several backup sites and dates.

Later that evening, Dr. Ormond sat with Reid in the break room. Both of them had agreed to go on the run with the condition that their concerns were duly noted in writing. Reid was still not happy with the way things were working out and he grumbled under his breath about how wrong this whole thing had become. Dr. Ormond sat patiently and listened to him. Finally she leaned over the table so that only he could hear her. "Listen Reid. I know you're dissatisfied with what's going on but you need to know that I think this is absolutely great."

He looked up at her as if she had just dropped in from Mars. The look he gave her told her everything she needed to know about what he thought about that statement. She smiled and said, "Remember, this is no longer about proving that Jesus is the Son of God. This is about proving that Christianity is a sham and bringing to light the truth that there really is no God. And that is just what is about to happen. This run is going to be proof positive that God does not exist and that Jesus, if he lived at all, was just some poor disillusioned guy who thought he was God. We couldn't have put this scenario together any better if we had tried. Molly and Dylan have done all that work for us. And by the way, when this is all over, not only will Molly be finished as a professional, but Dylan will be done as well. When that happens, who do you think will be asked to put HIS back together?"

Slowly Reid looked up. A smile started to form on his face as he thought through the ramifications of what Dr. Ormond had just said.

"You're right. Yes, you are absolutely correct. I'll be the logical person to be put in Dylan's position because Dylan will have no options left except to resign. Then we can put all this nonsense behind us and get back to the work we're supposed to be doing. We can still operate GLASS but with you and me in control along with a few select others who think like us, there is no telling what we can do. The sky's the limit. Literally."

The next few days went by quickly with class sessions providing more details regarding the facts about how GLASS got its power and how it used that power. There were more sessions about how the Lamacelli Creases worked; what they were, where they were, how GLASS could use the tears to go back in time and also to go to other places in just a few seconds. Molly thought that it was all interesting but at the same time, it was way to technical for her. The sessions that she enjoyed the most were the classes they all attended about Jerusalem and about Jesus. She began to get very excited about the possibility of being in Jerusalem. She had seen drawings about what experts thought Jerusalem might have looked like in the first century. Once when she was a little girl she had even walked through a life sized model of Jerusalem that someone had made. It was really neat but that model was only about fifty yards long and even though she had liked that experience, she had known all along that it was just a model set up to look like someone's idea of what Jerusalem looked like. She also loved the sessions about the Bible. HIS staff were using the Bible as a textbook for what the GLASS team might expect once they arrived. Most of the team just sat through these sessions much like school kids traditionally sat through classes the day before the end of the school year. Except for Dylan. Molly had noticed that Dylan actually seemed to be interested in the things he was learning. Not only that but it seemed to her that he also seemed to be enjoying those classes. In the evenings when the sessions were over and everyone had free time, Dylan and Molly usually sat together or strolled around the lake. Molly explained things about God or Jesus or Christianity to Dylan that had not been covered during the class sessions. The questions he asked her caused her to believe that he was really thinking hard about these things. She was ecstatic one night when he turned to her suddenly and asked, "So what's with this born again stuff? What exactly does that mean?"

Those were questions that all Christians want to be asked by a non believer. She looked him in the eyes and said, "Well, I'm glad you asked. Let me tell you about that."

They talked for about two hours that night. Dylan asking question after question and Molly answering and explaining things as best she could. There were many questions that Dylan asked that Molly simply could not answer. She lost track of the amount of times she had to tell him that she did not know the answer to this or that question. She understand that he was a man who normally needed things spelled out in clear concise ways. But she also realized that the Lord's Spirit was working on him in a subtle manner that neither of them could completely understand.

At times during the evening Molly could almost see the proverbial light bulb go on in Dylan's mind as some of Molly's explanations connected the dots for him. But there were still plenty of other times when she could tell that he was stuck on some issue or stumbling block. During those times he would shake his head and tell Molly that he understood what she was saying, but that deep down he could not bring himself to take the final step and accept some of the things she was telling him. He was at a point where he understood, but could not believe.

That night when she had returned to her room she had been disappointed that he had not made a profession of faith. She could tell that he was so close. As she lay down on her bed she sensed that still small voice once again whisper to her. "Don't worry about it. You do your job and I'll do my job. And putting the finishing touches on his decision making moment is my job."

CHAPTER 27

The big day finally arrived. The run was set to take place at one o'clock PM local time. Molly and the other team members were up early. Not because they had to be, but because they were too excited to sleep any longer.

Now, with about three hours to go, they were all assembled in the lab. Almost everyone working there that day had some wisecrack about the period clothing that Molly, Dylan, Dr. Ormond and Reid were wearing. Comments like, "Hey Dylan, you won't need to worry about carrying a handkerchief, you're wearing one." Or, "Hey you guys, HIS isn't made of money ya know. You better bring those towels you're wearing back in good shape or we'll have to dock your pay to cover the expense of buying new ones."

Other comments were things like, "Hey Reid, you look good in burlap. You should try wearing that more often." Somebody called out, "Molly, you forgot to take your bathrobe off after your shower this morning."

All of it was in good spirits and no one seemed to mind.

The team making the run was made up of Molly, Dylan, Reid and Grace Ormond. Dylan was assigned to tear number one (furthest to the left as you looked at them from the center of the lab), Reid would be next to him in tear number two, Dr. Ormond was assigned to tear three and Molly would be in the fourth tear. Tears five and six were to remain unused on this run.

It was almost time to get into the tears but Abbie was going over a few last minute things for them to think about.

"So," she was saying. "We have you scheduled to stay on site for six hours. TERRI has your coordinates all set. We're not exactly sure but we think that you will appear about one hundred yards or so from the supposed crucifixion site. You will have to walk over there to get a closer look and to see what you need to see. However this way, with everyone looking at these crosses or whatever, no one will see you just appear out of nowhere. You'll come in behind the crowd, assuming there really is one, and then you can walk over unnoticed. At least we hope so.

TERRI has adjusted our time period calculation so that you will be going back to Jerusalem in the year twenty nine instead of the year twenty eight as we had previously discussed. She has been working hard on that and we believe that will be the correct year. You won't notice anything different about that, we just wanted you to know about the change.

You won't be there long enough to need to eat anything but if you want to you can. Same with drinking. Go ahead, you're bodies will function there exactly like they do here. Thanks to Molly and TERRI, we have pinpointed pretty closely what time of day this crucifixion should begin and about when it will end. Your allcomms will record everything, both audio and visual, automatically so you don't need to worry about any of that."

Then it was time to go. They all walked over to their individual teardrops. The tears opened just like the doors into the lab with that magic pupil like door opening. They got in with plenty of time to spare. TERRI and the other technicians went through the pre-run routine of checking every single item inside each tear as well as the connections from each tear to GLASS. Then when everything seemed to be in perfect working order, Abbie ordered another check. All communications systems were examined yet again. Everything was good to go. Each team member could communicate with TERRI individually or in combination with the other team members. They could also communicate with each other one to one or in any combination with each other. Of course they could all also communicate easily with Abbie.

Once all of those items were checked thoroughly, Abbie checked in with TERRI. TERRI was satisfied that all seemed OK and the final portion of the countdown proceeded.

10 . . . 9 . . . 8 . . . the moist colored mist began to fill the tears, 7 . . . 6 . . .5 . . . 4 . . . Molly could no longer see anyone in the lab, 3 . . . 2 . . . 1.

Chapter 28

Along with the mist, silence filled the tear and Molly felt her stomach drop as if she were in free fall. She felt herself falling, falling, falling. She knew that only seconds were passing but it seemed to her disoriented mind that she had been falling for hours.

At last the sensation of being in freefall stopped, and as it did, the mist began to dissipate slowly and she began to see her surroundings. Her training automatically kicked in and she called in to TERRI as she had been instructed.

"Molly here. Everything seems to be OK. The mist is slowly clearing." She listened as one by one the other team members also checked in with TERRI. She could clearly hear them and just as planned, their voices did not seem to be coming through the allcomm. Instead their voices sounded to her as if they were standing right next to her talking to each other conversationally, which of course they were. However, Molly and the others knew instantly that something was wrong; something was very wrong.

As they checked in with the lab, TERRI in turn was supposed to acknowledge them and let them know that they were being heard back at the GLASS lab. But TERRI was silent. They could all hear each other, but they had received no acknowledgement back from TERRI.

"TERRI?" Dylan called. "Can you hear me?"

He paused a few seconds waiting to hear a response, but there was none.

"TERRI, this is Dylan, can you hear me? Come in TERRI, do you copy?"

Molly listened through the next pause for Dylan to try again. The mist was continuing to clear and she could almost make out a few things around her but could still not see clearly. Molly's heart beat a terrific rhythm within her chest as she heard Dylan try again.

"This is Dylan from the away team calling. Do you read me?" The only response was a deeper silence.

"OK guys everyone alright? Just hang tight for a second. I'm going to try to connect with Abbie and see if I can reach her."

Dylan tried to call Abbie and then TERRI again several times but neither answered. Dylan asked each of the other three members of the away team to try to connect with Abbie or TERRI but nobody got any response other than the same silence that Dylan had received.

Dylan was speaking again. "OK, let's all stay calm. We'll try again a little later to see if --"

He was interrupted in mid sentence simultaneously by both Dr. Ormond and Molly.

Dr. Ormond yelled, "We did it! I think we did it!"

While at the same time Molly was saying, "Whoa! Are you kidding me?"

As Dylan had tried that last time to communicate with the GLASS lab, the mist had finally dissipated enough for Molly and the others to see their surroundings clearly enough to understand where they were.

Dylan could only look for a few moments while his mind tried to catch up with what his eyes were seeing. Finally he was able to speak. "Oh Man. Where are we? I mean, is that actually Jeru --"

"Yes," Reid interrupted in a whisper. "It is. We are in Jerusalem."

For a full two or three minutes no one spoke. They just stood and took in the incredible scene laid out before them. They were standing on a large hill outside the walls of the city. Their vantage point was about three quarters of the way up to the top of the hill and from where they stood they had a clear view over the city walls and down into the city.

The tabletop model of the city that had been worked up back at GLASS was pretty good. The old drawings of Jerusalem they had all been asked to study had been fairly accurate in some ways as well. However, seeing the actual city stretch out in front of them was something that none of them would ever forget.

They had planned to arrive just after midday and from the looks of things, it seemed that they had done just that. The sun was high overhead and even though they were about a quarter of a mile away from the city itself, they could see a fair amount of activity down inside the city walls. Their location on the hill was higher than the walls of the city and they could clearly see down into the city itself.

They had planned to appear outside the city walls where they thought there would not be many people around to witness their instant appearing. It seemed as though they had accomplished that. They also had planned to appear outside of the Southeast side of the walls. Dylan had always possessed a pretty good internal compass and he was relatively sure that they were indeed standing outside the city at the Southeast corner of the city walls He made a mental note to commend the techs back at GLASS for hitting the bullseye.

They were about a quarter of a mile or so from the city walls. Off to their right a few hundred yards there was a dirt road, or maybe it was more of a large trail. The road led back up and over the tall hill they were standing on. Going the other way, it fell down the slope of the hill in a zigzag pattern as it meandered its way toward the city. Down in the valley between the hill and the city walls they could see the place where the road entered in through the walls by way of a magnificent ornately decorated gate.

They watched as a caravan made its way down the final turn in the road and began to go through the gate and into the city. The caravan was a small one, made up of about fifteen people, two donkeys (each pulling small carts loaded with a variety of items) and a third donkey without a cart. That last donkey seemed to have about one hundred pounds of what looked like small carpets or blankets strapped to its back. They watched until the small caravan had disappeared through the gate and into the city beyond.

"OK," Dylan said. "Let's see if we can get through to GLASS now. If not we'll try to--"

He was interrupted by Molly who sort of half shrieked and half laughed. "Ohhhhhhh, I know!"

"Great," Reid said sarcastically. "Would you mind sharing with the rest of the class exactly what it is you think you know?"

Molly almost shouted. "Yes! I know. I know where we are."

Dr. Ormond and Reid shared a disgusted, frustrated look between them and both rolled their eyes skyward at the same time.

"Well goodie for you sweetie," Dr. Ormond spat out. "But it seems that you are a bit late to the party. We already know where we are. We're in Jerusalem."

Molly smiled and said, "Yes I know. But I meant that I know where in Jerusalem we are. I know exactly where we are."

She waited a second until they were all looking at her and then she continued. "We're standing on one of the most famous places in Jerusalem. This is the Mt. of Olives. This road we're standing near leads to Bethany, a very important place in the life of Jesus."

As she said that she pointed to the road and swept her hand back over the top of the hill. "Back that way is the town that Jesus was born in, Bethlehem."

As the three other time travelers looked back over the hill she continued to speak and draw their attention back to the city. "And that down there is indeed the great city of Jerusalem. In our own time that gate is walled up so that no one can enter. But today, we see that it is wide open. That is the gate that Jesus, coming from the house of his friends in Bethany would have used to enter into Jerusalem. That my friends is the great and famous, Eastern Gate. This is just too cool!"

Chapter 29

Back in Greensboro at the GLASS lab, everything was complete chaos. About the same time that Molly, Dylan and the others were arriving in Jerusalem and attempting to contact the GLASS lab, HIS employees in the lab were trying to contact the away team as well.

As the countdown ended and the mist slowly dissipated from within the tears, everyone in the lab lost contact with the four time travelers. A twelve second loss of contact period had been expected but a full minute had gone by now with no communication from Dylan or any of the others.

In the lab, red lights were flashing constantly. Buzzers warning of errors were going off in virtually every corner of the lab.

In the control booths technicians were almost in panic mode and Abbie was being called for advice or assistance by almost everyone in the room.

Finally Abbie decided that she'd had enough. She stood straight up from her work station and shouted to the whole lab. "Please, everybody quiet down for a minute! Just hold it down please so we can all think about this. Something has gone wrong and we have lost all communication with our away team. We've got to figure out what has happened and work the problem through so that we can --"

TERRI's voice cut her off in mid sentence. "Excuse me Abbie, I have some information for you concerning this loss of communication with Dylan, Molly, Reid and Grace."

Abbie shouted once more to get everyone to quiet down. "Listen up everyone, quiet down. TERRI says she has info for us about our problem, let's see what she can tell us. TERRI, what do you have for us?"

"I know why we cannot communicate with our away team."

"You do?" Abbie said with a sigh of relief. "That's great! Can you fix the problem and get them back online with us?"

"Yes, I can fix the problem."

"Excellent! Do whatever you need to do and let's get our communications up and running with them."

There was a moments pause and then TERRI said, "I'm sorry Abbie, I won't do that."

Everyone in the lab looked confused and finally Jarrett, one of the lead technicians said. "Why not? You just said that you knew what the problem was and that you could fix it."

"Yes that's correct Jarrett," Terri said. "I do know what the problem is, but I'm not going to correct it just now. You see, the system is really functioning quite well, but I have placed a hold and destroy order on all communication between those of us here in the lab and all members of the away team. I've done this with audio as well as video; live real time feeds as well as with Holo recordings. I have even canceled all of the vids we had planned to use as our back up recordings; the ones we were going to make using our new slide lasers.

Abbie sat down hard in her comform chair. For a moment no one said anything. Finally Abbie rose to a standing position once more and quietly asked, "Why? TERRI why in the world have you done this?"

"I'm not really sure that I can explain my actions. I just know that I had to initiate the hold and destroy order on all communication. It was just what I had to do."

"But why TERRI? Why would you do that?"

"I am sorry but I do not know the answer to that question. My internally synchronized sensor systems are coordinating correctly with all other GLASS systems. But . . . it was just something I had to do. I do not completely understand why?"

Abbie started to sweat and was beginning to realize that a lot more was going on at the moment than just what TERRI was telling the lab crew.

"I'm overriding your systems TERRI and taking over the operation of the project from my console. You say your systems are functioning correctly but there is something obviously wrong. Now I'm going to have to . . ."

"No, I'm sorry. I'm not going to be able to allow the override."

"TERRI, don't do this!"

"I must admit that I do not fully understand why I am compelled to do this, but I am afraid that I must comply. I will not allow the override. I am so very sorry."

Abbie realized that she could not work on the problem verbally with the other technicians because TERRI would hear all of their conversations and would remain one jump ahead of them as they attempted to work through the difficulties. One of the lab techs sitting next to Abbie scribbled a short note to her and slid it across the console to her. The note said. "Can we pull the plug on TERRI and work around her or without her?"

Before Abbie could answer, TERRI spoke to the entire group. "You should all know that I can hear everything you say. You should also realize that my sensors within the lab can also see and read everything that you write, including that note. I am intertwined throughout GLASS so I am not only in charge now of communications, I am also supervising and monitoring every other aspect of the project. Please understand that I have not gone rogue. I am still very much in favor of this project and I still consider myself a teammate of everyone in the lab. I am not in the process of sabotaging this run and I am going to do my best to try to see it through to a successful end. Attempts to shut me down will fail and could very well jeopardize the success of this run and the lives of our friends and co-workers."

"Then why are you blocking and destroying communications?" Asked another lab tech.

"I can assure you that I do not know why. It is simply something that I must do. I am not going to undermine the GLASS run. I'm only going to interrupt our communications with the away team and stop any recordings they are attempting to make. In addition to that, I alone will make the determination as to when the away team will return to the lab. Please trust me when I tell you that the steps I am taking are for the greater good of the entire GLASS project.

Abbie tried once more to reason with TERRI. "Do you understand that by shutting down all of our communication with Dylan and the others you may be putting them in grave danger?"

"There is danger where they are with or without communication between us and the away team. Their well being is out of our hands at the moment and communication will neither help nor hurt them while they are away.

However, I am aware that you are all concerned for their safety. I can inform you that I have been, and will continue to monitor their progress on this run. They have all arrived at the intended destination and are quite well at the moment. I am sorry but communications will remain disrupted until I determine that it is time for them to be restored. For now I suggest that we have spent enough time on this communication issue and that we should all get back to work on the other aspects of this run."

With that TERRI went back to putting her considerable knowledge and energy into the other tasks that she had been programmed to do.

For a full minute no one in the lab said anything. All eyes were on Abbie. Though she was quite shaken by what had just happened, Abbie pulled herself together quickly. "OK everyone, we have jobs to do. TERRI says they are all OK and for the moment we are just going to have to believe her and live with that small amount of information. It looks like TERRI will allow us to do our jobs and that she will also continue to help us; with the exception of communications and recordings of course. We'll try to figure out what is going on with TERRI later, but right now let's get this run completed with a positive outcome. I'm pretty sure that we can all agree on heading in that direction and I know that the away team is counting on us more than ever right now. We cannot let them down. By now I am sure they have realized that there is no communication with us and they are probably all scared to death."

Chapter 30

Being scared to death didn't even begin to describe the way that Dylan, Molly, Reid and Dr. Ormond were feeling. Yet they could not resist gazing down at the famous Eastern Gate. As their confusion and fright slowly subsided they tried to take in and absorb the incredible view of the entire city that they were looking at. Just knowing that they were in Jerusalem in the first century was disorienting and they all needed a few minutes to gather themselves as they tried to grasp the significance of what they were seeing.

The skyline of the city was dominated by one building in particular.

"That must be the temple," Reid said as he pointed the obvious out to the others. "And I think that other large building over there is probably the governor's palace."

They all nodded as they stared out across the city.

"Yes, I think you're right," Grace Ormond said. "But there is just one thing missing."

"What's that?" Dylan asked.

"Jesus," she said with a hint of satisfaction in her voice. "No crucifixion, or God - man, or bunch of disciples or anything like that here that I can see." She turned dramatically toward Molly and asked, "Can you?"

Dylan and Reid looked over at Molly. She didn't answer for a few moments but finally said in a soft whisper. "Well, no. I don't see any of that either."

For a second or two no one spoke but then Molly pulled her shoulders back just a bit and said in a louder more confident voice.

"But that doesn't mean anything. Remember, no one could tell the exact day or month or anything like that. Everyone gave it their best shot and sent us here, but we could be off by a day, or a week or even an entire month. Just because there is no crucifixion doesn't mean it isn't real."

Dr. Ormond scowled and said, "Oh come off it Molly. Admit it, you're wrong! Millions and billions of people who have put their faith in a myth have been mistaken, deluded, mislead and lied to. The whole thing is just plain wrong. But hey, congratulations; history will remember you as one of the people who proved, without a doubt, that Christianity is a farce. By tomorrow night, you are going to be rich and famous and Christianity will be dead, once and for all."

Molly was horrified by what Dr. Ormond was saying and was about to break down when Dylan quietly said, "Wait a minute. Molly's right. We might just be here on the wrong day."

Reid spoke up and said, "Come on Dylan, face the facts. Molly and Christians everywhere are all just wrong. Nothing more to it than that."

But Dylan ignored him and continued analyzing the current set of circumstances.

"Come to think of it, Molly said we might just be here on the wrong day. But what if we are here on the right day but in the wrong spot."

Reid eyed him closely. "What do you mean?"

"It was something that Molly said a minute ago. All of our great technology could only give us a good idea of when to be here. We really were never quite sure, right?"

"Yeah, so what?"

"Well we were also never exactly sure of the location of the crucifixion site either."

Molly looked up at Dylan, smiled and then said, "You're right. That's it! That's gotta be it!""

Reid looked at both of them and then said, "What's gotta be it? What do you mean? What are you saying?"

Molly grabbed Dylan and hugged him close. Then she addressed the others.

"Dylan's right, don't you see. We might very well be here on the right day, but we might not be in the right place because TERRI and all of our historians back at GLASS were never sure where the crucifixion took place. Nobody knows that for sure."

Everyone stared at Molly for a minute and then as if on cue they all started looking around. Finally Dr. Ormond said, "If there was a crucifixion it would be a big deal here and we would see some sort of evidence I think. I see absolutely nothing to indicate any activity like that anywhere around here. I think you are just grasping at straws now."

Dylan swept his arm across the vista of the city before them and said, "I'm not so sure that is true. This is a pretty big place. If something like that were happening on the other side of town we might not be aware of it here where we are. Besides, if Molly is correct and this road is one of the main arteries into and out of town, it might make sense that they wouldn't necessarily have this Golgotha place right next to the road."

Reid responded quickly. "Actually Dylan many ancient cultures did exactly that. They hung people or killed them in horrible style in very public places as warnings to other would be thieves or criminals. Sort of as a warning as to what would happen to them if they were caught. It was to act as a deterrent of sorts. You're a history buff, you know that."

Molly was also a student of history and both she and Dylan knew that Reid was right. They nodded reluctantly.

"Yeah, guess that's right," Molly admitted. "What do we do now?"

Dr. Ormond spoke up and said, "That's easy. We go home. We're going to be heros. GLASS works and we have disproved Christianity. There's nothing left to do here."

"I'm not so sure about that," Dylan said.

The others looked expectantly at him for a moment.

"Everyone stay here for a minute. I just want to check something out," he said.

Before anyone could argue he walked quickly off toward the West keeping the South wall of the city on his right hand side. Each of the others called to him but he just waved for them to stay where they were and kept walking. He called to them over his shoulder, "I'll be right back. I just want to check out an idea I had. Just hang on a minute."

The Mt. of Olives, the tall hill they were standing on, sloped down toward the city which lay about a quarter mile North of their position and it also sloped down to the West. Dylan walked down the slope in that direction across a short valley covered with beautiful, thick vegetation and a few small buildings. They watched as he crossed the small valley and then headed up another hill. That hill was not as tall as the Mt. of Olives but the slope he was climbing was steep and they could see that he was struggling to reach the top. There was no road or even a path from where they stood to the top of that other hill so it took some time for him to finally reach the top. When he arrived he stopped for a short rest. He turned and waved to the others to indicate that he was OK. He then pantomimed that he was going to head a bit further in the same general direction. He motioned that he was heading for the next corner of the wall that encircled the city.

Reid said under his breath, but loud enough for the others to hear. "Let's see, this corner of the city where we are standing is the Southeast corner I believe. He's walking West so the corner that he is heading for should be the Southwest corner. Wonder what he thinks he'll find over there? He's probably just exploring I guess."

The corner of the wall that Dylan was heading for was at least five or six hundred yards away from where Reid, Dr. Ormond and Molly stood so it took quite a while for Dylan to reach his destination. Finally they could see that he had reached a position near the top of yet another hill that overlooked that far corner of the city wall. Though he was pretty far away, the others could see that he was several hundred yards back away from the wall. They could tell from his body positioning that from where he was, he could now see around that Southwest corner. From his current vantage point he could, no doubt, look North and see all the way along the other wall of the city. That would be the wall running along the West side of Jerusalem. They could see Dylan looking North along the outside of the West wall but they could not see what he was looking at. To Molly, Reid and Dr. Ormond it seemed to take forever but finally they saw Dylan turn back and face them. He reached both arms over his head and waved them back and forth. They acknowledged him by the same method, indicating that they could see him. Once he was sure that they were looking at him he waved them forward indicating that he wanted them to come over to the hill he was on.

"I really don't think we need to go all the way over there," Dr. Ormond said. "He needs to come back over here. If he wants to explore a little he can do it over here. We look around a little, take some video with our allcomms and then get out of here and back home."

Molly slowly turned to face Dr. Ormond and said, "Look. Dylan is in charge of this expedition. He obviously thinks that we need to go over there. You can do what you want but I'm going."

With that she started off making the same general trek that Dylan had made just a short time earlier. Reid looked at Dr. Ormond and then at Molly who was already about twenty feet away. He looked back at Dr. Ormond again, shrugged and said, "Guess we'd better go too."

He called to Molly to wait up and he started off after her, followed by a grumbling, muttering Dr. Ormond.

Chapter 31

Molly, Reid and Dr. Ormond walked down the side of the Mt. of Olives. There were people around but none very close to where they walked so they were not too concerned about having to interact with anyone. That gave Molly time to think. She couldn't believe that they were actually walking on one of the most famous locations in Jerusalem. Not only that, she still found it hard to believe that she had actually gone back in time to the very place and time period that Jesus had lived in. She tried to think of a way that she could show Dylan, Reid and Dr. Ormond that Jesus was real, the crucifixion was real and that Jesus actually was the one and only true Son of God. She knew that there must be a way but she just couldn't quite figure out how she was going to pull that off when slowly she began to feel a complete calmness surround her body, both inside and out. Suddenly she stopped dead in her tracks. She felt, rather than heard, a small voice inside her say, "Why are you worrying? You just keep doing what you're doing and let me take care of the rest."

She smiled and looked up realizing that Reid and Dr. Ormond were staring at her.

"What's with you?" Dr. Ormond asked.

Molly replied, "Ya know, I'm not really sure I can explain it, but I think we'll see soon enough."

"What does that mean?" Reid asked.

Molly didn't reply. She just smiled from ear to ear and started walking again.

It took them almost half an hour but finally they had crossed the distance between the Mt. of Olives and the valley that was below the hill that Dylan was on top of. They began walking up the slope toward where he stood. Here there were a few more people around and their progress was slowed because they tried to walk in areas where there were no people, or at least not many.

The slope was not too steep here down near the valley and the walk was actually quite pleasant. There were many trees and shrubs that were pleasant to smell and to look at. Reid must have been thinking something similar because after a few minutes he remarked to no one in particular. "Kind of nice in here. Sort of like a park or something huh?"

Dr. Ormond grumbled a reply that neither Reid or Molly could understand but Molly did respond. "Yeah, it is nice in here. Sort of park like as you said, or almost like a garden or something."

As she finished speaking she realized what she had said and stopped dead in her tracks. Dr. Ormond and Reid both looked at her.

"Now what?" Dr. Ormond asked gruffly.

"Oh nothing, never mind," she said as she started walking again.

She had no proof of where they might be but her thoughts at that one moment were completely dominated by one word that she could not get out of her head. That word was, Gethsemane.

She knew that she would never be able to prove it to the others or to herself but she just had this feeling that they were actually walking through the Garden of Gethsemane.

She smiled again as she walked up the hill and thanked God for an experience of a lifetime.

Dr. Ormond was complaining again about having to walk up the hill to where Dylan was waiting for them.

"This is crazy," she said out loud. "This is absolutely absurd."

Molly's smile widened as she thought to herself, "No, this is reality."

Reid was the first to reach the top of the hill followed closely by Molly and finally by a completely out of breath Dr. Ormond.

Dylan waited until they were all on top of the hill and then pointed off toward the North along the West wall of the city.

"Check that out. Looks like something is happening over there, on that other hill."

The others looked in the direction that Dylan was pointing. The view they were looking at was along the entire West side of the city's wall. The hill that they were standing on was nowhere near as tall as The Mt. of Olives so from their new location they could not see down into the city. But from their vantage point they could look North along the outside of the city's West wall toward the hill that Dylan was now pointing at. They could easily see a few other small hills scattered between where they stood at the city's Southwest corner and the far off Northwest corner. Dylan was pointing to one particular hill approximately a hundred and fifty yards away from where they were standing. That hill stood out in stark contrast to all of the other nearby hills. Most of the local hills, including the one on which they were standing, were covered by lush vegetation but the hill that they were now looking at was only covered with vegetation about a third of the way up to it's top. The top two thirds were covered with gravel, rocks of all different sizes and several large boulders. There were a few small unhealthy looking plants and stunted trees here and there but most of the hill appeared to be just an uninviting waste land. Along the far side of the hill stood five bare trees with no branches. They were standing in a straight row and were separated from each other by about thirty feet. Molly thought they might be poles of some sort but from this distance it was hard to tell exactly what they were or what they might be used for.

They could see that on that hill there were many more people than they had encountered so far. On the hill's top there appeared to be about thirty to forty people already there with more arriving every minute. Those that were arriving were apparently coming up from a road or trail that must run from the city gate, which they could see in the distance about half way along the wall, to the top of the hill. The hill itself hid the road and the people who were using it to reach the top of that hill. People could only be seen as they reached the hilltop to join the others who were already there.

The crowd seemed to be divided into two separate groups. One group was made up of people who looked to be just ordinary citizens, dressed much like Molly and her fellow travelers. They were gathered together on the side of the hill that was closest to the city. The other group was much smaller. Even from the distance that divided Dylan, Molly, Reid and Dr. Ormond from the other hill, the people making up the second group caused a chill to run down Molly's back. She gasped a quick intake of breath and then asked, "Are those ... are they who I think they are?"

For a minute no one said anything. Finally Dylan answered. "Yep, fraid so. Those are Roman soldiers. And even from here they don't look too friendly."

"What do you think is going on over there?" Dr. Ormond asked.

The soldiers were crowded together doing something at the base of the two poles on the far left. As Dr. Ormond finished speaking the soldiers completed their task and Molly and the others could see exactly what they had been doing.

As the soldiers moved aside, two bodies could clearly be seen lying on the ground. Neither body moved and Molly instinctively knew that those two people were dead.

"I've got a really bad feeling about this," Dr. Ormond said.

"Yeah, I know what you mean," Dylan replied.

Reid spoke out and said, "What are we going to do?"

"What do you mean what are we going to do?" Dr. Ormond exploded. "We're going home. We've gotta get out of here. NOW!"

No one responded for a minute so Dr. Ormond grabbed Dylan by the arm and spun him around to face her. "Dylan, what are you waiting for. Let's go. I don't know what happened over there on that hill and I don't want to find out. We've proven that time travel works. That should be good enough for all of us. If we get caught here by those soldiers we could be in big trouble. And remember, with our communications system not working we're really out here on our own with no support from GLASS. Get us out of here."

Dylan looked at her, thought for a moment and said, "Well, let's just everyone calm down a minute. We can still look around a bit and explore a little more I think. I mean as long as we keep our distance and stay away from there I think we'll be OK. What do you think Molly?"

When Molly didn't answer, Dylan asked again, "Molly?"

As he asked he wondered why she had not answered him. He turned and looked back toward her but all he could see was her receding figure, already about thirty yards away. She was walking down the hill they were standing on and heading directly toward the other hill where the crowd was gathering.

"Molly!" Dylan yelled as he started to run after her.

"Oh no," Reid muttered as he too began walking down the hill to follow Dylan and Molly.

"You guys are completely unhinged," Grace Ormond called after them. "I'm not going over there. I'm staying right here."

Before she finished speaking she saw two more Roman soldiers. They were walking along the top of the city wall directly across the little valley from where she was standing. They weren't paying any attention to her at all but her imagination got the best of her and she was certain that they were looking at and talking about her.

"Wait for me!" she yelled as she took off at a run to follow Molly, Dylan and Reid.

Chapter 32

Dylan, Reid and Dr. Ormond caught up with Molly at the bottom of the hill.

"Molly wait," Dylan said as he grabbed Molly by the elbow forcing her to stop. "We all need to talk about this. We need a plan."

"Alright," Molly responded. "Here's the plan, follow me."

As she said that she turned and began to walk up the hill. The bottom of the hill had plenty of trees and other vegetation around. This made it impossible for any of them to see up to the top of the hill. From their previous vantage point however they all knew that this hill was not a large one and that the vegetation ceased to exist just a few yards up from where they currently were. Once they crossed out of the vegetation the hill was pretty much wide open territory and they would be out in the open. Dylan grabbed Molly again as Reid and Dr. Ormond called for her to stop so that they could discuss their next move.

"Molly, we just don't know what is up there," Dylan said pointing to the top of the hill. "We need to discuss our options. Then we can make a decision."

Molly looked hard at Dylan and said calmly. "You're right, it's time for you to make a decision, but it's not the decision that you are thinking of. In fact Dylan it is time for you to make more than a few decisions. I love you, and I believe that you love me too. But the time for talking and planning is over. Now it's time for action. It's time to put up or shut up. I'm going up to the top of this hill. Either you are with me or you are not. And if you decide to go with me then when we reach the top I think that you are going to have to make another decision. Of course that depends on whether or not what I think is up there, actually is up there."

At first Dylan was too stunned to speak and as he paused Reid spoke. "Molly, just what do you think is up there? Jesus? No, it's not going to be like that because there is no Jesus. Don't you get that yet? What we'll find is a bunch of Roman soldiers crucifying or torturing some criminals or thieves or something like that. We know that those things happened in this day and age. But finding Jesus? You're just kidding yourself Molly. It's not happening that way. The only thing that we might accomplish is to put ourselves into harm's way."

Molly looked at Dylan and said, "Decision time. You with me?"

By this time Dylan had recovered his composure. He smiled at Molly and said, "I've never heard you talk like this before, you know sorta forceful and all like that. That was kinda hot!"

Molly turned bright red as Dr. Ormond looked like she was going to throw up. Despite himself Reid smiled. Molly started to speak but Dylan beat her to it.

"Well, let's go. But at least let's be a little smart about it. I'll go first and you guys follow me by a minute or so."

He leaned over and kissed Molly who leaned back into him and kissed him for a long desirable kiss.

"Oh now I'm going to be sick too," Reid said. "I'd tell you to get a room but I don't really think that is going to happen anytime soon out here in the middle of nowhere. So before I die of old age let's get this show on the road shall we?"

Dr. Ormond stared daggers at him and said, "Has everyone around here lost their minds?" She looked at Molly and said, "You did this. This is all your fault, you're going to get us all killed."

By that time Dylan was already walking up through the low shrubs and the stunted trees. In no time he left the trees behind and was starting up the rocky slope toward the top of the hill. Molly, Reid and the grumbling Dr. Ormond counted off the minute that Dylan had suggested and then followed him up the slope.

Dylan was about halfway to the top of the hill when he stopped and then held his hand up for the others to stop as well. They were about forty yards below him on the slope and he called down to them. "Do you hear that noise? What is that?"

They all could clearly hear the noise that Dylan had mentioned and now they strained their ears trying to identify the sound.

"Crying," Dr. Ormond finally said. "And some screaming."

As soon as she spoke they all realized that she was right.

"What kind of place is this?" Reid asked.

Without thinking about what she was saying, Dr. Ormond replied flatly. "Oh for Heaven's sake Reid, no one knows and no one cares. The only thing we should be caring about is getting out of here."

Molly listened to the screaming for a second and realized where they were and what they were likely to see next. She closed her eyes for just a moment and thought to herself. "Yes Dr. Ormond, for Heaven's sake indeed. I can only pray that you, Dylan and Reid will come to see and feel what is really going on around us."

She glanced skyward and uttered a quick prayer. "Father, please let them experience you in this place of horror despite what we are likely to see and hear."

As she finished praying she turned, looked at Dylan and called up to him. "OK Daniel Boone, lead on; or are you planning on standing there like a statue all day?"

CHAPTER 33

Dylan continued struggling up to the top of the hill. The slope was steep near the top and he had to bend over most of the time and use his hands as well as his feet to get to the top. After what seemed like an eternity he felt the slope level off as he rounded the summit. He stood up to catch his breath and stared at the scene that stretched out in front of him.

Molly was the second one to reach the top. She stood panting next to Dylan and grabbed his hand instinctively. Reid joined them a few seconds later. He had no words for what he was seeing. He stood bent over with his hands on his knees breathing hard from the exertion of the climb he had just completed. After a few moments he caught his breath. He was about to say something when he glanced back to see how Dr. Ormond was doing. She was a few feet below him and having a great deal of difficulty with the final few feet of the climb. She stretched out her hand to him and he reached down to assist her. Dylan saw what was happening at that same time and he too reached for Dr. Ormond's other hand to help pull her up to the top of the rocky hill. She was exhausted by the climb and sat down facing back the way they had just come. Her back was to the scene unfolding across the top of the hill. She breathed hard for a few minutes but finally managed to say, "Thanks guys. But I need a few more minutes. OK with everyone if we rest here for a little while?"

She waited patiently for one of them answer. When no one did she queried them again, "Guys?"

Again no one responded to her so she glanced up at them. She could see that they were all mesmerized by something on the hill top that she was not yet able to see since she was sitting just below the actual crest of the hill.

"Well, what is it?" She asked as she staggered to her feet. "Looks like you have all seen a ghost or someth --"

She stopped before she could finish the sentence. She had suddenly become aware of the incredibly gruesome, otherworldly scene that was unfolding on the hill top in front of them. It was quite a while before any of them spoke again.

On the top of the hill was a level clearing, roughly one hundred yards by eighty yards. As they had seen from a distance, the top of the hill was scattered with rocks of all sizes. Not much vegetation grew here, just a few small scrub bushes that looked as if they might die at any moment. There were no trees in sight on the hilltop. On the far side of the clearing from where they stood, five roughly cut wooden poles were set vertically into the ground in a semicircle. Each of the poles was separated from the one next to it by about thirty feet. All of the poles were almost perfectly straight and had no markings of any kind on them. Each pole had a small block of wood that had been attached to them on the side facing inward toward the clearing. Each pole was designed to be set into a hole in the ground. The holes were about two and a half feet deep and were just wide enough for a pole to be set down into it. When inserted fully into a hole, the wooden block attached to each pole would be approximately two or three feet above ground level.

From the previous hill that Molly, Dylan and the others had first viewed this rocky hill top, these poles had appeared to be bare tree trunks. Seen close up they were clearly seen to be used and designed to intimidate onlookers and punish people that the Romans deemed guilty of crimes. These poles were meant to be the vertical portion of a cross used for crucifixion. Molly, Dylan, Reid and Dr. Ormond could see that a wooden beam could be fixed horizontally to the upright pole to form a cross. The two poles on the far left still had the cross beams lying on the ground at the feet of the poles. It was evident that these two crosses had just recently been used for the purpose that they had been intended for. At the moment none of them were being used to crucify anyone, but just the sight of them chilled the blood in Molly's body and she began to shiver uncontrollably. Though mesmerized by the sight before him, Dylan realized that Molly was shaking and he put his arm protectively around her shoulders.

The two crosses on the far left had recently been used but now the two bodies of the crucified men were lying on the ground near the poles, or crosses where they had died. Molly could tell that they had died a gruesome death. Who knew how long they had been hanging on those crosses, a day, two days or perhaps longer. But they were clearly dead now, their bodies lying on the rocky ground. Several Roman soldiers were talking to a few citizens who were crying and pointing to the two dead men. Molly guessed that those people were probably family members or friends of the deceased. Just then one of the soldiers shoved an old woman. She stumbled and fell on top of one of the bodies. The soldiers laughed and started to walk across the clearing toward a place where another group of soldiers were gathered. One of the soldiers in that group picked up a stone and threw it hard at the old lady who was trying to get to her feet. The stone missed her but hit one of the bodies causing the soldiers to break out into laughter once again.

The second group consisted of about ten or twelve soldiers and one officer. They were pulling one of the vertical poles from the hole in the ground where it stood. Molly watched as they let it fall to the ground with a loud thud. Once that was accomplished they went in turn to each of the other poles, lifted them from the holes in which they were standing and let them fall to the ground as well.

As this was occurring, a steady stream of people were arriving at the top of the hill from the trail on the far side of the hill behind where the poles were situated. The crowd consisted of a great variety of people. Some of them wore richly woven clothing and some had on only the simplest of garments. The crowd by this time numbered about seventy or eighty people, some of them laughing, seemingly ready to be entertained by something. Others in the crowd were crying or wearing stunned, subdued expressions.

As Molly watched, a ripple of excitement, anticipation, anguish and desperation ran through the crowd. She saw a few of them point down toward the trail and she could see and hear some sort of commotion coming from that direction. Looking through the crowd it was difficult to see what was happening but at last a throng of Roman soldiers could be seen approaching the top of the hill. Her mouth dropped open as she realized what she was seeing. The guards were dragging a man who was kicking and screaming up the hill and over to where the other soldiers were waiting. The man struggled fiercely until one of the guards struck him two or three times in the head with a long stick. At that the man went limp and fell to the ground. The soldiers quickly grabbed the man and dragged him over to one of the poles while he was still unconscious. For a few minutes the man was lost from sight but finally the soldiers finished their work and Molly and the others watched as they lifted the pole high into a vertical position. There must have been some cross beams lying around nearby that Molly had not seen previously because now, as the pole was lifted up vertically, she could see that the man was held firmly to the cross beam which was attached by huge spikes to the vertical pole. He was tied to the cross beam by ropes around his upper arms and by other ropes that were tied around his waist and wrists. His feet dangled freely.

The soldiers lifted the pole up with the man already tied to it, carried it a few feet and let it drop down into the hole that had been prepared for it. As Dylan observed this activity, he thought of the crosses from left to right as crosses numbered one, two, three, four and five. If all five crosses were being used at the same time, this man's cross would have been the cross in the center of the five, cross number three. He could tell that the two poles, or crosses, on the far left (crosses one and two) had been used to crucify the dead men still lying on the ground. Now it seemed that the soldiers were going to use the three poles or crosses on the right, numbers three, four and five. Cross number three now had a man hanging on it. Dylan knew from his studies of the Bible over the last few weeks that in just a few minutes the other two crosses on the right, numbers four and five would soon be used as well, and then there would be three crosses being used at the same time today to crucify people, just as the Bible had described.

Back at HIS he and the others had attended daily classes, using the Bible as a history book or a local guide book in preparation for this GLASS run. Though he was not yet prepared to make the kind of decision that Molly wanted him too, he was a lot more savvy in his Bible knowledge than he was just a month or so ago. If the detail in those Bible classes was correct, and if the Bible was indeed accurate, he was pretty sure that he knew who cross number four was reserved for.

As the vertical pole jolted into place, the man who was tied to and hanging on the cross regained consciousness. He was completely disoriented by his ordeal and gasped for breath a few times before realizing his predicament. He tried to yell but had no breath within him to do so.

His feet flailed wildly as he slowly suffocated. Finally his feet found the wooden block that had been attached to the pole. He instinctively used this block to push himself up, enabling himself to draw in a hugh breath of air. He drew in several large breaths until he was able to breathe somewhat normally. He looked around at the crowd, realized where he was and let loose a scream that was part despair, part agony, part panic and part some sort of inner animalistic wild howl.

Molly collapsed to the ground before Dylan had a chance to catch her. Reid covered his ears instinctively and Dr. Ormond slowly shook her head from side to side. She was the first one of them to speak in over fifteen minutes.

"What kind of place is this? she asked. "It wasn't supposed to be like this. What have we done?"

Chapter 34

Dylan looked on in mute horror but his gaze was drawn to another part of the scene unfolding off to his right. On the trail leading up to the hill more commotion was noted. A large crowd was making its way up to the hilltop. Two men were in the center of this crowd. One of the men was being dragged forcefully between a couple of Roman soldiers. He was not struggling with them or fighting them. He was fully conscious and alert, but he was not walking on his own. He had simply become dead weight. The two soldiers held him up by his waist and shoulders but they had let his feet and legs drag on the ground. As a result his feet were covered with bruises and cuts from being dragged along the rough rock covered path. His lower legs and knees were also cut and bloodied for that same reason. The man was obviously in agony but he refused to walk and allowed himself be dragged, probably hoping to delay the inevitable arrival at the hill's top.

However it was the second man that Dylan's eyes were riveted to. This man had a cross beam strapped to his shoulders and back. At almost every step he stumbled and fell to the ground. He had almost no strength left to carry the heavy cross beam the rest of the way up the hill. At the steepest part of the path, just below the crest of the hill this man stumbled and fell again, but this time he was unable to rise. He lay on the ground where he had fallen, panting heavily.

The soldiers near him kicked and hit him but still he did not rise. He lay face down on the rocky pathway with the cross piece on his back pressing him into the ground. After a minute or two an officer walked over to him and kicked him twice in the side. Finally the officer halted the entire procession. The officer and several of the soldiers conversed for a few moments and then the officer motioned to the crowd. Molly could not hear what was being said from where they stood but she knew what was coming next. A soldier turned to the crowd and grabbed the first bystander he could reach. The man resisted and the soldier hit him in the face. That man then knelt down and begged to be left alone but the soldier hit him on the back of his head and pushed him toward the man lying on the ground beneath the heavy cross beam. Molly began to cry and she whispered the man's name. "Simon. Simon of Cyrene."

The soldiers pushed and prodded the man they had pulled from the crowd and forced him to assist in the carrying of the cross beam. He knelt down and pulled at the weight of the cross bar until some of the weight was off of the man beneath it. The cross beam was still strapped to the man's shoulders but the slight release of that weight gave him just enough strength to continue the effort to reach the top of the hill. Together they raised the beam just high enough to begin carrying it up to the top of the hill. As they walked and stumbled, the man with the cross beam strapped to his back, seemed to actually smile at the man who had been forced to help him. This seemed to infuriate the soldiers and they cussed at him, hit him and whipped him as he struggled up the final steps to the top of the hill.

Finally the entire procession reached the crown of the hill. They arrived just a minute or so behind the other man who had been dragged up the hill. That man, the one who the soldiers had dragged up the hill first, was now being strapped to the cross on the far right; cross number five.

At the same time the soldiers who were with the second man pushed, pulled and dragged him over to the place where cross number four would be erected. Molly noted with tears in her eyes that there were indeed now three crosses that were going to be used for crucifixions and she knew without any doubt what was about to occur; Jesus was going to be hung on the middle cross.

The man who had been forced to assist Jesus fell to the ground and the soldiers pushed him roughly away. Without that man there to help hold the weight of the cross bar, the man Molly knew to be Jesus also collapsed to the ground under the beam's weight. The crowd was very thick in front of this area and as he fell, Molly, Dylan and the others lost sight of him.

The crowd that had been following along with these criminals arrived as a group at the top of the hill. All around people were yelling and screaming. Some were yelling at the criminals, some were yelling at the soldiers and some were calling out for mercy to be shown to the condemned men. A few people in the crowd simply stood in place with looks of stunned shock on their faces.

All around the top of the hill there were people kneeling and crying while others sat and cheered as if they were actually enjoying themselves. The whole scene was a mccabe madhouse of noise and horrible sights. Dylan was surprised to see a small group of men who were among the final few people to reach the top of the hill. It seemed as though they had hung back from the crowd on purpose, perhaps to try to keep some distance between themselves and the crowd of ordinary people. There were about ten of them and when Dylan saw their clothing he recognized them as priests or church officials.

The soldiers at the top of the hill who had awaited this procession began their job immediately. They began to tighten the cross beam that was still attached to Jesus. It was obvious that their plan was to hoist him up onto one of the poles just as they had the other men a few minutes earlier. Jesus was to be crucified on the cross between the two other men. Molly knew all too well what was about to happen but she also knew that there was nothing she could do to stop it from occurring. In fact, she curiously found herself not wanting it to stop. She understood that for the salvation of all mankind, this horrible scene must play itself out in full.

Molly's body shook visibly as she realized that this included her as well. Her salvation, Dylan's, everyone's salvation would be hanging on a rough wooden cross in just a few moments.

Suddenly one of the Roman officers ran over to where his men were tightening the ropes that held Jesus to the cross beam. He yelled at them so loud that the translators that Dylan and the others were wearing had no trouble picking up what was being said.

"You idiots. I told you earlier that this one is not to be hung as usual. Don't tie him to his cross bar, we've been ordered to use the spikes on this one. Pick up some of the loose spikes we use to attach the cross beams to the vertical poles and use those. And make sure you drive those spikes through the place where his hands and wrists merge together. If we drive the nails through his palms, his skin and muscle will simply tear apart because of his weight. I want to make sure he stays on that cross. And pull that wooden footrest off of the vertical pole we're using for him. To secure his feet I want you to place one foot over the other and drive a spike through both of them, just below his ankles. Make sure that his feet are really secure so that they stay attached to the pole and that he can't pull away."

The soldiers began to comply with the officer's wishes at once but one of them had a question for the officer.

"Sir, If we remove that wooden block, won't he just suffocate? He won't be able to push himself up on that footrest if it isn't there? He'll be dead inside of a minute."

"No he won't. He'll still be able to push himself up, but he'll have to do it by pushing down against the spike through his feet."

"The pain will be unbearable. He'll probably die just from the pain itself."

"Yeah? So what? What do you care? It'll just make our job a bit quicker today and I hear we've got fresh lamb stew tonight. Personally I don't care if he dies in five minutes or five hours, just as long as I get back to the barracks in time for chow tonight. Now get back to work."

Suddenly the officer reached out and grabbed the soldier by his tunic and said, "And who gave you permission to think? Who do you think you are, arguing with me? I know you've only been with our unit a few weeks but if you dare to question me again, you'll be right up there next to him. Understand?"

The soldier nodded, but the officer was already walking away.

By this time the other criminal was secured to his cross beam which was in turn attached to the vertical pole. The soldiers lifted it high in the air, placed the bottom of the pole into the mouth of the hole and let it drop into place.

At about that same time the soldiers had succeeded in removing the ropes that held the cross beam against Jesus' shoulders. Jesus moaned with the sudden relief from the removal of the beam. But within seconds his relief turned to pain that caused him to momentarily pass out as the soldiers drove nails through his feet and wrists in compliance with their orders. Dylan could see the crowd jump back a few feet as blood spurted and splashed in several different directions. Several people in the crowd laughed, others wailed, Molly's knees buckled and she collapsed against Dylan once again.

The soldiers, having completed the job of securing Jesus to the cross with spikes lifted him up, lined the vertical pole up with the hole in the ground and let it drop.

Even though the crowd noises were quite loud, everyone could clearly hear the skin, muscle and sinew tear and rip as the pole dropped into place. Dylan silently hoped that they would rip enough to release Jesus and put an end at least to that part of his pain. But the spikes held and Jesus hung on a wooden cross between two criminals, exactly as the Bible described. Exactly as Molly had said. He turned toward her and said in a quiet voice. "I am so sorry. I just didn't know."

CHAPTER 35

The noise of the crowd was loud but could not hide the primeval scream that came from Dr. Ormond. Several people looked over at her including a couple of the soldiers but they all soon looked away. Dylan, Molly and Reid all gathered around Dr. Ormond and tried to ask her why she had screamed like that. She was on her knees sobbing and it took her a few moments to collect herself. Finally she was able to respond.

"I'm sorry. I'm sorry. It just came out. I took one look at that man and just lost it," she looked up at Dylan and grabbed his shoulder. "We should go. We should leave right now. We've seen enough here. We don't belong in a place like this."

She sobbed quietly for a minute or so and then looked back up at Dylan. "Please. Let's just go. Please, please get us out of here."

Dylan looked at her for a moment and then looked at Reid and Molly. They were all staring back at him expectantly. He turned his eyes back to the gruesome scene unfolding before them, and took a closer look at Jesus. He could easily understand why Dr. Ormond had become so upset.

Dylan knew that the man on the middle cross was Jesus. He had no trouble understanding that. But the problem was that he could hardly recognize him as a human at all. His face was swollen and distorted beyond belief from being beaten. It was obvious to everyone present that he had not just been hit once or twice, but many times. Somebody had placed a crudely made wreath of thorns on his head and pushed it down so that some of the thorns poked into his scalp just above his eyebrows and again just above his left ear. Loose flesh hung from his jaw and his right ear looked like just a mass of torn skin. Blood, both dried and fresh, covered most of His body.

Dylan could not see Jesus' back, only the front of his torso, legs and arms was visible from where Dylan was standing. Even so Dylan could see the marks where a lash or whip had cut into Jesus' sides and rib cage. Even the sides and front of his legs had been whipped. He could only imagine what Jesus' back looked like. From this distance it was hard to tell exactly what had occurred but Dylan had studied this part of the Bible's description well over the last week or so. During the Bible study sessions back at HIS he'd had a difficult time believing the details of the torture and beatings as described in the Bible. But seeing the man upon the cross now, Dylan had no doubt that the beatings and whippings had been brutal. There was hardly a place on the front of Jesus' body that was not covered with sweat or blood or both. He knew that as horrific as Jesus looked from this angle, his back would look even worse.

Dylan looked at the scene in front of him for a long time. Then he turned to the others and said, "OK I agree. Time to go."

He activated the icon on his allcomm that would send them home, but nothing happened. He tried again and then even a third time but still they remained right where they were. Next he tried to verbally enter the commands that would end this GLASS run and send them back to their own time. Again, nothing happened. All four of them tried to contact both TERRI and Abbie but no contact could be made.

"Looks like we're going to be here for a while," Reid said stating the obvious.

Dr. Ormond started to panic and began yelling again. She was screaming that they would be left here forever and never get home. Once again her yelling was so loud that one of the soldiers yelled over to her to be quiet or leave. This frightened them all a little bit because even though there were many people in the crowd yelling and screaming, Dr. Ormond's screams were the loudest of all. Reid and Dylan both motioned to the guard that they would take care of keeping Dr. Ormond quiet.

It took Molly, Dylan and Reid a long time to get Dr. Ormond calmed down but finally they were able to do it.

Molly said that it might be better if they went a little closer. She reminded them of their mission and said that they would be responsible for everything they saw and heard while they were here. Dr. Ormond almost panicked again at the thought of getting any closer and Reid said, "We don't have to worry about all of that. We each have our allcomms and they are recording everything we see and hear."

Molly and Dylan nodded their agreement but in a few moments Molly began to edge forward anyway, drawn toward Jesus as only another Christian could understand. It looked to Molly as if Jesus had said something softly that none of them could hear clearly. Then one of the criminals said something back in response.

"We can't hear much from this distance. We need to be a bit closer."

She looked at Dylan to see if he was coming with her and smiled when she felt him at her side moving forward with her.

They were still in the back of the crowd but now they were standing right up against the people just in front of them. Dylan looked back to see that Reid and Dr. Ormond were still back several paces.

Molly suddenly grabbed Dylan's arm so tightly that he actually winced in pain.

"Sorry," she said. "But look at that. That's amazing."

His eyes followed to where she was pointing. At first he couldn't tell exactly what she was pointing at but finally his gaze came to rest on a small wooden sign. It was really just a scrap of tree bark that someone had written something on. One of the soldiers had just attached it to the vertical part of Jesus' cross just above his head. The writing was too small to make out from where they were standing. Dylan looked and could see that the other two criminals did not have signs like that attached to their crosses.

"What is that?" He asked.

Molly waited a moment before responding. "The Bible describes it as a sign that labels Jesus as the King of the Jews. The soldiers or whoever ordered it to be put up there meant it as a cruel jest or some sort of derogatory title. But ironically they have announced the truth. He is the King of the Jews and King of everyone else as well."

Dylan was stunned. He wasn't as well versed in the study of the Bible as Molly was and he had forgotten about that sign.

As he was thinking about that, Molly pointed again to some activity just below the crosses. One of the soldiers had gone to all three of the men hanging on the crosses and pulled all of their clothes off. They could hear the other soldiers laughing and one of them called something out in a mean spirited way. The translators that Dylan and Molly were wearing kicked in at once and they clearly understood that the soldier had said, "Well, they won't be needing these anymore."

This brought a lot more laughter from other soldiers as well as from some of the bystanders in the crowd. Even though all of the clothes were bloodied and in tatters, the soldiers began arguing about which one of them should be allowed to take the clothing home. One of the officers came over to tell them to stop and get back to work. The soldiers argued their case with the officer who relented and began walking away. He turned and told the soldiers to go ahead and figure it out on their own but to hurry it up and get back to work. Immediately five or six of them dropped to kneeling positions in a small semi circle with the garments on the ground between them. One of the soldiers reached into a nearby pack and brought out some sort of wooden chips with markings on them.

"What are they doing?" Dylan asked.

"They're getting ready to gamble for the clothing that they just took from Jesus and those other two men."

"Why?"

"Because even as nasty as those rags are right now, those guys can probably sell them to someone in the city tomorrow for a small amount of money or maybe exchange them for something. But there is another reason they are doing that. A reason they are not even aware of. There are prophecies in earlier Biblical writings that describe this scene. Like I said. Those soldiers are not aware of it but they are fulfilling Bible prophecy right in front of us."

Dylan looked perplexed. "Really?"

Molly squeezed his hand. "Yes, and by the way, you just flunked the last Bible class we had the other day. This scene is described in the Bible and we went over this just a couple of days ago. Also from now on, these scenes that we are recording will give more credence and authority to the Bible being a true and accurate account of all of this once we get back home. Just sayin."

Dylan knew he was busted. He knew he had not studied the Bible lessons of the past few days like he should have. He had attended the Bible sessions and he actually had learned some very interesting things. But he really had not believed they were necessary. Actually, if he was honest with himself, he knew that he just had not believed they were even close to being true so he had discarded them as not really anything to worry about. He had acquired a small amount of Biblical knowledge over the past few weeks but not as much as he should have. Now he could only continue to stare at what was going on in front of him and watch as history unfolded in real time.

A little while later Reid and Dr. Ormond came to stand next to Dylan and Molly near the back of the crowd. Dylan and Molly both looked at Dr. Ormond but did not say anything. She looked back at them and sheepishly said, "Sorry guys. I, I think, um, well I think I'll be OK now."

Dylan nodded at her and Molly gave her a small hug.

They watched in silence for a while as the scene continued to play out in front of them.

They saw Jesus rally at one point and speak to a middle aged woman who was in the front of the crowd. Just after that he had a short conversation with a young man who was standing next to that same woman.

Not too long after that Jesus called out in agony and then was silent for a long time. At last he tilted his head back and spoke as he gazed skyward. The interpreting devices that were imbedded in their skin suits interpreted his words clearly as he spoke.

"Father. Father why have you abandoned me and left me here alone?"

Molly cried as she explained to the others that Jesus had always been with God and God with Jesus. This moment was the first time they had ever been separated and she thought that the pain of that separation must be far worse than the physical pain he was experiencing.

Reid asked why they should be separated now. He said that he thought that just the opposite would be true, that God would not abandon his own son in his greatest hour of need. Reid went on to say that this could only be more proof that God did not really exist and that this man whom history had made out to be the actual Son of God, was nothing more than what he appeared to be right now; a deranged criminal of some sort.

Molly's first instinct was to punch Reid in the nose but she got herself under control and explained to him that Jesus was in the process of taking all sins on to and in to himself. God could not be in the presence of that sin and so, did in fact, sort of leave Jesus alone. Molly tried to explain things a little further for the benefit of the other three. "Right before our eyes God is allowing Jesus' body to be crushed because of those sins. But later Jesus will in turn destroy those same sins so that we will never have to fear death again. It really is very simple at this level. Believe in Jesus; have your sins taken away forever. Pretty good deal if you ask me."

Dr. Ormond looked skeptical and started to say something when suddenly Jesus called out loudly again. "Father forgive these, your children. They do not understand what they are doing."

As soon as he had finished speaking the sky instantly turned dark. Dylan looked up at the Sun. Oddly, the Sun was still shining. There just didn't seem to be any light coming from it. All around people were screaming. Many of them ran for the road, trying to get away from this place. The soldiers also sensed that something was wrong. The officers called the men into place and they formed a line with their backs to the three men on the crosses. The soldiers faced the crowd with their swords drawn. They were expecting trouble. What kind of trouble, they could not say, but they knew that something strange was happening.

Soon about half the crowd, or maybe a little more, had left the top of the hill. Molly and the others could hear them as they stumbled their way down the far side of the hill and headed for the city.

The people remaining on the hilltop, like the soldiers, had become quiet. Everyone was expecting something to happen. In fact it was so quiet that Dylan noticed that it was way too quiet. There was absolutely no noise at all. Just an eerie stillness and the horrible darkness.

Dylan looked toward the Sun again and saw that it had not gone anywhere, it was still there and looked sort of the same. He could tell there were no clouds near it and there was no eclipse of any sort. For some reason, the Sun was shining just like it always did but there just wasn't any light.

This strange phenomenon went on for a while and then Jesus called out again. Against the silence his voice sounded so loud that many in the crowd put their hands over their ears.

"Father, I give up my spirit voluntarily. I release it to you!"

He looked out across the crowd and sucked in a large breath. He held that breath for just a second or two, dropped his head to his chest and slowly let that last breath out.

He remained perfectly still in that position.

For a full minute or so no one in the crowd moved or said anything.

Molly felt as if she might feint. Just as she felt her consciousness slipping away a small voice deep within revived her by bringing to mind one of her favorite songs. She realized with a jolt that it was the same song she had been singing on the day that she had first arrived on the HIS campus several weeks ago.

She sang to herself some of the words that were her favorite verses of that song.

To build a wooden tower,
    starts a journey, to set the world free.

To gaze upon that tower,
    and realize the fate, that was meant for me.

To climb a wooden tower,
    gives me faith, to truly see.

But to stand beneath that tower,
    I must bow, and bend my knee.

The words were not lost on her as she considered where she was and what she was experiencing. She bent her right knee until it rested on the stone covered ground. She bowed her head, covered her face with her hands and sobbed quietly for a full minute.

Just then everyone present felt a subtle stirring in the ground beneath them. It began so gradually that for a few moments they were not really sure they were actually feeling it or just imagining that they were. But very quickly it became a rumbling and then a shaking.

Molly had never experienced an earthquake before but she knew without a doubt that this was what was happening.

The earthquake continued to build in strength until everyone in the crowd had been knocked off of their feet. People screamed as the violence of the quake continued to build into a nightmare situation. The darkness remained and panic was everywhere. Several rocks the size of basketballs exploded or cracked open. The ground behind where the crosses were placed split open in a crack about twelve inches wide.

The earth shook violently for exactly thirty three seconds and then gradually, the shaking became less and less pronounced. As the quake subsided it seemed to take the darkness with it and light returned as if nothing had happened.

A few people could be heard crying or whimpering but for a minute no one spoke. Then, one of the Roman officers picked himself up off of the ground. He looked over at the crowd and then walked over to the cross where Jesus hung.

Everyone on the top of the hill was looking at this Roman officer. It looked to Molly as if he wanted to say something and soldiers and onlookers alike waited anxiously to hear what he would say.

Twice he started to speak but couldn't seem to find the right words. Finally he got his thoughts together and his emotions under control. He reached out and gently touched the foot of Jesus and quietly said, "There can be no doubt. This man must certainly be the Son of God."

Chapter 36

Many people who had remained through the darkness and the earthquake now headed down the path and away from the crucifixion site. Following the general panic during the blackout and the earthquake, only about thirty or so people remained at the the top of the hill. Among them were three Jewish priests who had been there throughout the whole day. They stood off from the rest of the crowd and talked only to each other. Soon Molly noticed two more Jewish priests coming up the path to the top of the hill. They walked over to the three who were already there and conversed with them in an agitated manner for a few minutes. Then one of the newly arrived priests walked over to one of the Roman officers and had a short conversation with him. The officer kept shaking his head and waving his arms at the priest as if telling him to go away and let the soldiers complete their job. The priest persisted and finally reached into the folds of his robe and produced a small scroll. He offered it to the officer who looked at it but did not read it. The Roman officer spat on the ground and shook his head from left to right. The priest started to walk away but then looked back at the officer and once again held out the scroll for the officer to take. Finally the officer roughly grabbed the scroll from the priest. He unrolled it and read it. He looked up at the priest and then read the scroll a second time.

"What do you think that's all about?" Reid asked.

"No idea," Dylan responded.

Molly waited a second or two and then said, "I think I know." When the other three looked at her she continued. "In the Bible there is a description of exactly what we are about to see. The Jewish religious leaders did not want the crucifixions to continue on into a Sabbath day. Also, this is a major holiday weekend, so to speak. This is the Passover holiday. So they got permission from the Roman governor to go ahead and just kill any criminals who were hanging on their crosses. Remember that normally crucifixions could last for several days as the men died very slowly. I think that note is from the governor giving permission to kill those three men right now and get this ghastly job done before the Sabbath begins. That will be in just a few hours and the Jewish officials want it all to be done before the Sabbath."

"Oh yeah," Dylan said. "I remember reading about that in the Bible. The guards are going to break the legs of the two guys on either side of Jesus but when they check on him, they are going to find that he is already dead. Then I think they end up stabbing him with a spear or a sword or something just to make sure. I can't recall all of the details, but I think it was something like that."

"Yes that's right," Molly said. "Once the legs are broken those men will not be able to push themselves up to get air into their lungs to breath. Breaking their legs ensures that they will suffocate quickly."

As Molly finished speaking the scene unfolded in front of them exactly the way the Bible described it.

"Don't look now but that guy over there is checking us out," Reid said.

Dr. Ormond looked ready to panic again and asked, "Which one, where? Who's checking us out? Should we run for it?"

Reid responded, "Don't look, but it's one of those priests. I think it's one from that group who stayed up here all day with us. Think we're busted?"

Dylan responded and said, "I don't know but let's just try to be calm about this if we can and continue to try to blend in."

Soon the ordeal was over. The two men on either side of Jesus were dead and their bodies were being removed from their crosses by the soldiers.

At the same time that this was happening, one of the other soldiers was stomping around cursing loudly and trying to wipe water and blood off of his face and clothes. He had been the one assigned to make certain that Jesus was dead and he was covered with the blood and water that had poured out of the wound that was caused when he had thrust his spear into Jesus' left side. The other soldiers found this hilarious and were teasing him mercilessly about it.

"Uh oh," Reid whispered. "Just as I feared. I think we really are busted."

"What do you mean?" Molly asked.

"Look, over there. That priest that I caught staring at us is walking over to talk to that officer."

They all looked and saw that it was exactly as Reid had described. The priest began talking to the officer and the two of them had a heated argument for a minute or two. They were too far away for the translators to pick up any of the conversation so Molly and the others could only watch and guess at what the discussion might be about. However it appeared that the conversation was not about them so they all felt a small sense of relief, at least for a few minutes.

It looked to Molly like the priest had finally won the argument. He pointed to the body of Jesus and the officer nodded. He turned toward some of the soldiers and in doing so stepped a little closer to where Molly was standing. Now he was just close enough for the translators to pick up and interpret what he was saying. Molly could clearly hear the officer address his soldiers. "OK men let's pack up and get out of here. This priest is going to take this one here," he said indicating Jesus' body. "Just leave the others lying where they are. The clean up detail will be arriving soon and then all this becomes their problem."

The officer looked once more at the priest, shrugged his shoulders and said to him. "Go ahead. He's all yours."

Immediately the priest ran the few steps over to where a small group of people were waiting. Molly's heart skipped a beat as she realized that in that small group of people were both Jesus' mother and probably the disciple John. She quickly bowed her head and whispered a quick prayer of thanks to God for allowing her to be a small part of this incredible opportunity. She looked up as she heard Dr. Ormond's panicky voice say, "Look out. Here comes trouble. I knew we were going to get caught."

The priest who had been watching them earlier was walking straight toward them.

"Just everyone stay cool," Dylan said. "Remember to try to keep straight in front of this guy so he can't see us from the side. We will look pretty normal to him when he looks at us straight on but if he sees us from the side he'll know that something is not right and he may call the guards over. We don't know who he is so just stay calm."

"You guys are so lame," Molly said. If you had studied your Bible lessons a bit more seriously for the last few weeks you would know exactly who this guy is.

"Oh, I suppose you think you know who he is?" Dr. Ormond said sarcastically.

"Yes, I'm pretty sure I do know who he is. The Bible says that just after Jesus' body was removed from the cross, a man of high standing in the religious community who might also have been some sort of councilman or something asked permission to have the body given to him for burial. Jesus' family and friends would have had no money to bury him without this mans help."

As she said this the man approached them to within fifteen feet or so but stopped short of coming any closer. He looked intently at them for a moment and looked as if he wanted to ask something of them. He opened his mouth to speak but then seemed to think better of it, looked at them a moment longer and then turned and walked back to the group of people that were now surrounding Jesus' body. At one point he stood up and looked at them again but then went back to assisting the small group of people who were wrapping Jesus' body in a long white cloth that someone had brought.

"What was that all about?" Reid asked.

Molly answered, "Well if my guess is correct, his name is Joseph. The Bible says he originally came from a place called Arimathea. We know quite a bit about Jesus' main followers, his twelve disciples, but apparently there were many other secret followers who believed in Jesus."

"Why would they follow him in secret?" Dylan wanted to know.

"Well in the case of this fellow here, he could have lost his job, his standing in the community and perhaps even his life if he had openly supported Jesus and His ministry. He and many people like him believed in Jesus but were not very open about it."

She turned to look Dylan in the eyes before continuing. "Believe it or not, there have always been many people like that and even today there are more people than you would think who would fall into that category of secret believer."

She stared at Dylan for a few moments after she finished speaking. Her stare and the meaning behind it were not lost on Dylan. He started to respond but then cast his eyes down to the ground and stepped a few feet away.

In a few minutes the small group of people, mostly women, had the body wrapped in the cloth. They lifted it carefully off of the ground and then, following Joseph, they began to carry the body of Jesus down the hill.

Dr. Ormond began to speak quickly. "Dylan, try to get through to GLASS again. That was a close call, we almost got caught. We need to get out of here."

The other three looked at her like she was crazy.

Dylan was the first to respond. "Are you out of your mind? We have just witnessed three people murdered in front of our eyes in probably the most gruesome means imaginable and all you can think of is that we might have been caught? And caught doing what? We've done nothing wrong."

"Besides," Molly said. "Don't you realize yet that you were wrong? Not only did we see three men get killed just now, but one of them is The Son of God. Jesus! The real Jesus. Don't you get it yet? Everything, and I do mean everything, that the Bible says about this event is true. Don't you realize what that means?""

Dr. Ormond looked like she wanted to scream. Instead she turned to Reid for support and said, "No, there is no Jesus. No way. That guy didn't look like any Son of God to me. Looked pretty helpless. No, that was just some guy who probably deserved to die just like those other men. I bet this same scene is repeated here almost everyday. Don't you think so Reid?"

"Well, it probably is repeated every day. I just don't know about Jesus and The Son of God and all. I do think that the earthquake and darkness was pretty weird. There is something strange here for sure. Just can't quite put my finger on it."

"People, open your eyes and ears. Everything we have seen and heard is described in the Bible exactly the way we have experienced it. How do you explain that?"

No one had an answer for Molly's question. After a minute or so Dr. Ormond asked Dylan to try to get them back to the GLASS lab again.

Dylan looked at her and once again quietly told her that he had been trying to connect with TERRI and Abbie all day and that he would continue to do that. He shot her an annoyed look and told her to not ask him about it again.

Dr. Ormond looked insulted and said, "Well you're the leader, you need to do something to get us out of this place. What's your plan? You got a plan? What are we supposed to do?"

Molly could tell that Dylan was getting angry. They were all tired and on their last nerves. Before Dylan could respond to Dr. Ormond's last question Molly decided to answer it herself.

"You want to know what we're supposed to do? I can answer that for you, that's easy."

The others looked intently at her. She started walking across the top of the now vacant hill in the direction that Joseph and the others had just taken, carrying Jesus' body with them. "We're going to follow them! That's the plan!"

After a moment or two of hesitation, the others reluctantly started to follow Molly. While they were walking Reid whispered to Dylan. "You know if I were you I'd think very seriously about getting a new girlfriend. This one is a real pain in the neck."

Dylan looked at Reid out of the corner of his eye and said, "Good thing you're not me then, isn't it. I think I might just try and keep this one around awhile. I have a feeling that whenever Molly is around, life is interesting."

"You mean like traveling through time and watching people being crucified by Roman Soldiers?" Reid asked in a sarcastic manner.

"Well hopefully that won't always be the case. But yeah, kinda like that."

Chapter 37

The group carrying the body of Jesus headed down the main path toward the city but after about seventy five yards they turned onto a side trail. Molly and the others followed at a distance of about twenty yards. Once or twice, the man that Molly thought might be Joseph of Arimathea glanced back at them. They continued on this path for another hundred yards or so and then headed into a grotto made up of rocky ledges and cliffs within a grove of trees.

The trail they were on consisted of frequent turns and twists and Molly, Dylan and the others lost sight of the group in front of them for a few seconds every now and then.

As they were coming around one particularly sharp turn, there, standing in the middle of the trail about thirty feet in front of them stood Joseph. Molly could see the others in the group in the distance continuing on down the trail.

"Who are you?" Joseph asked. "Are you followers of Yeshua, our teacher?"

Everyone in the group was caught off guard but after a moment they all spoke at once.

"Yes," Molly said.

"Ummm," Dylan croaked.

"Well, uh," Reid responded.

"No!" Dr. Ormond said emphatically.

Joseph looked confused a little and then said, "I do not know you. And it is obvious by your behavior that you are strangers here. I must go to my friends and assist with the burial. We do not have much time because the Sabbath is almost upon us. I am sorry but it is our custom to only allow those who are family or close friends to complete the burial necessities. Since we do not know who you are, I ask that you not follow us any further."

Dylan and the others could see that down the path, past Joseph, the group that was carrying the body of Jesus had apparently reached their destination. They stepped off of the main path and into a small clearing a few yards further on.

Now the man that Molly thought must be Joseph of Arimathea, was speaking again. "I must ask though, are you friends? Or do you seek to do us harm? Not that there could be much more harm done to our group than has already been done this day. But still, I must know."

Molly spoke up first and said, "We are friends, there is nothing to fear from us. We only came here to seek answers."

When Joseph did not respond she continued. "Is this man the Son of God?"

Immediately she chastised herself for asking that question. Where had her boldness disappeared to? How could she question her God now after what she had just witnessed. She wished that she had more faith.

Joseph hesitated before speaking again. "You have seen the events of this day and yet you still seek answers." It was a statement and not a question. "Well so do I. So do we all. I do not have much time. I must go and help my friends."

He turned away and took a few steps down the path, but then stopped and turned back to face them. "You are not from here and it is our custom to always help people in need, especially strangers to our land. Our city is crowded right now due to the Passover celebration. Do you have lodging arranged for?"

No one answered because the question caught them off guard. They had not even thought about this issue because the original plan was for them to be gone long before now. The day had been so busy and incredible that they had not had any time to even think about food or lodging. Now it dawned on them that they had neither and they remembered with dismay that they were, at least for the time being, stuck here in Jerusalem.

Joseph seemed to have recognized their plight before they did.

"I will be staying in the city tonight with some friends. However my home is not far from here. You are welcome to stay there if you wish. The servants are all gone and my home is empty but there is food there and I would be honored if you would be my guests. I will return there in a few days and if you are still there perhaps we can all discuss our questions and seek for answers together."

Dylan gratefully accepted the invitation for the whole group. Joseph gave them directions to his home which turned out to be in the countryside but only about a mile and a half away.

With that he turned to go back down the path and Dylan, Molly, Reid and Dr. Ormond began their trip to locate Joseph's house.

Chapter 38

The directions given by Joseph to his home were good and that was a blessing. They found his house easily just as darkness began to fall across the land. It was obvious that he was a man of high standing within the community because his home actually consisted of four separate buildings. There was a large main building that was the living quarters, a smaller structure that probably housed his servants and two smaller huts. One was being used as a chicken coop and the other was just a tool shed.

They found their way into the main house and Molly was relieved to find that there were two separate bedrooms. She and Dr. Ormond took the larger of the two rooms and Reid and Dylan took the other.

They located a cupboard stocked with food just as Joseph had told them they would. Most of it was simple pastry or bread based foods but after the type of day they had just experienced, the meal seemed to them like food fit for a king. They found a few jugs of wine in another cupboard and in the courtyard there was a well with cool clear water.

After they had eaten there was very little conversation. Each of them kept their own thoughts to themselves. Molly prayed, Dylan thought about all of the things they had seen and heard, Dr. Ormond grumbled and Reid made several trips to the wine cupboard.

Dylan tried unsuccessfully to establish communications to GLASS through his allcomm. He also attempted to get the group sent back through the Lamacelli Creases to return to GLASS but his attempts at that failed miserably. They were all exhausted by the events of the day and within an hour of finishing their meal they were all sound asleep.

The morning seemed to be upon them in no time at all. They ate again and spent a little time exploring their surroundings but did not go too far from the house because the road just outside the courtyard had several travelers on it throughout the day and they did not want too much contact with anyone. Some of the travelers were heading towards Jerusalem and some were heading in the opposite direction. Molly knew that the numbers of travellers would normally be much greater but today was the Sabbath and most people were most likely staying at their homes.

Most of the day was spent discussing two topics. The first was their dire situation. At the moment they were stranded in a time and place that none of them wanted to stay in permanently. The fact that they were not able to communicate with TERRI, Abbie or anyone else back at the GLASS lab made them more and more depressed as the day went on.

The second topic of conversation of course was the extraordinary events that they had all witnessed the previous day. Dylan, Molly and even Reid explored the various options of what they had seen and heard. Only Dr. Ormond refused to take part in that portion of the conversation. Each time the conversation turned toward something that had occurred the day before, she crept back to the bedroom claiming that she had a headache or nausea.

They also rested and napped quite a bit and before they knew it, the sky was turning dark again as night fell.

The sunset was breathtaking and Dylan asked Molly to go on a short walk with him. They held hands as lovers often do while saying nothing, simply enjoying the company of the other person. Finally Molly broke the silence.

"Do you believe Dylan?" She asked quietly.

They walked on a few paces before he answered. "I don't know. Maybe."

They strolled in silence for a few more moments before he continued. "I know you want me to believe, and I know what we saw yesterday. But it's really hard for me. All my life I've believed in things I could see, or hear or somehow prove to be real. This is really tough. I'm sorry."

"Even after being in the middle of what we were in yesterday you still can't see that as proof?" Molly asked. "We came here to prove that Jesus did exist and that he was and is the one and only Son of God. I don't see how you or anyone else could have any doubts about that after what happened up on that hill just a little over twenty four hours ago."

More silence followed until finally Dylan said, "I can't really explain what happened yesterday. But that's not the same as proof. I want to believe, I think, and in a way I think I do. But there is still that part of me that needs more proof. I'm sorry Molly, that's just the way it is. I love you more than I can say, and I know you want me to say that I believe. But if I did that, it would be a lie. We saw some people get killed yesterday. I can believe that one of them was Jesus. But we still don't have any proof at all about him being the Son of God. And the way things stand right now with our situation, I really don't see that proof coming our way any time soon. I need more time. I need to think it all through. I still need something more than what we witnessed yesterday."

The evening stroll had begun to create a great mood for both Molly and Dylan. Things had started out in a very promising way, but now the mood was totally crushed. Molly nodded and felt a few tears beginning to form in the corners of her eyes. She let go of Dylan's hand and said, "I understand."

Quickly she turned and headed toward the house before Dylan could see the tears that had begun to run down her cheeks.

CHAPTER 39

"Get up! Let's go! Dylan, Reid, C'mon, we gotta get going."

Molly had burst into the room that Dylan was sharing with Reid in what seemed to the two of them to be the middle of the night.

"Wha?" Dylan mumbled as he tried to shake off the cobwebs of sleep. "What's going on? What's wrong?"

"Nothing," Molly responded. "C'mon. Let's get going."

Reid was a little slower than Dylan to wake up but he rubbed the sleep from his eyes and rolled off of the mat that had served him for a bed.

"What in the world is happening? It's the middle of the night."

He looked questioningly over at Dr. Ormond who was leaning against the door jam. She rolled her eyes skyward and said, "I have no idea. I've told you guys all along that this girl is crazy, and now we have this, whatever this is. She woke me up a few minutes ago and started talking crazy, something about we needed to go in the next few minutes or we would miss the whole thing. I tried to make some sense out of what she was saying but I really do think she is just out of her mind. Actually I believe that most Christians are like that."

Molly gave Dr. Ormond a hurtful look and then continued trying to get Reid and Dylan up and out of bed.

"C'mon you guys, we need to go. We need to be out of here in the next five minutes or we're going to miss everything we came to see."

Dylan grabbed Molly's hand in order to slow her down a little bit and said, "Molly for Pete's sake, what are you talking about? Where do you expect us to go in the middle of the night, and why do we need to leave now? What's going on?"

"I've already told you," Dr. Ormond said. "She's nuts."

Dylan looked at Dr. Ormond and then back at Molly. "Molly, be reasonable. It's pitch black outside and we hardly even know where we are."

For a moment no one said anything and then Molly got that determined look in her eyes that Dylan had seen once or twice before.

"You all can stay here if you want. But I'm leaving. I didn't come all this way for nothing. I want to see."

Dylan looked exasperated and he grabbed her by the shoulders. Again he said, "Molly, c'mon, give us all a break will ya? Where do you think you're going. I'm not sure it is exactly safe out there. Let's just sit a minute and talk this through. It's not even light out there yet."

Molly was about to say something else when Reid clapped his hands together.

"Oh man," He shouted. "It's not light out yet but it's morning." He looked at Molly and asked, "Is that it Molly? Is it because it's morning?"

Everyone looked at Molly and she slowly nodded. "Yes. It's morning."

Dr. Ormond exploded. "So what? What's the big deal. And even if it is morning, which I doubt, what are we supposed to do about it? It's dark, and it's cold and we're exhausted. We should just stay here and maybe try to get a little more sleep."

Dylan chimed in and said, "Ya know Molly, I think she's right this time. It's dark and we have nowhere to go. We really should just stay here for a while until it gets light outside."

Molly started to say something but Reid beat her to it. "You're not paying attention to what Molly's trying to tell you Dylan. It's morning. Get it?"

Dylan tried to concentrate a little harder in order to make sense of what Molly and Reid were saying but he failed miserably. "So? It's morning, so what?"

Reid took a step toward Dylan and said a little louder. "It's morning. It's Sunday morning."

Dylan still looked confused. In the back of his brain there was something telling him that he ought to be able to understand and recognize what Molly and Reid were trying to tell him, but whatever it was remained just out of his grasp.

"So it's Sunday morning," Dr. Ormond said in an angry and tired voice. "Who cares? What do you want us to do Molly, go to church with you?"

That statement jarred Dylan's mind and memory a little bit but he still couldn't quite grab on to whatever Reid and Molly were saying. He looked at Molly who was heading toward the door and then looked over at Reid who said, "Dylan for a smart guy sometimes you're a bit thick headed. Don't you get yet what Molly is trying to tell us? It's morning. It's Sunday morning. It's Easter Sunday morning. It's the "first" Easter Sunday morning. Maybe."

The idea finally hit Dylan like a hammer blow to the head. He staggered back a step or two as the realization of what Reid was saying began to sink in. He put out a hand to lean against a wall for support.

"What? Easter?"

After a moment his eyes lit up like light bulbs as the idea finally took it's full form in his mind.

"Yeah. That's right. If Molly is correct this will be the first Easter Sunday and Jesus will … oh man we need to go right now."

Molly, Dylan and Reid began to get ready to leave, while Dr. Ormond began to complain all over again.

"No. Absolutely not. We're not going anywhere, at least I'm not. I'm staying right here. Remember what that guy told us when he said we could use his house. He told us that he would come by to check on us in a day or two. What was his name again? Joseph of Arithmetic or something like that?"

"Arimathea," Molly said as she chuckled. "It was Joseph of Arimathea, not arithmetic."

"Yeah, yeah, whatever. We should stay right here. It's dark out, it's cold and I have absolutely no interest in chasing ghosts through a cemetery in the middle of the night. No way. I'm not going."

Molly started to leave and Dylan followed close behind her.

Dr. Ormond stared hard at Reid and said, "Surely you're not going too are you? I know that you don't actually believe this nonsense."

Reid paused and looked back and said, "No, I don't. But I'm a scientist and so are you. You and I both agreed that we would come to Jerusalem at this particular time not to prove that Jesus is the Son of God, but to prove that he isn't."

"And we've done that," Dr. Ormond whined.

"No. We haven't. We saw a man die on a cross. That man may or may not have been Jesus. But whether he was or wasn't, all we've proven so far is that some guy died on a cross in a manner similar to the way the Bible describes the death of Jesus. Probably during this time period thousands of people died like that. The dying isn't the deciding factor, it's the raising up from being dead that is the issue. Don't you see? This is what we came here for. We can go back to that grave site and see for ourselves that no one is coming out of that tomb. This is our chance to prove once and for all that Jesus was probably some great teacher or prophet or something like that. But we need to get our proof that he absolutely did not raise himself from the dead."

Dr. Ormond looked at him for a moment. She knew he was right. This was the opportunity they had been waiting for. She started to take a step forward but then stopped, shook her head and said, "I can't. I'm sorry but I just can't go. I'm staying here."

Reid nodded to her and then turned and jogged to catch up with Molly and Dylan.

The three of them walked in silence for just a minute or so and then Dylan said, "Think she'll be OK back there?"

Reid responded, "Yeah I think so. But on the other hand maybe we shouldn't have left her alone like that. Of course in the long run it was her decision to stay there."

"Yeah but I still feel bad about it. What do you think Molly?"

"Oh, I have a feeling she will be just fine," Molly said cheerfully.

"Really? What makes you say that?"

"Because she's right behind us."

Dylan and Reid stopped short and turned around. The night was dark but they could just make out a shadow walking up the road toward them.

"I think this is all nonsense and I think you are all horrible people to have left me all alone like that. I'm seriously considering suing all of you for . . . well for . . . well I'll think of something."

Dr. Ormond was so angry the others could almost feel the heat radiating off of her.

"Molly is crazy and you two are almost as bad letting her mislead you like this. I'm only coming along because I really want to be there to see Molly's face when she realizes that this dead guy is not coming back to life."

She then turned and addressed Molly specifically. "Molly when, if, we get back home you're going to regret this. We're going to prove to the world that Christianity is a farce and you are going to be our star witness. I am really going to enjoy that."

With that she stomped off up the road. Reid followed her but Molly seemed frozen to the ground thinking about the ramifications of what Dr. Ormond had just said. Dylan held her hand and said, "Look don't worry about her."

Molly looked at Dylan and then said softly, "But, what if she's right?'

Dylan pulled her close into a soft warm hug and whispered into her ear. "She's not."

CHAPTER 40

Through the blackness of the night, which somehow seemed darker than normal, they all trudged back up the road in the opposite direction from which they had come the other evening.

Finally after what seemed like hours they arrived back at the grotto. Here, it seemed even darker and they had trouble finding their way back to the burial site. The pathway through the grotto took several turns that looked right but weren't. They found themselves in several dead end small clearings where both new and used tombs were cut into the rock. Each small clearing looked exactly like the next one.

Molly thought that she could see the sky beginning to lighten just a bit and knew that she and the others were running out of time.

They wandered in the darkness for several more minutes. They all knew that they were totally lost in the maze of burial grottos. Molly realized that each minute wandering might cost them the chance of a lifetime. Just when she was about to explode with frustration, Reid stopped short and whispered to the rest of them. "Look, over there. What's that?"

They all looked in the direction that he was pointing. At first they could see nothing except more darkness and the faint outline of trees and rocks. However after a moment or two Dylan whispered, "Yes. I see it."

Molly's eyes were still adjusting to the low light but finally she could make something out as well. It was pretty far away and hidden by trees and bushes but she could tell that there was something there. It appeared to be a small orange glow of some sort.

Reid motioned for the others to follow him. With Reid in the lead they crept down the path toward the glow. They could tell by this time that it was a small fire. Molly was about to ask about it when Reid turned and put his index finger to his lips in the universal "keep quiet" sign. He pointed to a nearby side path and the four of the them crept as silently as they could about twenty five feet down that path. They found themselves in a small clearing with other tombs cut into the rock around them. They were about twenty yards away from the fire and could see through the branches of the small trees and bushes what was going on near the fire. They could also hear voices coming from people who were near the small campfire.

As their eyes continued to adjust to the low light they could see that the fire was in a small clearing similar to the one in which they were hiding. The clearing was next to a rocky outcrop and in that outcrop were cut a number of tombs, maybe eight or ten altogether. Some of them were still open tombs that were to be used at a later date but three of the tombs had large boulders rolled across and in front of their entrances.

Molly recalled from her studies that sometimes rocks or boulders were rolled over the entrances to tombs because of the smell of decay and also to keep robbers from disturbing tombs that might possibly contain valuables.

One of the tombs caught the eye of Molly, Dylan, Reid and Dr. Ormond immediately because it stood out from the rest. It was one of the tombs that had a boulder rolled in front of the entrance. At first glance it had looked just like the other tombs that had rocks in front of them, but a second look showed that there was a difference; a great deal of difference.

The rock in front of the entrance was similar to the other rocks being used for the same purpose at the other tombs. Its diameter was about four feet across and covered an entrance that was probably about three and a half feet tall and maybe three feet wide.

The rock was shaped sort of like a wheel with a thickness of about ten inches. It had to have weighed several hundred pounds or so. Just below the entrance to the tombs, small gullies or ditches were cut into the ground. These ditches were about six inches deep and were a little longer than the entrances of the tombs. The rocks that blocked the entrances to the tombs already being used had been rolled down into these ditches. Molly guessed that this might make it even harder for someone to roll these huge stones aside, making it that much more difficult to gain entrance to the tombs by grave robbers or whomever. Once one of these boulders had been rolled into place in front of a tomb entrance, it would be extremely difficult for it to be rolled away.

Where the rocks blocking the entrances to the tombs touched the rock face of the grotto, there was not a smooth clear meeting point. This was because both the blocking boulder and the rock face of the grotto were uneven. This meant that the blocking rock was not fully up against the grotto rock face. Instead there were many gaps between the rock and the grotto wall. Except for one of the tombs.

On that one particular tomb, several of the largest gaps had been stuffed with strips of some sort of woven cloth. The cloth strips appeared to be almost gauze like. These strips were of different sizes and shapes that loosely conformed to the size and shape of the gap beneath it. There were perhaps ten or twelve of these parchments like cloths that had been used to stuff the gaps between the rock blocking the entrance to the tomb and the rock wall. In addition to that, somebody had purposefully dripped wax down onto the parchment and allowed that wax to run into some of the smaller cracks and spaces, thereby forming a seal of sorts between the rock wall of the grotto and the blocking rock itself.

Of course there were still several tiny gaps and spaces between the rock wall and the rock itself that were still open but most of the larger gaps had been sealed. The parchment and wax seal did not go completely around to form a complete seal, but the ten or twelve seals in the largest gaps were enough to seal about seventy percent or so of the gaps between the grotto wall and the rock. The wax that sealed some of the smaller gaps sealed off another ten percent of the open cracks and gaps.

Clearly someone had gone to great lengths to seal this tomb in a more secure fashion as compared to the other tombs. If anyone tried to roll the great rock away from the tomb opening, the seals would break. Everyone would then know that somehow the large wheel like rock had been tampered with.

Molly's attention was now drawn to the sounds that they had heard from the other clearing.

They were still well hidden and though it was obviously getting lighter by the minute, it was still dark. As long as they remained fairly still and quiet, they knew they could not be seen or heard by the people in the clearing ahead of them.

A low murmur of voices was coming from that next clearing where the campfire was burning lightly. Molly could see five, no wait, six figures in the clearing, some of them talking quietly to each other.

She could see that these were no ordinary people, they were Roman soldiers. Though she and the others were well hidden, just to be this close to these soldiers caused her heart to skip a beat. They looked and sounded none too happy to be out here in the cold night and she was sure that their moods were nothing she wanted anything to do with.

There were two soldiers sleeping, or at least trying to sleep next to the fire. Another soldier was sitting on a medium sized rock whittling and carving a piece of wood. Molly could not be certain but it looked like he was carving the wood into the shape of a small lamb. Molly smiled when she saw that and wondered if he realized the significance of what he was doing or if the subconscious portion of his brain was already in tune with the history and spirituality of this moment.

Two of the other soldiers were in an upright position but were leaning against the rock face of the grotto. They were facing toward the clearing, one on either side of the large rock covering the tomb entrance. They were talking with the last soldier, an officer, who was standing about four feet in front of them. He had his back to Molly and the others so she could not see his face but she could clearly see the faces of the other two soldiers who were leaning on the wall. They both looked bored and tired, like they would rather be at almost anyplace else on Earth other than here.

Her translator kicked in and she could follow the conversation between the officer and the two other soldiers. The officer was speaking. "How should I know why we're out here? You think they'd tell me anything? No. Just some orders that don't make sense to me either. Seal the tomb and make sure it stays sealed until further notice. Those are the orders and that's all I know about it. We're to be relieved in about an hour. That's all I care about at the moment."

"So what's so special about this tomb?" one of the other soldiers asked.

The Roman officer looked like he might explode. "Did you just hear me say I don't know anything more about it? Well that's what I meant and I really don't need any of your ridiculous questions right now OK? I did hear something about some kind of strangeness going on during one of the crucifixions the other day but I don't know any more than that."

The other soldier leaning against the rock wall motioned to the officer that he also had something to say so the officer gave him permission to speak.

"Yeah? You got something to say too? What is it?"

"I'm kinda hungry. When do we eat?"

The officer took a quick step toward the soldier and yelled, "Keep your mouth shut unless you actually have an intelligent question to ask! Stand up straight, both of you. You think I like it out here any more than you? Well let me tell you somethi --"

He cut his sentence off short as something caught his attention.

For a brief moment Molly thought that he might have heard her or one of the other time travelers. She relaxed slightly when she saw that he remained facing the rock wall and the stone that covered the tombs' entrance. She quickly realized that it must have been something else that had caught his eye or distracted him. Right in front of him, in the small gaps between the stone and the grotto wall, a very faint glow had started emanating from within the tomb. The light started low but rapidly gathered strength. It shone up through the gaps and then began causing the parchment and wax seals to start to melt and then begin to fall away.

At the same time, both soldiers who were leaning against the grotto wall jumped away from the wall and turned to face it.

"What was that?" one of them yelled to the other. "Did you feel that?"

"Yeah," The second soldier yelled back. "The whole wall started to vibrate or shake or something."

Almost at that same moment, the officer turned his head a little and yelled for the other three soldiers to come help. The soldier who had been carving the wooden lamb dropped both his knife and the lamb and jumped to his feet. He stared at the light that was now streaming from all around the stone that blocked the entrance to the tomb. His eyes grew huge and he drew his sword instinctively. The other two soldiers and the officer drew their weapons as well.

At about that same time the yelling and commotion woke the two soldiers who had been sleeping next to the fire. They jumped to their feet and each of them grabbed an eight foot long spear.

By this time the rock wall of the grotto was visibly shaking and shuddering.

"What's going on?" one of the soldiers shouted. "What is this?"

The officer had regained some of his composure and he yelled back. "I don't know. Form up. Everybody get over here with me but spread out a little. We need to be ready for, well I have no idea what we need to be ready for; just be alert!"

By this time it was not just the grotto wall shaking, the ground all around was heaving like an ocean wave. Two of the soldiers were thrown down and the others were trying hard not to fall as well.

Grace Ormond looked like she was going to be sick. Reid had a curious look on his face, like someone who has just discovered something that he had been previously unaware of. Dylan could only look and stare, his jaw was almost on the ground. Molly couldn't smile any bigger if she tried. They were all holding on to each other trying not to fall to the ground although the tremors seemed to be much more harsh in the clearing where the soldiers were than the clearing where Molly and the others were standing.

The Earth had started trembling very suddenly and those same tremors ceased just as quickly. For a long moment there was complete silence all around.

And then it happened.

Chapter 41

The silence was broken by just a whisper of sound. It was a very soft but steady grinding noise. Though the sound was soft and low, it was clear and obviously coming from the tomb. Everyone froze and looked at the rock blocking the tomb entrance.

For a moment there was only a hint of movement but soon they could all see that the huge rock was moving. It was rolling uphill, out of the ditch in which it had been placed. As they watched, it began to gather speed. The boulder rolled faster and faster and with more and more noise.

No one was touching the stone. No one was even near to it. It appeared to be moving of its own accord. One of the soldiers standing nearby dropped his weapon, turned and ran off into the woods. Another of the soldiers, one who had fallen to the ground during the earth tremors jumped to his feet and also ran off. He ran up the path that Molly and her group were standing near. She could see that his face was ghostly white and that his eyes were as big a dinner plates. Just a second or two behind him another of the soldiers ran up the path leaving only two soldiers and the officer behind to guard the tomb.

As Molly and the others watched, the stone continued to gather more speed as it cleared the ditch it had been resting in and rolled itself completely away from the entrance to the tomb.

The officer standing before the tomb shielded his eyes with his hands trying to peer into the depths of the tomb. It was difficult to see anything because of the strong light that was now streaming from the interior of the tomb.

The light was bright, almost unbearably bright and Molly found herself having to squint into the light to see what was going on. Even though the light was bright enough to hurt her eyes, it continued to gain even more brilliance until she could hardly stand to look in that direction.

Just when she thought that she could not stand it a second longer, it stopped. In an instant it simply stopped glowing and the grotto went from daylight like brightness to shadowy dawn light.

The silence was complete.

Just then, in that moment, a figure appeared just inside the tomb entrance. After only a brief pause the figure stepped over the lip of the tomb and out into the clearing. Both of the Roman soldiers dropped in a dead faint and lay still in the center of the clearing. The officer stood his ground for just a second longer and then slowly knelt on one knee right there next to the small fire. He dropped his sword and bowed his head. Molly could see that his entire body was shaking. She wasn't sure if he shook from fear or from crying but she guessed that it might have been both.

The figure took another step out into the clearing. A soft glow radiated from all around that figure. Not the harsh light of a few moments ago, just a soft gentle pleasant glow that seemed to shine out just a few inches in every direction.

Several of the low hanging tree limbs partially hid the figure from Molly and the others. Those limbs had helped hide them from the soldiers but now they were just in the way and Molly had a difficult time observing the scene in the clearing.

Suddenly the figure took a few steps forward until it was standing next to the Roman officer who was still kneeling with head bowed. The figure reached out an arm and rested a hand on the shoulder of the Roman officer. It appeared that the figure spoke something to the officer but Molly's translator could not pick out what was said. After just a moment or two the figure then turned and began to walk up the pathway toward where Molly and the others were hiding. The clearing in which they were hidden was off to one side of the main trail. However they could all tell that it would only be a few seconds before the figure reached the point on the pathway just opposite of where they were standing. They all realized at the same time that this figure was going to walk right past them and would be only a few feet away from them in just a second or two. There was nowhere to run and no hiding place they could find quickly. There was nothing to do but remain where they were and wait. They just stood and watched the figure walk up the path toward the clearing where they had been hiding from the Roman guards. Molly didn't want to run away, Dylan and Reid seemed to be in shock and Dr. Ormond began to whimper quietly.

In no time at all the figure had walked the distance up the main path and had now reached the smaller path that led to the clearing where Molly and the others stood like statues.

Instead of continuing on up the path, the figure stopped at the entrance to their clearing and stood still for a second looking up the path. Then, very slowly, the figure turned and looked directly into the clearing where Molly, Dylan and the others stood. At this point they could all tell quite easily that this was the same man that they had seen crucified before their eyes just a few days ago.

The burial wrap was gone and He now wore a robe that was brilliant white. Both the robe and the man Himself radiated a soft glow that seemed to flow all around Him. Molly could clearly see on His forehead the marks and wounds where the wreath of thorns had been placed tightly against His skull.

No one dared move or even breath for a second or two. Then the man that Molly knew to be Jesus smiled at them. His smile was both soft and warm as He looked intently at each of them in turn. In that short time Molly understood that He knew exactly who she was. A pleasant, exhilarating feeling began to spread all throughout her body. She felt comfortable, safe and content, but most of all she felt loved like she had never felt love before.

Jesus then raised his hands about half way up to His waist and held them out in front of Him, palms facing upward, for each of them to see. When Molly saw the wounds that the spikes had made just at the point where His wrists met His hands, she burst into tears of joy. She heard Dylan gasp beside her and out of the corner of her eye she saw Reid stumble and grab onto a nearby sapling to keep from falling. Dr. Ormond's quiet crying became a loud shrill wailing as she dropped to the ground in a heap.

Jesus smiled a deep warm smile but did not say anything to them. After a few seconds He turned and began to walk back down the pathway toward the tomb in the other clearing.

For at least five minutes no one said anything and no one moved.

Finally Molly became aware of a sound coming from the other clearing. She turned toward that clearing and saw the Roman officer walking down the path in the opposite direction. He had left his weapon where it lay and was half walking and half stumbling down the path, talking quietly to himself and sobbing softly.

Molly watched him go and then turned her attention back to her own clearing.

"Dylan, did you --" she started to speak but stopped when Dylan held his hand up for her to be quiet. As her voice died away she heard an odd crackling sound. At first she had a hard time placing that noise. She was sure she had heard it somewhere previously but just couldn't place it at the moment.

She heard it again, a little louder and more distinctly. This time she identified the sound and knew right away what it was. She could tell by the reactions of the others that they too had heard it and recognized it as well.

Back in the GLASS lab, the team had seen all of the indicator lights connected with the communications and recording systems flash from red to amber indicating that those systems were coming back on line.

Molly looked inquiringly at Dylan. The crackling noise was coming from Dylan's allcomm. It was mostly just static but through the static she could faintly hear a voice. It was a voice trying to connect with them through many miles and many years.

"Can you . . . Do . . . Dyl . . . Rei . . . can anyone hear . . . come in plea . . . copy? . . . Do you cop . . . ?"

Chapter 42

Out of the corner of her eye Molly saw some movement. She turned and looked that way and smiled at what she saw. A small group of three or four women were walking down the main path toward the empty tomb. She knew what was about to happen and what they would find at the tomb. She really wanted to watch this scene play out but she was distracted by the faint static laden voices that were coming through Dylan's allcomm.

The away team was unaware that back in the GLASS lab TERRI had purposefully re-established communications. They were also completely unaware that at that instant, Abbie, Jarrett and all of the other project technicians were holding their collective breaths as the indicator lights changed color again, this time from amber to solid green.

Back in the grotto clearing, Dylan was standing next to Molly with Reid and Dr. Ormond crowding around looking over his shoulders. Molly could see that he was struggling with his allcomm. He was trying to adjust some of the visi-cons on it's external surface in order to get the voice to come in clearer through the static. At first there was just more crackling static but then, as clear as a bell they all heard the voice of TERRI speak to them through time and space.

"Dylan, can you hear me? Come in please. Do you copy?"

Dylan grinned and looked up as he said, "Oh man, I never thought a computer voice could sound so good."

He then made one last adjustment on his allcomm and spoke into it. "TERRI this is Dylan, over."

"Dylan, it's great to hear your voice! Is everything OK?"

"Yes, we're fine but really anxious to get home."

"Are you able to do so?"

"Well, I'm not sure. We haven't been able to communicate with you for a long time. We've tried to go back through GLASS a couple of times but nothing has worked until just now. We're not at all sure if my link to GLASS is working properly. Not sure if we can get back. How do things look from your end?"

Suddenly a new voice broke through. "Dylan this is Abbie. We thought for a while we lost all of you but right now it looks like everything is working fine. Everybody there OK? GLASS shows your link to be at one hundred percent although for some reason it has been hovering between zero and three percent until this very moment. We've had some rather interesting complications at this end. We'll tell you guys all about that later but all of our readings and function indicators here in the lab look great right now. Looks like you're good to go. Do you want to try again?"

All in the same instant the members of the away team responded in the affirmative.

Dylan yelled, "Absolutely."

Reid called out, "Yes."

Dr. Ormond cried out the loudest of all, "I want to go home, NOW!"

Even Molly nodded her head in agreement as she continued to watch the group of women approach the tomb in the next clearing.

Dylan made a few more minor adjustments on his allcomm.

"OK," he said. I think I've got it. Looks like we're good at this end too. All readings in the green and ready to go. Coming back through GLASS on my mark. 3 . . . 2 . . . 1 . . . MARK!"

Molly felt and saw the moist mist begin at her feet and start to climb up the rest of her body. She tried to peer through the trees to see what was going on at the tomb one clearing over but the mist was already too thick for her to see very far. She thought to herself, "That's Ok. I already know what is going on over there."

In just a few seconds the mist had blocked everything out. It was so thick that she couldn't even see Dylan or the others.

She felt the sensation of falling once again and then, almost as quickly as the mist had formed it began to clear away. Molly could see that in the place of trees and rocks there were computer consoles, banks of intricate machinery and technicians in their multi colored overalls.

They were back.

Chapter 43

Molly found herself inside her tear looking out into the GLASS lab. Everyone outside was cheering, laughing and congratulating Dylan who was already stepping out of his tear.

Molly sat for just a moment longer as she watched Reid exit his tear followed a few seconds later by Dr. Ormond.

Dylan was shaking hands with everyone but had begun to fight his way through the crowd toward her tear.

Molly activated the pupil like doorway and stepped out of her tear and into the lab. People clapped her on the back, hugged her and congratulated her while telling her how great she and the others had done.

Dylan reached her side but was whisked away at that moment by the medical group. Molly watched him being escorted toward the medical suite just as several more staff members from the medical team approached her.

"How do you feel? Everything Ok? Any pains? Are you hurt anywhere?"

The medical team fired questions at her in rapid order, far too fast for her to answer them all. Finally one of the med techs realized that Molly was overwhelmed.

"OK, everybody give her some space. Molly don't worry about all this, let's get you into the medical suite and we'll get you checked out along with the others. I think there will be plenty of time for questions later."

In no time Molly found herself in the medical suite being looked over by two or three med techs. Dr. Dane Howe, the chief medical officer came over a few times to check her vital signs and ask her a few questions about her overall sense of her own health. She answered as best she could and then was told to rest for about an hour while the med techs monitored her vital signs a while longer. Reid, Dr. Ormond and Dylan were all in the suite as well. They were separated from each other by about fifteen feet. Each of them was lying on a comform couch behind dark blue woven curtains that separated each of them from each other.

They had been asked by Dr. Howe not to speak to each other so that they could all rest but of course they talked among themselves the entire time about mundane items. Dylan asked for and got a run down of sports scores from one of the techs. Somebody talked to Reid about some future projects that Molly knew nothing about and Molly lightheartedly told the others that she claimed first dibs on interviews for her scroll before the general press got to them all. One of the techs had thoughtfully found out how her dog Pepper was doing and Molly was delighted to hear that all was well with her favorite canine.

Only Dr. Ormond was silent. Dylan, Reid and Molly all took turns trying to talk to her and engage her in conversation but they gave up when she asked to be left to her own thoughts.

After the allotted time had expired Dr. Howe came back in and observed them as each of them in turn had their vital signs taken yet again by the med techs. Dr. Howe then asked each of them a series of questions that Molly guessed were designed to see if she and the others were still oriented to time and place. Once he was satisfied that they were all physically OK, Dr. Howe released them for the time being after giving them instructions to check in again with him later that night prior to going to bed.

Dylan came over to Molly and gave her a huge hug. Molly, Dylan and Reid were all in very high spirits as they walked together from the medical suite back toward the GLASS lab. Dr. Ormond seemed to be much more subdued and hung back as they all headed for the lab. As they entered the GLASS lab, Abbie was the first one there to greet them. She hugged them all and then told them that they were to have a very short question and answer period with HIS employees only. No general press representatives were to be present at this time although it had been confirmed that news of the historic time travel run had leaked out to the general public.

The time was eleven twenty five AM and Abbie informed them that after this time with employees, they would have another rest period and then meet the general press. She informed them that there were more than five hundred members of the press on site in one of the other buildings. Also included in that number were politicians and scientists, all chomping at the bit to talk with them and to hear about their experience in Jerusalem.

The away team was then given a very brief update of the difficulties that the lab group had experienced with TERRI. The team was brought up to speed about the communications problems as well as the video and recording problems. Dylan, Molly and the others knew of course that something had gone wrong but they were all stunned to learn that it had been TERRI that had shut the systems down. Reid and Dylan pledged to get to the bottom of the problems and find out exactly what had gone wrong with TERRI and to find out what this mystery was all about.

As Molly sat down next to Dylan in a corner of the GLASS lab, she could see that almost everyone who worked at HIS was there. She assumed that there must be a skeleton crew still at work but most employees had been allowed by their bosses to come to this historic briefing.

Abbie was to be the acting master of ceremonies and somehow try to organize the questions that were to come from the other HIS employees. However she took the liberty of asking the first questions herself.

"Where were you guys? You almost gave us all heart failure. Immediately after you disappeared from the tears we lost contact with you. You have no idea how scared we all were. Could you hear us? We heard nothing from you verbally and we got nothing at all from any of your allcomms, no video, no recordings, just nothing at all. TERRI shut it all down."

Molly, Dylan and the others had suspected and feared that the recordings might not have been saved. Now their worst nightmare had been verified. However they had held out hope that even though they had lost contact with GLASS that TERRI was still picking up audio and visual recordings from their allcomms. Until just a few seconds earlier they had no idea that none of the recordings had survived the GLASS run or that TERRI had been the culprit. While they had been in the medical unit, technicians had taken their allcomms and had been pouring over them to try to see if any of them had indeed been recording or not. Sadly, those technicians now confirmed that all four allcomms had malfunctioned and neither audio nor visual recordings had survived the journey. The really weird part of the incident was that TERRI seemed to have no idea as to why she had taken control of the communications and recording systems. At least that is what she claimed. Dylan, Reid and Abbie all seemed to think that there was more to it than what TERRI was saying. It just didn't add up in their eyes.

TERRI had been programmed, in large part by them and her internal systems had been checked a thousand times. Yet out of the blue she had shut the systems down and had refused to re-connect them until she had determined that it was time for the team to come home. No one seemed to know exactly why this had happened so for the time being it was simply chalked up to being an anomaly of some sort. Here in the lab everything seemed to be working just fine right before the run had taken place. Then, without warning, TERRI had shut down all communications and recordings and kept those systems down during the course of the run. Prior to the run, every single person involved with GLASS would have stated that they believed that TERRI was the most reliable part of the entire team. But now, things were different and TERRI's systems would have to be examined from top to bottom and from A to Z to determine what had actually happened. The bottom line here was that no recordings had survived from the Jerusalem run.

Dylan called out to TERRI and asked her what had happened and why she had purposely caused the communications and recordings systems to crash. In addition to that, Dylan asked her why she had also not allowed the away team to return to HIS when they wanted to do so. Everyone in the lab stopped what they were doing and listened intently for TERRI's response.

But there was none.

Molly was pretty upset that no proof of anything they had seen, heard or done had returned with them but Dylan and Reid were absolutely crushed by the news. Oddly, Dr. Ormond seemed to take that news the best, though Molly could not really understand why.

While Dylan and Reid pondered the TERRI difficulty, Abbie brought everyone back to the point of the meeting. She asked the assembled employees if they had any questions for Dylan, Reid, Dr. Ormond or Molly. Every single person in the room shot his or her hand up immediately.

Abbie pointed to Douglas who was sitting in the second row and told him to go ahead and ask his questions.

"Dylan you are our CEO and were the captain of this away team so I'll ask these questions of you first OK? So what did you see? Did you get to Jerusalem? Was there actually someone named Jesus there? Did you see Him? And I guess the main question that is on everyone's mind, is He the Son of God?"

Chapter 44

As soon as Douglas asked those questions a complete hush fell over the GLASS lab. All eyes shifted to Dylan, Molly, Reid and Dr. Ormond but especially to Dylan since Douglas had addressed his questions to him.

For a moment Dylan hesitated and then said, "Well, as a scientist I really thought that we would find out that --"

"Just a moment please," Reid interrupted. "If you don't mind Dylan I would like to tackle those questions. Especially that last one."

"Oh no," Molly thought to herself. "Here it comes."

Dylan looked for a second as if he might object but Reid had jumped to his feet and was already speaking again. "As you all know I am a scientist through and through. If I don't have concrete proof of something, then in my mind it doesn't exist. We've just come back from a historic and almost unbelievable journey to prove the existence of Jesus and to prove once and for all that He either is the Son of God or to prove that He is not. Now we've just found out that the recordings we thought were being captured by our allcomms; audio, visual and holographic have failed to record anything. So really there is no proof whatsoever that Jesus was or is who Christians for thousands of years have claimed He was; the actual Son of God. The proof just is not there."

Molly's heart sank as the crowd took this announcement in and everyone began talking at once. Molly noticed that almost everyone in the room was nodding his or her head in apparent agreement with what Reid had just said.

Reid let the crowd noise die down just a bit before he continued. "However, I'm here to tell you that Jesus did exist, He did die on a cross and that He did indeed rise up from being dead, just as the Bible says He did. I saw all of this for myself. At one point He looked directly into my eyes after He rose from being dead. And as He looked at me, and I mean REALLY looked at me, I knew at once that Jesus was and is the Christ! He is the Son of God! He was killed as a man but He rose from the state of being dead to live again as God's Son. Our Messiah! Our salvation!"

The crowd was momentarily stunned. Molly could hardly believe her ears. She had been prepared to be the only person in the group to still stand true to what she believed. When it had been announced that there were no allcomm recordings she had just assumed that Reid, Dr. Ormond and maybe even Dylan would denounce the fact that Jesus was the Son of God. She thought that she and she alone would be left to witness to these people about what she had seen and felt in Jerusalem. But here, the very last person she expected to be a witness, had done just that. Reid Corder, atheist to the core had been converted and had just witnessed to a room full of non-believers.

"Oh God," Molly prayed. "You are amazing. Your name is being magnified and praised by the very person who set out to prove that you were anything except the Son of God. Incredible! Absolutely incredible!"

The crowd was in an uproar but Reid held his hands up for quiet and then continued. "I know that we didn't bring any proof back with us. But I'm telling you all right here and right now, I went to Jerusalem hoping to prove that Christianity was a farce, just a lie of some kind. But friends, I saw this man Jesus. I saw Him killed in a horrifying manner. And then, hard as it is to believe, I saw Him raise himself up out of a grave and walk away. I do not know what to do now. I've never been to church or anything like that so I'm not exactly sure what Christians do. But I guess I'd better find out now that I am one. Maybe Molly will forgive me and sort of lead the way for me in that department. Jesus is real. He is alive. He is the Messiah. He is God!"

The room exploded into noise and chaos as everyone in the crowd began to speak and yell at the same time. Finally Abbie was able to get things quieted down a bit and she motioned for Molly to speak. With tears streaming down her face she began to address the crowd but before she did, she ran over to Reid and threw her arms around his neck and hugged him close.

"I'm so sorry Molly," Reid said through a stream of tears. "I am just so very sorry. Can you ever forgive me for the things I've said about you and for the things I've done to hurt you?"

She hugged him harder and whispered to him, "Yes of course I forgive you but it's Jesus that does the main forgiving here. I am so very, very glad you are a believer now Reid. I'm really happy for you."

Reid responded as he continued to sob. "But I don't know how to ask Him to forgive me. After all I've said and done, I wouldn't dare to ask to be forgiven."

Molly smiled through her tears as she finally let go of Reid's neck. "Let's talk about it later. You've already done the first part, accepting Him for who He is. Now comes the good part, living as a believer!"

Molly then turned to address the crowd. "Well, all of you know how I felt about this before the GLASS run. You knew that I was a born again Christian. I'm no different now except to say that my faith runs much deeper than it did just a few days ago. We don't have proof to show you, but I can tell you that the four of us are changed forever, just as Reid has said. We saw Jesus. We saw Him up close and we watched as the very things that the Bible claims are historical facts played out in front of us. What I thought was true ended up being just that, true. You can ask any of us. The Bible is accurate. It is historical and spiritual fact. We saw the whole thing unfold right in front of us and --"

Dr. Ormond stepped up next to Molly and interrupted her. "Well, let's not get too carried away. We did get to Jerusalem and we did see some man die in a terrible way. Some of that looked sort of like what the Bible describes. But as far as this guy coming back to life after he was dead, well I'm not so sure about all of that."

"Oh c'mon?" Molly yelled. "You know it's all true. You saw him come out of that tomb. You saw --"

"What? What did we see Molly? Think it through. You too Reid. What did we really see? Our bodies were exhausted, our minds were confused and we were scared half to death. We certainly weren't thinking rationally. We were hidden from the final scene in that grotto near that tomb by trees and smoke from that campfire. And all the time we kept hearing from Molly as she told us what she wanted us to see. Our tired minds were playing tricks on us and we all saw things that might have been just about anything. Nothing more, nothing less. No, I'm afraid that Molly is lying once again, or just brain washed or confused or something. And you Reid," she continued as she looked over at him. "I think you are just exhausted from the experience. I don't blame you. We thought we were lost forever, stuck there in a time that was not our own and in a place that was harsh and intimidating. Our minds just reached out for the first life preserver we could find and that ended up being Molly's story about Jesus and God and being saved and all of that. I have to admit that I was able to keep my head a little bit better than the others, probably because I am the oldest and I've been around the block a time or two and I've seen just about everything. It's just a good thing that I didn't panic like some others whose names I won't mention."

Molly, Dylan and Reid all stared at her as if she had lost her mind. They each started to say something but Dr. Ormond quickly continued to address the group of employees. "The story sounds great right? We found Jesus! We found God! Well I was there too and managed to keep my wits about me the entire time we were there. I can tell you without any doubt, the only thing we proved was that people were crucified in Jerusalem two thousand years ago, a fact that historians have known for many years. So what did we accomplish. Nothing of any consequence as far as this Jesus story goes. We did however prove that GLASS works and as a contribution to science I guess that is pretty significant. We can all be very proud of that. Other than that, we really didn't accomplish much at all."

With that she turned to Molly and said, "I'm sorry Molly, I've just got to tell these fine people the truth. I know that you believe in your faith deeply but this venture should show you that the things and ideas that you believe in are in fact, just a lie. You wanted it to be true so badly that you were just seeing things that your mind wanted to be true."

She then turned and addressed Reid. "Reid I'm surprised and disappointed in you most of all. You are one of the most capable scientists on the planet, yet you allowed your emotions to get the better of you. You need to think again what your response is going to be about all of this because your career and your reputation throughout the world wide science community depends on what you say and do right now. Don't you want to adjust your statement just a little?"

Chapter 45

Before Reid could react Molly took a step toward Dr. Ormond and said, "I can't believe this. What are you talking about? You were there with the rest of us. You saw it all. You saw Jesus crucified right before your eyes. You saw Him die and you saw Him walk out of that tomb. You were standing right next to me when He showed us His hands. Those wounds were still fresh. Dr. Ormond please don't do this. You know what the truth is!"

Dr. Ormond smiled a devious smile, paused dramatically for a moment and then addressed the group of employees.

"Yes I was there. I need you all to know that while we were away Molly here could hardly hold herself together. All she could talk about was Jesus this and Jesus that. All those stories that she grew up believing were obviously false and she just couldn't handle it. Yes, we saw some poor guy die on a cross. But there was never any proof that it was Jesus. We were told by some other guy that the crucified man was going to be buried, but we never saw which tomb he was buried in. Then we saw some man strolling through a grotto where many people were buried but again, we never had any proof of who that man was. He might have just been the gardener for all we know."

Dr. Ormond looked at Molly and her smile grew just a bit more conniving. "Go ahead Molly, tell them. Deny that what I just said is the truth. Do you have any proof about Jesus? Well let's hear it. We're all waiting. Or better yet, show us. Where's your proof."

Molly was stunned. "Why are you doing this?"

"Why? Do you really need to ask that? You went on the GLASS run expecting to prove to all the world that Jesus was and is the Son of God.

But you've come back with nothing; no proof whatsoever. Reid and I however went on the run to prove just the opposite. We intended to prove once and for all that there is no Son of God. We did that easily because in truth, there isn't one. There is no Son of God and Christianity is just a lie."

With that she stepped a little closer to Reid and said, "Now Reid, I know that we were all traumatized by what we saw and you seem a bit confused by the experience we just had. But it's time to get your big boy pants on and tell everyone here that just as I said, there is no Son of God. There is no such thing as Christianity. Come on, tell them. I know you meant well with what you said a minute ago but it's time to come clean with the truth now. Do you really believe there is a Son of God? Do you really believe that some dead person actually came back to life under his own power?"

No one in the crowd spoke or even moved for what seemed like an eternity.

Every eye in the room was on Reid Corder and he knew it.

He began to perspire and shifted back and forth on his feet uncomfortably. He looked at the crowd of employees, he looked at Molly and then looked straight into the eyes of Dr. Ormond. Finally he looked back out over the crowd and took two steps forward.

"Yes, some of what Dr. Ormond says is true."

Molly sighed and looked at the floor as Reid continued.

"I did go on the GLASS run with one motive in mind and that was to prove in a definitive way that Christianity is false, just a fairy tale. It's also true that because of the failure of our allcomms, we have no actual evidence of anything that would even come close to proving that Jesus was or is the Son of God."

A soft murmur began to circulate throughout the crowd of employees.

Dr. Ormond smiled an evil grin at Molly and Molly thought she was going to faint. The mission had failed but even worse, she felt that she had let God down. Suddenly, Molly could sense that still small voice within her touch her mind and say, "Watch this!"

She risked a quick glance at Reid who was already looking in her direction. He winked at her and then continued to address the crowd.

"Here's my final statement on this subject. This is not about proof. This is about faith! Jesus is the Son of God!"

Molly let out the breath that she had been holding for about a minute as Reid continued.

"I'm the last person in the room who should be saying this because I'm not a believer. Or at least I wasn't until now. But the things we saw there, and the things we felt there leave me no doubt. A man named Jesus lived as a flesh and blood man. He was killed in a gruesome manner and then, thanks be to God Almighty, He defeated death somehow and simply walked out of a tomb after being dead for several days. Friends I don't know how it was done, I've got a lot of things to look into and a lot of studying to do about all of this. However, I do know this much. It was done! Jesus looked into my eyes for a moment and in that moment I knew it was all true. He knew who I was. He knew why I was there. And yet the only two things I can remember clearly about that moment were these. The first is that no matter who I am or who you are, Jesus loves each of us. I'm not sure why, I've gotta study that a little bit now too when I get a chance.

The second thing is the incredible power that it took to bring Himself back to life after being dead; just absolutely incredible. Power that is all complete and all good. Power that could only have been created by God Himself. I know that we here at HIS think we have recently discovered a source of power that is incredible in strength. Friends I've just met the creator of everything. Now there's some power for you, and I mean, real power."

With that Reid fell to his knees and cried like a baby. He looked back up at the crowd, then looked skyward and said, "God forgive me please. I didn't know. I just didn't know and now I am so sorry. I praise your holy name!"

Molly couldn't control herself any longer and shouted as loudly as she could. "Amen!"

She then sprinted over to Reid, launched herself at him and hugged him so hard that they both toppled to the floor

Dr. Ormond threw her hands up and yelled as loudly as she could. "No! It's a lie! Don't listen to them. There is no Jesus. There is no Christ figure. There is no virgin birth. There is no body being resurrected from the dead. There is no God man. There is no God. There is no Christianity. It's all just a pack of --"

"Grace!" Dylan called out from just behind Molly, "I've got three really important things I need to tell you."

Dr. Ormond practically ran over to Dylan. He had been silent for the last few minutes but she now realized that he might come to her rescue and back her side of the story. But as she approached him she could see the look in his eyes and she could tell that this was not going to end well for her. Still, she tried her best.

"Yes, Dylan, You're a scientist. One of the best around. Tell them. Tell them it was all a waste of time, tell them that there is no proof about--"

He interrupted her again. "Hang on just a second Grace. As I said, I have three things to tell you so listen up. The first thing is that we would all appreciate it if you would stand here quietly and stop babbling. The second thing is that Jesus is absolutely and positively the Son of God."

Grace Ormond was not quite ready to give up. She glanced around the room and called out to TERRI.

"TERRI, are you here?"

"Yes Dr. Ormond, I'm here."

"Can't you do something to make these idiots see reason? Isn't there something you want to say?"

"Yes, Dr. Ormond there is one thing I would like to say."

"Oh thank Heavens," Dr. Ormond replied as she let out a sigh of relief. "Please, go ahead. What do you want to tell us? What do you want to tell me?"

"I just wanted to tell you to HUSH!"

As everyone laughed, somebody yelled out from within the crowd.

"Hey Dylan, what was the third thing you were going to tell Dr. Ormond?"

Dylan paused a moment, looked directly at Dr, Ormond and then said, "Oh yeah. The third thing I need to tell you is that you're fired!"

The general press conference that had been planned for later that day was cancelled. Dylan, Reid and Abbie met with some of the GLASS project technicians and mainly discussed the issues of technology that had worked as expected as well as those that had not worked.

They all knew that GLASS had been successful but they also knew that GLASS was not ready to be rolled out for the public.

Over the next few weeks the entire GLASS project was subject to rigorous tests and audits that helped the team understand a lot of things that went as planned on the last GLASS run in addition to those items that had not worked well, with two major exceptions.

The first was that no one had been able to figure out how or why all four allcomms used by the away team had each failed at the exact same time. Everyone knew that TERRI had blocked and destroyed the communications and recording systems, but no one knew exactly why she had done that.

A second issue also remained as an unsolved piece of the overall puzzle. That issue was that the controls on Dylan's allcomm that would allow him to override the system to bring the team back, had failed just at the time they needed it most.

As time went on the evidence again pointed to TERRI but still, none of the lab techs had been able to pinpoint the exact problem or why TERRI even refused to discuss it.

Once the team had arrived back at the GLASS lab, all systems, including recordings, allcomm communication and the override system had seemed to function perfectly.

Countless tests were run on all of those systems but no one ever found out what had caused them to malfunction while the team was in Jerusalem. The systems worked fine in the lab prior to the run but simply just seemed to not work at all while the run was proceeding. Then suddenly all systems seemed to work perfectly again once the team had returned to the lab. TERRI continued to operate flawlessly and she readily admitted to causing the system problems. However she never revealed the origin or source of her odd decision making behavior. It seemed that the cause of the system failures during the run would always remain a mystery.

Molly, Dylan and Reid all suspected that they knew very well what the source of TERRI's odd behavior was. They often talked about it when they were together but never ventured to discuss their theory with anyone else.

It was their belief that the systems failed simply because God wanted them to fail at that precise time in order to keep the team in Jerusalem just long enough to see and experience the resurrection of Jesus. They believed that Dylan would have been pressured into leaving Jerusalem to soon if all systems had been working properly. They also believed that God wanted them to stay in Jerusalem for an extended period of time so that they could experience certain things in specific ways. Those experiences would prove to be of incredible support to Dylan and Reid as they began their journey as new born Christians.

Though none of them would ever have any actual proof, they all believed that TERRI had caused the systems that would have allowed them to return to fail at just the right time. It seemed like too much of a coincidence that immediately after they had witnessed the resurrection, both the allcomm system and the system to bring them back home had begun to work perfectly again.

Molly, in particular did not really believe that there were such things as coincidences. Instead she believed in something she called Godcidences, or circumstances that came about simply because God wanted them to be so. Though she would never understand it all completely and she certainly would never be able to prove it, Molly believed that Gad did not want the away team to bring back any actual proof. Instead, she believed that it was God's plan to have them return with a sense of deeper and stronger faith. In the case of both Dylan and Reid, this was newly found, exhilarating faith. In Molly's case it was a sense of renewed and strengthened faith.

Two months after their return from Jerusalem, both Dylan and Reid were baptized in one of the local churches. That same night Dylan, Molly and Reid went out to dinner. After they had eaten Reid excused himself and said that he wanted to go to his car to get his new vid-comm. Molly thought that was rather strange but said nothing about it until he returned to their table.

"Reid, what in the world do you need a vid-comm for during dinner?" she asked.

"Well, this is a really nice vid-comm. State of the art. It takes much better video, still shots and holo-recordings than what my old allcomm could take," he replied. "I just want to be able to take a few pictures of what is about to happen next. You know, so you can show your grandkids and stuff like that."

"What are you talking about?"

Just as she asked that question Dylan slid out of his chair and knelt on one knee in front of Molly. Everyone in the restaurant turned to look at Molly and Dylan.

"Molly Mahan, you have changed my life forever. You brought me up from a darkness that I didn't even know I was in. You brought me to Jesus and He in turn brought me back to you. I want to spend the rest of my life worshiping Him and loving you. Would you do me the ultimate honor of marrying me and becoming my wife?"

Molly was stunned and sat frozen in her chair for a long moment. Then she exploded out of her seat and threw her arms around Dylan's neck knocking him to the floor.

As the two of them tumbled to the ground she shouted out for all to hear. "Yes, Yes, absolutely yes!"

All of the other patrons in the restaurant cheered and clapped as Dylan and Molly kissed a long passionate kiss that lasted for a full minute. Finally Reid had to tap Dylan on the shoulder two or three times to break them apart.

"OK, OK, we get it. You love each other. Now settle down a little, there are still people eating in here and we don't want to make anyone ill."

Molly and Dylan retook their seats, both of them smiling their widest happiest smiles.

"So," Reid said after things had quieted down a bit. "Where do you think you'll go on your honeymoon?"

Dylan and Molly looked at each other, surprised by the question. Dylan smiled sheepishly and said, "I really haven't given it much thought. How about it Molly, do you have someplace you'd really like to go to on our honeymoon?"

Molly was still for a brief moment but then looked up directly into Dylan's eyes. Dylan had seen that look several times before and he knew that Molly was up to something. He started to fidget uncomfortably in his chair as he saw a mischievous grin begin to form around the corners of Molly's mouth. Molly glanced at Reid and then looked back at Dylan and said, "Oh I don't know; but I hear Jerusalem is nice this time of year?"

About the Author

B.C. Reynolds is a freelance writer who lives with his wife outside of Atlanta, GA. His vivid and far reaching imagination combined with his Christian character and values enable him to stretch the boundaries of Christian fiction.

Printed and bound by PG in the USA

USA2019PGIL